THE HEART'S FRONTIER

THE HEART'S FRONTIER

LORI COPELAND AND VIRGINIA SMITH

CHRISTIAN LARGE PRINT
A part of Gale, Cengage Learning

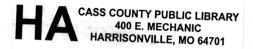

GALE
CENGAGE Learning·

Detroit • New York • San Francisco • New Haven, Conn • Waterville, Maine • London

GALE
CENGAGE Learning

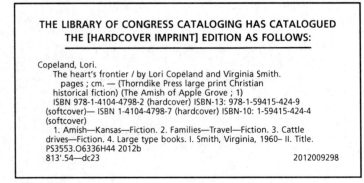

THE LIBRARY OF CONGRESS CATALOGING HAS CATALOGUED THE [HARDCOVER IMPRINT] EDITION AS FOLLOWS:

Copeland, Lori.
   The heart's frontier / by Lori Copeland and Virginia Smith.
      pages ; cm. — (Thorndike Press large print Christian historical fiction) (The Amish of Apple Grove ; 1)
      ISBN 978-1-4104-4798-2 (hardcover) ISBN-13: 978-1-59415-424-9 (softcover)— ISBN 1-4104-4798-7 (hardcover) ISBN-10: 1-59415-424-4 (softcover)
      1. Amish—Kansas—Fiction. 2. Families—Travel—Fiction. 3. Cattle drives—Fiction. 4. Large type books. I. Smith, Virginia, 1960– II. Title.
PS3553.O6336H44 2012b
813'.54—dc23   2012009298

[CIP data for the hardcover edition without any alterations]

Published in 2012 by arrangement with Books and Such Literary Agency, Inc.

Printed in the United States of America
1 2 3 4 5   16 15 14 13 12

FD101

Whether you turn to the
right or to the left,
your ears will hear a voice
behind you, saying,
"This is the way; walk in it."

ISAIAH 30:21

ACKNOWLEDGMENTS

A NOTE FROM LORI AND GINNY
When we set out to write *The Heart's Frontier,* neither of us considered ourselves experts on cattle drives or the Amish lifestyle. We devoured a lot of books on the cattle drives of the 1880s, and we spoke with many people who helped us understand the Amish approach to a simple life.

We're so glad we did! What a fun period of America's history, and what an incredibly interesting lifestyle we were privileged to learn about. We're grateful to those who helped us tell our story with authenticity.

We owe a debt of gratitude to our agent, Wendy Lawton, who introduced us and made this coauthor arrangement possible. We're also deeply grateful to the good folks at Harvest House who have worked alongside us to bring this story to you. Thanks to Bob Hawkins, Kim Moore, Terry Glaspey, Shane White, Barb Sherrill, LaRae Weikert, and all the others who believed in this book.

We're each thankful for our supportive families, and especially to our Lord, without whom we could produce no book worth reading.

God bless,
Lori Copeland and Virginia Smith

PROLOGUE

El Paso, Texas
May 1881

"Hot diggety!" Shep Carson whipped off his hat and flung it in the air. "I knew I'd make a man outta you yet!"

Grinning, Luke watched his father make a fool of himself in front of the other wranglers. El Paso teemed with cattle this morning as the cowhands loaded the herd into pens. He'd expected as much, but watching Pa grinning like a possum eatin' a yellow jacket wasn't easy. "I don't know why you find my decision surprising. Haven't I spent the last few years riding herd over your drives?"

Pa's gaze softened. "You have, and I'm not surprised but a little baffled. It took you long enough to make up your mind."

The older man sat tall in the saddle. The years had been kind to the cowboy who had spent most of his life driving cattle to market. Until he was old enough to ride with him, Luke barely knew the man, but over the years he'd developed a deep bond with his father, and the proud look shining in his pa's eyes made him feel good.

"So. Who signed you on?" Cattle jostled the men's horses while they worked. Sharp whistles and wranglers' shouts pierced the air as the milling beef bumped flesh.

Luke cut his chestnut to the left and called back, "Simon Hancock."

"That a fact? What trail?"

"Chisholm."

Pa's grin lengthened. "Got yourself a fine trail and a decent boss. It says a whole lot that a man like Hancock would hire you on for your first drive."

It was Luke's first drive in the sense that he would be foreman. He had close to twenty drives under his belt but always as point rider. Every cowhand in Texas knew Hancock's reputation — a quiet man who managed his herds from a nearby hotel — but most wranglers would give an arm and a leg to take Hancock's beef to market. His stock was the finest around.

"You didn't happen to have anything to do with his decision, did you?" Luke headed off another stray.

Pa was waiting for the steer. With one

nudge to the horse, the bull slid through the shoot. "Not me. I haven't worked Hancock's herd in years. He made me mad as a peeled rattler once, and I refused to work for him again."

The news didn't surprise Luke. He'd ridden with Pa since he was fourteen, and he couldn't recall seeing a Triple Bar brand in the herd, but he'd never thought to ask why. Didn't matter. Luke was sure he could take whatever Hancock dished up. He must have gotten wind that Shep Carson's boy was looking for his first foreman job and decided to contact him. Hancock and Pa might have crossed swords in the past, but the cattle baron gave Luke's father the highest compliment. When the young man hired on with a handshake and a thanks, Hancock grunted and merely said, "I don't have any concerns about Shep Carson's boy."

And he was right about that. Luke might have taken his time to decide what he wanted to do with his life — punch cattle or buy land and settle down — but when he obligated himself to a cause he stuck to it. Now that he was in charge of this ride, he'd see there wasn't a single hitch. There wasn't much he didn't know about cattle. Over the years he'd eaten enough dust and survived enough dry drives to make him one of the best in the business, but until recently he'd been content to follow. Now he wanted to lead.

When the horses pulled up beside one another, Luke took off his hat and wiped his brow. He glanced up when he felt his father's eyes on him. Eyes brimming with pride.

"What?"

"I'm proud of you, son. Your ma would have been proud."

"No, she wouldn't. She hated your job, Pa. And she hated even more that I rode with you. She wanted you home."

Glancing away, Shep focused on the milling cattle. "Can't deny your words. I wasn't much of a husband or father." His eyes roamed the herd. "The trail gets in your blood, and I had to put food on the table."

Luke traced his gaze. He didn't want to be like Pa, not in this way. He liked the work, but someday he knew as certain as he was sitting in the saddle that he'd leave the job. Maybe buy a Texas ranch and raise a family. But for now he knew cattle like the back of his hand, and the good Lord willing, he still had a lot of years ahead of him before he had to decide exactly what he wanted out of life. He'd yet to meet a woman he'd give up bachelorhood for, and with Ma dead and his two brothers scattered, he was free to wander for as long as he wanted.

"It's a hard life." Pa's quiet words broke into his thoughts.

"Driving cattle? I can do it with my eyes closed. And I get along with others, but I can also be tough as nails if necessary." He figured he'd make a fine trail boss, one any man could respect. Life was as simple as setting your mind to something and following through.

"No, I meant life can get confusing. A man might think he knows all he needs to know, but he'll soon find out he's about as dumb as a stump in some matters."

Chuckling, Luke shook his head. "You're gettin' old, Pop. You need a hot bath and a T-bone steak. Life's only as worrisome as a man makes it."

The older man's eyes fastened on him. "Think you got it all figured out, do you? Got your first big job. Feeling mighty good about yourself."

"Am I certain I can drive cattle as well as my old man?" Luke flashed a grin. "Maybe not as well, but pretty durn close."

"You think that's all there is to life? Knowing when to push, when to water, and when to let up?"

13

"That about sums it up, doesn't it?"

Shep shook his head. "Young'uns. All fire and stink water." Reining his horse, he winked. "Have a fine drive, son. And once you get those cattle to Hays, your old pa will buy *you* that T-bone." A chuckle rumbled deep in his throat. "Oh . . . and you can tell me how you've managed to hog-tie and lasso life into a tidy little bundle."

Giving another chuckle, he rode back into the herd.

ONE

Apple Grove, Kansas
July 1881

Nearly the entire Amish district of Apple Grove had turned out to help this morning, all twenty families. Or perhaps they were here merely to wish Emma Switzer well as she set off for her new home in Troyer, fifty miles away.

From her vantage point on the porch of the house, Emma's grandmother kept watch over the loading of the gigantic buffet hutch onto the specially reinforced wagon. Her sharp voice sliced through the peaceful morning air.

"Forty years I've had that hutch from my dearly departed husband and not a scratch on it. Jonas, see that you use care!"

If *Maummi*'s expression weren't so fierce, Emma would have laughed at the long-suffering look Papa turned toward his mother. But the force with which *Maummi*'s fingers dug into the flesh on Emma's arm warned that a chuckle would be most ill-suited at the moment. Besides, the men straining to heft the heavy hutch from the front porch of their home into the wagon didn't need further distractions. Their faces strained bright red above their beards, and more than one drop of sweat trickled from beneath the broad brims of their identical straw hats.

Emma glanced at the watchers lined up like sparrows on a fence post. She caught sight of her best friend, Katie Beachy, amid the sea of dark dresses and white *kapps.* Katie smiled and smoothed her skirt with a shy gesture. The black fabric looked a little darker and crisper than that of those standing around her, which meant she'd worn her new dress to bid Emma farewell, an honor usually reserved for singings or services or weddings. The garment looked well on her. Emma had helped sew the seams at their last frolic. Of course, Katie's early morning appearance in a new dress probably had less to do with honoring Emma than with the presence of Samuel Miller, the handsome son of the district bishop. With a glance toward Samuel, whose arms bulged against the weight of holding up one end of the hutch, she returned

Katie's smile with a conspiratorial wink.

Emma's gaze slid over other faces in the crowd and snagged on a pair of eyes fixed on her. Amos Beiler didn't bother to turn away but kept his gaze boldly on her face. Nor did he bother to hide his expression, one of longing and lingering hurt. He held infant Joseph in his arms, and a young daughter clutched each of his trouser-clad legs. A wave of guilt washed through Emma, and she hastily turned back toward the wagon.

From his vantage point up in the wagon bed, Papa held one end of a thick rope looped around the top of the hutch, the other end held by John Yoder. The front edge of the heavy heirloom had been lifted into the wagon with much grunting and groaning, while the rear still rested on the smooth wooden planks of the porch. Two men steadied the oxen and the rest, like Samuel, had gathered around the back end of the hutch. A protective layer of thick quilts lined the wagon bed.

Papa gave the word. "Lift!"

The men moved in silent unity. Bending their knees, their hands grasped for purchase around the bottom edges. As one they drew in a breath, and at Papa's nod raised in unison. Emma's own breath caught in her chest, her muscles straining in silent sympathy with the men. The hutch rose until its rear end was level with its front, and the men stepped forward. The thick quilts dangling beneath scooted onto the wagon as planned, a protective barrier from damage caused by wood against wood.

The hutch suddenly dipped and slid swiftly to the front. Emma gasped. Apparently the speed caught Papa and John Yoder by surprise too, for the rope around the top went slack. Papa lunged to reach for the nearest corner, and his foot slipped. The wagon creaked and sank lower on its wheels as the hutch settled into place. At the same moment Papa went down on one knee with a loud, "Ummph."

"Papa!"

"*Ach!*" *Maummi* pulled away from Emma and rushed forward. Her heart pounding against her rib cage, Emma followed. Men were already checking on Papa, but *Maummi* leaped into the wagon bed with a jump that belied her sixty years, the strings of her *kapp* flying behind her. She applied bony elbows to push her way around the hutch to her son's side.

She came to a halt above him, hands on her hips, and looked down. "Are you hurt?"

Emma reached the side of the wagon in

time to see Papa wince and shake his head. "No. A bruise is all."

"Good." She left him lying there and turned worried eyes toward her beloved hutch. With a gentle touch, she ran loving fingers over the smooth surface and knelt to investigate the corners.

A mock-stern voice behind Emma held the hint of a chuckle. "Trappings only, Marta Switzer. Care you more for a scratch on wood than an injury to your son?"

Emma turned to see Bishop Miller approach. He spared a smile for her as he drew near enough to lean his arms across the wooden side of the wagon and watch the activity inside. Samuel helped Papa to his feet and handed him the broad-brimmed hat that had fallen off. Emma breathed a sigh of relief when he took a ginger step to try out his leg and smiled at the absence of pain.

"My son is fine." *Maummi* waved a hand in his direction, as though in proof. "And so is my hutch. Though my heart may not say the same, such a fright I've had." She placed the hand lightly on her chest, drew a shuddering breath, and wavered on her feet.

Concern for her grandmother propelled Emma toward the back of the wagon. As she climbed up, she called into the house,

"Rebecca, bring a cool cloth for *Maummi's* head."

The men backed away while Katie and several other women converged on the wagon to help Emma lift *Maummi* down and over to the rocking chair that rested in the shade of the porch, ready to be loaded when the time came. *Maummi* allowed herself to be lowered onto the chair, and then she wilted against the back, her head lolling sideways and arms dangling. A disapproving buzz rumbled among the watching women, but Emma ignored them. Though she knew full well that most of the weakness was feigned for the sake of the bishop and other onlookers, she also knew *Maummi's* heart tended to beat unevenly in her chest whenever she exerted herself. It was yet another reason why she ought to stay behind in Apple Grove, but *Maummi* insisted her place was with Emma, her oldest granddaughter. What she really meant was that she intended to inspect every eligible young Amish man in Troyer and handpick her future grandson-in-law.

Aunt Gerda had written to say she anticipated that her only daughter would marry soon, and she would appreciate having Emma come to help her around the house. She'd also mentioned the abundance of marriageable young men in Troyer, with a suggestion that twenty-year-old Emma was of an age that the news might be welcome. Rebecca had immediately volunteered to go in Emma's place. Though Papa appeared to consider the idea, he decided to send Emma because she was the oldest and therefore would be in need of a husband soonest. *Maummi* insisted on going along in order to *"Keep an eye on this horde of men Gerda will parade before our Emma."*

As far as Emma was concerned, they should just send *Maummi* on alone and leave her in Apple Grove to wait for her future husband to be delivered to her doorstep.

Rebecca appeared from inside the house with a dripping cloth in hand. A strand of wavy dark hair had escaped its pins and fluttered freely beside the strings of her *kapp.* At barely thirteen, her rosy cheeks and smooth, high forehead reminded Emma so sharply of their mother that at times her heart ached.

Rebecca looked at *Maummi's* dramatic posture and rolled her eyes. She had little patience with *Maummi's* feigned heart episodes, and she was young enough that she had yet to learn proper restraint in concealing her emotions. Emma awarded her sister with a stern look and held out a hand for the cloth.

With a contrite bob of her head, Rebecca handed it over and dropped to her knees beside the rocking chair. "Are you all right, *Maummi?*"

"*Ach,* I'm fine. I don't think it's my time. Yet."

Emma wrung the excess water from the cloth before draping it across the back of *Maummi's* neck.

"Danki." The elderly woman realized that the men had stopped working in order to watch her, and she waved her hand in a shooing motion. "Place those quilts over my hutch before you load anything else! Mind, Jonas, no scratches."

Papa shook his head, though a smile tugged at his lips. "*Ja,* I remember."

The gray head turned toward Emma. "Granddaughter, see they take proper care."

"I will, *Maummi.*"

Katie joined Emma to oversee the wrapping of the hutch. When Samuel Miller offered a strong arm to help Katie up into the wagon, Emma hid a smile. No doubt she would receive a letter at her new home soon, informing her that a wedding date had been published. Because Samuel was the bishop's son, there was no fear he would not receive the *Zeugnis,* the letter of good

22

standing. Rebecca would be thrilled at the news of a proper wedding in tiny Apple Grove.

But Emma would be far away in Troyer, and she would miss her friend's big day.

Why must I live there when everything I love is here?

She draped a thick quilt over her end of the hutch and sidled away while Papa secured a rope around it. The faces of her friends and family looked on. They filled the area between the house and the barn. She loved every one in her own way. Yes, even Amos Beiler. She sought him out among the crowd and smiled at the two little girls who hovered near his side. Poor, lonely Amos. He was a good father to his motherless family. No doubt he'd make a fine husband, and if she married him she wouldn't have to move to Troyer. The thought tempted her once again, as it often had over the past several weeks since Papa announced his decision that she would live with Aunt Gerda for a while.

But she knew that if she agreed to become Amos's wife she would be settling. True, she would gain a prosperous farm and a nice house and a trio of well-behaved children, with the promise of more to come. But the fact remained that though there was much to respect about Amos, she didn't love him. The thought of seeing that moon-shaped face and slightly cross-eyed stare over the table for breakfast, dinner, and supper sent a shiver rippling across her shoulders. Not to mention sharing a marriage bed with him. It was enough to make her throw her apron over her face and run screaming across Papa's cornfield.

He deserves a wife who loves him, she told herself for the hundredth time. Her conscience thus soothed, Emma turned away from his mournful stare.

"That trunk goes in the front," *Maummi* shouted from her chair on the porch. "Emma, show them where."

Emma shrank against the gigantic hutch to give the men room to settle the trunk containing all of her belongings. An oiled canvas tarp had been secured over the top to repel any rain they might meet over the next week. Inside, resting on her dresses, aprons, bonnets, and *kapps,* was a bundle more precious to her than anything else in the wagon: a quilt, expertly and lovingly stitched, nestled within a heavy canvas pouch. Mama had made it with her own hands for Emma's hope chest. The last stitch was bitten off just hours before she closed her eyes and stepped into the arms of her Lord.

Oh, Mama, if you were here you could convince Papa to let me stay home. I know you could. And now, without you, what will happen to me?

Yet, even in the midst of the dreary thought, a spark of hope flickered in the darkness in Emma's heart. The future yawned before her like the endless Kansas prairie. Wasn't there beauty to be found in the tall, blowing grasses of the open plain? Weren't there cool streams and shady trees to offer respite from the heat of the day? Maybe Troyer would turn out to be an oasis.

"Emma!"

Maummi's sharp tone cut through her musing. She jerked upright. Her grandmother appeared to have recovered from her heart episode. From the vantage point of her chair, she oversaw every movement with a critical eye.

"Yes, ma'am?"

"Mind what I said about that loading, girl. The food carton goes on last. We won't want to search for provisions when we stop at night on the trail."

An approving murmur rose from the women at the wisdom of an organized wagon.

"Yes, ma'am." Emma exchanged a quick

25

grin with Katie and then directed the man carrying a carton of canned goods and trail provisions to set his burden aside for now.

A little while later, after everything had been loaded and secured under an oiled canvas, the men stood around to admire their handiwork. Samuel even crawled beneath the wagon to check the support struts, and he pronounced everything to be "in apple-pie order."

Emma felt a pluck on her arm. She turned to find Katie at her elbow.

"This is a gift for you." Her friend pushed a small package into her hands. "It's only a soft cloth and some fancy-colored threads. I was fixing to stitch you a design, but you're so much better at fine sewing than I am that I figured you could make something prettier by yourself." She ducked her head. "Think kindly of me when you do."

Warmed by her friend's gesture, Emma pulled her into an embrace. "I will. And I expect a letter from you soon." She let Katie see her glance slide over to Samuel and back with a grin. "Especially when you have something exciting to report."

A becoming blush colored the girl's cheeks. "I will."

Emma was still going down the line, awarding each woman a kind smile and a farewell nod, when Bishop Miller stepped up to the front of the wagon and motioned for attention.

"It's time now to bid Jonas Switzer Godspeed and fair weather for his travels." A kind smile curved his lips when he looked to *Maummi* and then to Emma. "And our prayers go with our sisters Marta and Emma as they make a new home in Troyer."

He bowed his head and closed his eyes, a sign for everyone in the Apple Grove district to follow suit. Emma obeyed, fixing her thoughts on the blue skies overhead and the Almighty's throne beyond. Silence descended, interrupted only by the snorts of oxen and a happy bird in the tall, leafy tree that gave shade to the porch.

What will I find in Troyer? A new home, as the bishop says? A fine Amish husband, as Papa wishes? I pray it be so. And I pray he will be the second son of his father so that he will come home with me to Apple Grove and take over Papa's farm when the time comes.

A female sniffled behind her. Not Katie, but Rebecca. A twist inside Emma's rib cage nearly sent tears to her eyes. Oh, how she would miss her sister when Rebecca left Troyer to return home with Papa. She vowed to make the most of their time together on the trail between here and there.

Bishop Miller ended the prayer with a blessing in High German, his hand on the head of the closest oxen. When the last word fell on the quiet crowd, *Maummi*'s voice sliced through the cool morning air. "Now that we're seen off proper, someone help me up. We'll be gone before the sun moves another inch across the sky."

Though she'd proved earlier that she could make the leap herself at need, *Maummi* allowed Papa and the bishop to lift her into the wagon. She took her seat in her rocking chair, which was wedged between the covered hutch and one high side of the wagon bed. With a protective pat on the hutch, she settled her sewing basket at her feet and pulled a piece of mending onto her lap. No idle hands for *Maummi*. By the time they made Troyer, she'd have all the mending done, and the darning too, and a good start on a new quilt.

Emma spared one more embrace for Katie, steadfastly ignored Amos's mournful stare, and allowed the bishop to help her up onto the bench seat. She scooted over to the far end to make room for Papa, and then Rebecca was lifted up to sit on the other side of him. A snug fit, but they would be okay for the six-day journey to Troyer. Emma settled her black dress and smoothed

28

her apron.

"Now, Jonas, mind you what I said." *Maummi*'s voice from behind their heads sounded a bit shrill in the quiet morning. "You cut a wide path around Hays. I'll not have my granddaughters witness the *ufrooish* of those wild *Englischers*."

On the other side of Papa, Rebecca heaved a loud sigh. Emma hid her grin. No doubt Rebecca would love to witness the rowdy riots of wild cowboy *Englischers* in the infamous railroad town of Hays.

Papa mumbled something under his breath that sounded like *"This will be the longest journey of my life,"* but aloud he said, *"Ja, Mader."*

With a flick of the rope, he urged the oxen forward. The wagon creaked and pitched as it rolled on its gigantic wheels. Emma grabbed the side of the bench with one hand and lifted her other hand in a final farewell as her home fell away behind her.

Two

After three long days on the trail, the jostling wagon had jarred Emma's body until every muscle ached. She couldn't bear one more day sitting on the hard wooden bench and took to walking beside the wagon, as Papa did.

The July sun beat down mercilessly from a clear blue sky. A refreshing wind had swept across the prairie only the day before, but today the air gathered like a stagnant pool around her. Oh, how she wished she could shed the heavy black dress and apron the way Papa shed his coat. She glanced to where he walked up at the head of the oxen, at the line of his suspenders fastened to the back of his trousers and up over white-clad shoulders. His shirtsleeves had been rolled up to the elbows, exposing the tanned skin of strong arms. Even that relief from the sweltering heat inside her dress would be welcome, but the *Ordnung* forbade women to bare their arms in the open.

"I'm hot." Rebecca's whine came from the bench behind the oxen. "And the sun is coloring my face. By the time we get to Troyer I shall be beet red. Papa, can I wear one of your hats to shade my face?"

"*Ach,* what a question." *Maummi* straightened in her rocking chair to scold her younger granddaughter. "We're not three days from home, and already you're throwing aside the Plain ways. Put on your bonnet, girl."

"My head will bake inside that black cloth." If Emma hadn't been walking near the bench, she wouldn't have heard the rest of Rebecca's sullen answer. "When I have my *rumspringa,* I'll wear hats if I choose."

Emma was confident her sister would do that. She hoped Rebecca would find nothing more troublesome to do in Apple Grove than wearing hats during her *rumspringa.* No doubt that was why Papa insisted that Rebecca return with him while Emma and *Maummi* stayed in Troyer. The opportunities to get into trouble during her time of running around before she was baptized would be far fewer in Apple Grove than in a larger community.

Emma made a practical suggestion. "Cover your head with a light-colored cloth, like your apron."

A playful dimple creased Rebecca's cheek. "You mean like this?" She picked up the skirt of her apron and pulled it up over her face and head.

Emma laughed. "You look like you did when you were little and *Maummi* hung your favorite blanket out to dry. You'd pull a stool beneath the laundry line and sit with your face and head covered in wet blanket."

A muffled chuckle came from beneath the white fabric. "A fine fool I'll look riding into Troyer this way. But at least the sun can't find me here."

The sound of horse hooves reached Emma almost at the same moment she saw eight mounted men top a ridge to their left. Alarm zinged along her nerve endings. They looked road weary, and she didn't spot a single smile among them. Papa saw them too, and he put a hand out to stop the oxen. The wagon rolled to a halt, and Emma stepped closer, her back against the wooden side rails. *Maummi*'s hand gripped her shoulder, while Rebecca uncovered her head and scrambled over the back of the bench to crouch in the space at *Maummi*'s feet.

The horses galloped toward them without hesitation. When they arrived, four of the men crossed to the other side of the wagon, and then they all spread out until they formed a menacing circle of horseflesh around them. The expressions of the men were not kindly as they inspected the women and the wagon. Fastened to the sides of their saddles were rifles, and Emma caught a glimpse of a pistol at the belt of the man closest to her. She shrank backward, and Rebecca let out a whimper.

The man in the lead halted his horse near Papa. "Where you headed, mister?"

"My family and I are going to Troyer."

Admiration for Papa's calm voice filled Emma. Wasn't he afraid of these rough men? She couldn't have forced a single word through her teeth, much less spoken in such an even tone.

The cowboy pushed his hat back off his forehead. "Folks there are some kind of religious sect or something, ain't they?"

Papa's straw hat moved up and down with his nod. "We are Plain people. Amish. Troyer is the home of our kin."

"Is that why you dress in them weird clothes and shave your mustache while your beard grows wild?"

Papa merely nodded again.

The horse in front of Emma skittered sideways, the man on its back staring into the wagon behind her head. "What have you got under that cover?"

Maummi's grip tightened on her shoulder. Emma raised a hand and covered her fingers.

Papa answered in the same even tone as before. "Household belongings."

The man jerked a glare back at him. "Any weapons?"

"None. We are a peaceful people."

"Hey, I've heard of the likes of them," one of the men behind the wagon shouted. "They don't believe in fighting, even if someone steals from them."

The leader stared at Papa for a long moment. Then he pulled a revolver from the holster at his side. Emma's breath caught in her chest and blood pounded in her ears. *Please protect Papa, Lord!*

The man's voice held an insult. "Do you mean if I point this here gun at you and tell you I'm meaning to take your wagon, you wouldn't try to stop me?"

For a moment Papa didn't answer. Would he defy them? Though part of Emma, an unrighteous part hidden way down inside, wished he would do that, she knew he would not. The Plain people were peaceful. If struck, Papa would turn the other cheek, as was right.

After a long moment during which the cowboy's eyes narrowed, Papa held himself a little straighter. "We believe and confess that the Lord Jesus has forbidden His disciples and followers all revenge and resistance, and has thereby commanded them not to return evil for evil, nor railing for railing."

The words came straight from the Amish Confession of Faith. A proud smile curved Emma's lips.

Papa's voice then took on a less formal tone. "I will not raise a hand against you, but I will ask, from one man to another, for mercy. My mother is elderly, and my daughters are young. If left to wander the prairies on our own, I fear for their safety."

The man cocked his head sideways, his lips pursed as he considered. Then he nodded. "No reason to be uncivilized if we don't have to be, I figure." He returned his pistol to its holster. When the weapon disappeared, Emma slumped with relief. The man intended to let them go.

He spoke to his men. "Earl, take charge of those oxen. Lester, you and Porter give them your canteens."

Lester wasn't happy with his boss's order. He spat at the ground by Emma's feet. "What fer?"

"Because I'm being merciful, like the man asked. Now get them women out of our wagon and give them your canteens. And mind your manners, you hear? These ain't no saloon girls."

Our wagon. Emma's heart fell. He was planning to steal their wagon and leave them on the trail with nothing but a couple of canteens. A strange brand of mercy these *Englischers* practiced.

Lester grumbled as he and another man dismounted and approached the wagon. Emma turned to give her sister a warning glance. *Don't make trouble. Do as they say.* Her message reached its mark and Rebecca nodded, and then she allowed herself to be lifted down to the ground by the man's rough, dirt-encrusted hands.

For a moment Emma feared *Maummi* wouldn't be as pliable. The spirited woman's jaw jutted forward, and her lips gathered into a furious pucker. When Lester held his hands toward her to lift her down, she clasped the arms of her rocking chair with a white-knuckled grip and glared.

"Young man, with his own hands my dearly beloved made this hutch forty years ago. You've never see a finer piece of furniture in all your born days."

A smirk twisted Lester's lips, revealing a

set of crooked, blackened teeth. "I'll keep that in mind. Ought to bring a good price when I sell it. Or, when the weather turns cold, it'll make me a good fire to keep my backside warm while I sleep." His laugh rolled over the plains around them.

A purple-red flush suffused *Maummi*'s face, and Emma feared for her heart. But after a moment the old woman set her jaw and rose from her chair with the air of one who deigns not to answer a taunt. She allowed herself to be lifted down from the wagon, and when Lester had set her on her feet, she straightened a wrinkle from her apron.

When she accepted the canteen from Lester's hand, she looked up into his eyes. "I'll keep you in my prayers, young man."

Even though their situation was dire, Emma bit back a smile. No doubt the Almighty would get an earful about Lester and the others tonight, and she doubted if *Maummi* would be praying for their souls.

Emma stood beside Rebecca, *Maummi*, and Papa off the side of the trail and watched the thieves turn their oxen around to head in the direction they had come. No doubt they were heading for Hays, where they would sell all their possessions. She reviewed the contents of her trunk. Her

37

clothes wouldn't fetch much of a price, but *Maummi*'s hutch certainly would. The only other thing she possessed worth anything was —

Tears stung her eyes. Mama's quilt.

No!

A lump swelled in her throat. A stranger's hands would finger those beloved stitches and rub across the beautiful squares, the quilt made especially for her, meant to adorn her wedding bed.

It's wrong to become attached to a possession. The loss of a quilt doesn't mean a thing. Mama's love in making it is what matters.

She swallowed back a sob and blinked to clear her eyes in time to see the wagon disappear behind a ridge where the trail curved behind them.

"This is the way of the *Englisch*." Papa put a hand across her shoulders in a rare display of affection. "Come, daughter."

He turned them around with their backs toward their wagon, and they began their march.

Dinnertime had come and gone when Emma spied a settlement up ahead. Rebecca saw it too.

"Look!" She pointed toward the small cluster of buildings nestled in the center of a swell in the surrounding prairie. "It's a town."

"Where?" *Maummi* shielded her eyes with a wrinkled hand. "My eyes are failing me after all the harsh sun. Is it a big town?"

Emma glanced down at her. *Maummi*'s eyes had started to fail her long before today, but she stubbornly refused spectacles. Not for reason of vanity, Emma was sure. At least, not vanity of looks.

She slipped a supportive arm around her grandmother's waist. "Not too big, I think."

"Big enough." Papa gave a decisive nod. "The Lord has brought us here, and He will provide."

Papa increased his stride, his eyes scanning the buildings in front of him as he walked ahead. They hurried to keep up with him.

A carefully lettered sign at the edge of the settlement announced that they had arrived in Gorham. Emma had never heard of such a place. The town consisted of one wide path carved through the center of a dozen or so buildings. A cluster of saddled horses were tied to posts in front of a building halfway down the dusty street. Beyond that, at the far end of the settlement, a wagon had been pulled up long-ways near a wide covered porch in front of a general store. A man appeared carrying a crate. He loaded it onto the wagon and then disappeared back inside.

"We will ask for help," Papa said.

They started in the direction of the store, dust swirling around their feet with every step. Emma inspected her apron. The white cloth was covered with dirt from the trail. Rebecca's skin had, indeed, turned a rosy red from the sun, and a smear of mud covered one cheek. Emma knew her face appeared no better, as trail dust had mixed with perspiration for the past several hours. A tendril of hair waved free at her temple, and she smoothed it back into place beneath her prayer *kapp.*

Music drew her attention to the building where the horses stood clustered. A pair of half-length wooden doors swung in a wide doorway. She'd heard a piano once, long ago when she was a child and had traveled to Hays with Mama and Papa. She'd hovered outside a window and peered inside, watching a man bang on a black-and-white keyboard while the air was filled with a magical sound. Like now.

The roar of men's voices drifted to her from inside. A woman's laughter tinkled above them. Rebecca drew to a halt, her wide eyes fixed on the doorway.

"It's a *saloon*." An alarming note of awe deepened her whisper.

Maummi stopped to spear her with an outraged look. "*Ach!* Where did you hear the name of such a place?"

She lifted a hand and pointed at Emma. *Maummi* rounded on her, hands planted on her hips. Emma nearly took a step backward, but she managed to hold her ground.

"Hearing is not the same as visiting." A lame defense, to be sure. She couldn't help adding one mischievous observation. "The music is pretty, don't you think?"

Maummi placed a hand over her heart and staggered where she stood. "Jonas, this is not a good place for us. My heart hurts. We must leave immediately, lest the evil ways of the *Englisch* lure our Emma and Rebecca away."

Above his beard, Papa's lips twitched as he suppressed a grin. Then, with an effort, he sobered. "The Lord has led us to this place for a purpose. He will send us help —"

The saloon doors swung outward and a body sailed through. Emma jumped back, a hand over her own heart. A man landed at their feet with a gigantic *poof* of dirt.

When the dust cleared, she stood gaping down into the face of a cowboy, his wet hair plastered to his head.

A grin broke across Papa's face. "See? The Lord has sent us help."

Emma searched the dazed face at her feet. Disappointment stole any consolation Papa's words might have offered.

The Lord might at least have cleaned him up first.

THREE

Stars exploded behind Luke Carson's eyes when his skull cracked against the hard-packed road.

That low-down, no-good . . . I'll wring his scrawny neck!

He lay on his back, eyes closed, breathing dirt and planning retribution on his best friend and top cattle wrangler. He'd taken falls trying to break ornery wild stallions and landed softer than this. He planned on giving Jesse a whupping he wouldn't forget. But that had to come later. Right now he had to fish him out of that saloon and sober him up, or they would never get the herd back on the trail this morning.

When Luke's ears stopped ringing, he opened his eyes and found himself surrounded. Four people stared down at him, their heads silhouetted against the bright blue sky. The old woman had a puckered-up face like one of those potatoes McCann fried up for the men a couple of days ago. Beside her a young girl stood with her mouth gaping wide. An older girl stood directly above him, her face flushed and damp, her narrowed eyes fixed on him with a speculative stare. She and the other females were covered up with black dresses despite the heat, and they wore skimpy little white hats on their heads with dangling laces. The man beside them looked even stranger, with a clean-shaven lip and a bushy beard covering his chin. He wore suspenders over a white shirt and had a wide-brimmed straw hat.

White teeth showed between the man's smiling lips. "Thank the Lord. Help has landed at our feet."

Luke frowned. "What?" The fall had knocked the breath right out of him, and he was preoccupied trying to force gulps of air into his lungs.

"The Lord has saved us," the man repeated. "Thanks be to thee."

Worried creases appeared between the older girl's eyes. "We may need to help him first, Papa. He isn't breathing properly."

"Don't . . . need . . . help . . ." Luke panted as he rolled to his side and then struggled up to his knees. His lungs finally relaxed, and he drew in a couple of deep breaths. He'd get Jesse for this if he had to hog-tie him in his sleep first.

The oddly dressed people watched as he climbed to his feet. The moment he was vertical, the man stepped in front of him. "Will you help us, sir?"

Luke shook his head to clear the last of the fuzz away. He didn't have time for beggars. He had two thousand head of Texas longhorns to drive to market and little time to do it.

"Sorry. Can't help," he mumbled. Dusting off his hat, he jammed it on his head and turned to walk away.

The man lifted his forefinger. "Sir!" Luke ignored the call and left them standing in the street while he headed for the saloon. When he stepped inside, he paused for a moment while his sun-dazzled eyes adjusted, and then he located Jesse, who had moved to a corner table and had a woman on his lap.

When he spotted Luke, a wide grin split his youthful features. "You back for more? Leave me alone. Better yet, how about a pay advance so I can have another drink?"

Apparently he'd drunk enough whiskey to pickle his brain. The fight seemed to have left him, but Luke was going to have his satisfaction with the numskull. He was tired of dragging him out of every dance hall and saloon they passed. Disgusted, Luke shook his head. "You don't need another drink."

Jesse spoke in a whiskey-slurred voice to the frill-covered woman in his lap. "My friend here doesn't drink, which means he doesn't approve of me drinkin' either." He appeared to find that funny. He threw his head back and guffawed.

Luke heaved a sigh and held out a hand to the saloon girl. "If you'll excuse us, ma'am, I need to get him back to camp while he's in good health."

"Has he been ill?"

"He's about to be."

She slid off Jesse's lap and then bent to lift his hat and plant a kiss on his forehead. "Stop by next time you're through these parts, sugar — and collect your pay first." She winked and turned with a flounce of her bustle and crossed the room to a table full of poker-playing cowboys.

Jesse grinned up at him. "Didja hear that, Luke? She called me sugar."

Luke shook his head. "Come on, num-skull. It's time to go."

"Where're we going?"

"I'm going to beat the living daylights out of you, and then we're going back to camp."

"That'll be nice." He grinned lopsidedly.

"Let's drink to that."

Luke helped Jesse to his feet and held on to the back of his vest when he wobbled on unsteady legs. "Is he paid up?" he asked the barkeep.

"Nope. Owes thirty-five cents for that last bottle."

Luke dug the coins out of his pocket and tossed them on the polished mahogany bar, and then he hauled Jesse through the doors and out into the sunlight.

The four black-and-white-clad people had not moved.

Now that he was no longer dazed from his fall, he recognized their clothing. He'd passed through settlements of similarly dressed folks a few times. They belonged to some religious group. He stopped short.

Stirring, Jesse slurred, "Luke, do you see what I see? We're being overrun by nuns."

He gave Jesse a shake that would have knocked him off his feet if he hadn't had a good grip on his shirt. "Watch your mouth. They're God-fearing folk."

The man approached, and the females followed behind. The soft lilt of an accent gave the words a foreign sound. "Sir, our wagon and oxen were taken by thieves. Will you help us?"

Luke met trusting brown eyes and felt a

stirring of discomfort. "Sorry, mister. I have a herd of two thousand head milling around a couple of miles from here, and I'm running behind on getting them to market."

The smile faded, replaced by a forlorn countenance, complete with sad eyes.

Jesse took a step toward the ladies and spoke to the taller girl. "You're kind of young to be a nun, aren't you?"

"I'm not a nun. I'm Plain."

Jesse's head cocked sideways as he stared at her face. "Aw . . . you wouldn't be so plain if you'd smear on a bit of rouge and put on a pretty dress instead of wearing that black sack. You ain't ugly." He flashed a grin.

The younger girl giggled, and the old woman drew herself up with a sharp intake of breath and a look that would have seared a rock.

Luke smacked the back of Jesse's head and knocked his hat down over his eyes. "Not that kind of plain, you numb wit. That's what they call themselves. They're . . ." He searched for the word.

"We are Amish." The bearded man extended a hand. "I am Jonas Switzer. These are my mother and daughters."

The old woman continued to scowl and the younger girl giggled again. The oldest daughter dropped her head demurely in acknowledgement of the introduction. Long dark lashes lay for a moment against the soft curve of her high cheekbones. Jesse was right about one thing. This particular woman was a far sight from ugly.

Luke shook Jonas Switzer's hand. A strong grip, his skin rough and calloused. The hand of a man who has known hard work. "Luke Carson." He jerked a nod toward Jesse. "This disrespectful knothole is Jesse Montgomery."

"Hey! Is that any way to talk about your best point rider?" Jesse jerked away from his grip, wavered on his feet for a second, and then caught his balance.

If it hadn't been true, Luke would have been quick to correct him, but besides being a pain in the backside, Jesse *was* the best point rider in his outfit and a longtime friend.

"You say thieves took your wagon?"

"*Ja.* They went that way." Jonas pointed toward the western horizon. "They left us with nothing."

Luke took off his hat and scratched his head. "I understand your dilemma, mister, but I don't have time to help. I'm being paid to get Simon Hancock's cattle up to the railhead in Hays. We've been on the trail for two months. Our lead group got spooked

49

yesterday, and we rode a hard stampede right up until dark and then spent half the night gathering strays. We're at least a dozen miles off course, and I have less than a week to get the herd to market."

True, the train wouldn't leave until Monday, and at the pace they had kept they would arrive by Friday if nothing else delayed them, but there was no sense cutting it closer than he had to.

The younger daughter stepped up beside her father. "Papa said the Lord would send help, and when we saw you we knew for certain that He'd answered our prayers."

The old woman plucked at her sleeve. "Still your tongue, Rebecca."

" 'Tis the truth. Isn't that right, Emma?" Despite her protest, she stepped back beside her grandmother and lowered her head demurely.

"She does speak the truth." Emma's soft, low voice fell on his ears like a warm breeze on a chilly night. "What we've lost are only things, but without them we have nothing. If the Lord places it in your heart to help us, you will have our gratitude."

Dark blue eyes rose to meet his. The trust he saw in them, and also in her father's, stirred something in his chest. Something he didn't like.

The voice of reason came from an unlikely source. "Sorry, folks. We don't have time to chase down a wagon and steal it back from a bunch of thieves." Jesse plucked off his hat, smoothed his hair, and put it back on his head. The slur had become less pronounced, but his movements were still slow and overly careful.

Once again, Luke couldn't argue with him. These seemed like nice people, but he didn't have time to spare. "I'm sorry," he told Jonas. "I wish I could help."

"Ach!" The grandmother slapped a hand to her chest and wilted against her elder granddaughter. "My hutch will end up as firewood for the man with black teeth." The girls each took an arm to support her, and she sagged between them.

Jesse inspected her. "Your ma doesn't look so good," he told Jonas. "You want me to get the doc? He's inside the saloon playing poker."

The woman's eyes went round as she cast a startled glance toward the establishment. She drew in an outraged breath and straightened, giving an offended sniff. *"Danki,* no."

"You're welcome." The cowhand staggered sideways a step.

Luke steadied him. What he needed was a

couple of hours of hard riding to sweat the whiskey out of his blood, but they couldn't leave the Switzers stranded in the middle of the street with nothing. Especially when they thought the Lord had sent him to their aid. Luke didn't think it all that likely the Lord would send him here to retrieve a drunk cowhand *and* rescue a stranded Amish family, and he certainly didn't think the Lord expected him to desert his herd long enough to deliver them forty miles east to Troyer. Still, he wouldn't feel right walking away without doing something.

He dug cash out of his vest. "I really am sorry I can't help." He pulled out some folding money and thrust it into Jonas's unresisting hands. "Here's enough to pay for a couple of nights lodging and to send a message for someone to come get you."

Jonas stood looking at the money as though he'd never seen cash before. Luke touched two fingers to his hat brim and nodded a farewell to the women, and then he grabbed Jesse by the arm and marched him away. With a minimum of trouble, he got his unsteady buddy in the saddle. When he'd mounted himself, he pointed Bo toward the eastern edge of the settlement. Jesse fell in beside him, though he was starting to look a bit pasty, and his hat sat unevenly on his head.

At the end of town, Luke glanced over his shoulder. The Switzers had not moved. They stood watching him leave, looking for all the world like lost children. Guilt knifed him in the gut. They looked as though they had no idea what to do with the hand they had been dealt.

Chances were, they didn't.

From what he could recall, Amish folks kept pretty much to themselves. Had Jonas and his womenfolk ever stayed in a boardinghouse before? Did they even know what a telegraph was?

Ride on, Luke. You've done all you can, and more than most would. You can't spare the time to help them find their wagon.

But at the sight of the girls in long black dresses with their white head coverings, and of Jonas in his suspenders, his conscience refused to be soothed. With a sigh, he halted.

"Wait here."

Jesse drew his horse up to a stop. "Where you going?"

"Don't ask questions. I won't be a minute."

He turned Bo and headed back toward the waiting family. They watched his return with fixed gazes. When the horse stopped in front of them, all four heads turned upward,

53

their eyes fixed on him expectantly.

"The boardinghouse is there." He pointed at a building down at the western end of the short road.

They looked but didn't move.

He spoke slowly, as if to children. "You go inside and ring the bell. The owner's name is Mrs. Minerva Gorham. Tell her you need a place to stay and that you want to send a *tel-e-gram.* She'll help you out."

Emma's head shot upward. An angry flame erupted in her eyes, and her lips tightened. "Come, Papa. We need to get *Maummi* out of the sun." She gripped her grandmother's arm, turned, and set off toward the boardinghouse at something short of a march, pulling the old woman along with her.

Luke stared after her. What had ruffled her fur? She looked as mad as a barn cat in a rain barrel.

Jonas followed their progress for a few seconds and then turned back to him. "I thank you, Mr. Carson. The Lord truly did send us help." He folded the money, removed his straw hat, and tucked it carefully inside. When he'd replaced the hat on his head, he looked back up at Luke. "After you deliver your cows in Hays, go a few miles farther to Apple Grove. Ask for the farm of

Bishop Miller. He will see your money returned to you."

Luke chuckled. "Just like that? I walk in and say, 'I helped Jonas Switzer over in Gorham, and I'm here to get my money back,' and he'll hand it over?"

A small smile curved the man's lips above the bushy beard. "We are Amish. We repay our debts."

A sound from behind Luke drew his attention. He turned in the saddle in time to see Jesse waver, and then tip sideways and tumble out of the saddle. He landed in the dirt with a thud.

Jonas chuckled. "It appears your friend needs your help too."

Disgusted, Luke shook his head. Yesterday he'd chased a stampede as bad as he'd ever witnessed and then spent the night rounding up strays, and now he had to play nursemaid to a drunken cowhand. "Yeah. It appears so."

He touched his hat in farewell again and rode off.

Anger buzzed in Emma's ears as she marched down the street, dust swirling around her feet with every step. That rude *Englischer,* sitting tall on his horse and staring down at them as though they were stupid. The Lord certainly would not send someone like him to help. If he'd given his money to her, she would have thrown it back at him. How could Papa stand to take it?

"Granddaughter, you'll walk my legs off my body and pound my heart through my apron," *Maummi* complained.

Contrite, Emma slowed her pace. Her grandmother's face did look flushed, and her chest heaved with exertion. Perhaps they really should call for the doctor.

But what kind of doctor must be retrieved from a saloon?

Rebecca ran up from behind and fell in step with them. "Weren't they handsome?"

Alarmed, Emma gave her sister a startled look. Dark tendrils of hair clung to her damp forehead, and her eyes sparkled with something that should not be there. "They are not handsome. They are *Englisch*."

Even as the words left her tongue, she admitted privately that they were untrue. Though he was arrogant and rude, she could not deny that Luke Carson was a handsome man. Or he would be, if he would wash away the dirt and cut his hair in a proper manner, like Papa's. And those dark eyes, the rich deep color of chocolate.

Straight seeing too, unlike poor Amos Beiler's.

"My dearly departed, Carl, was *Englisch*." *Maummi's* mouth curved into a smile at a memory only she could see. "A more handsome man you never saw."

Emma had heard the tale many times, how *Maummi* met a handsome young *Englisch* man while on *rumspringa* and had chosen marriage to him over church baptism. Their marriage was short lived, for Grandpa Carl had been killed less than two years later, leaving *Maummi* with a toddler and a baby on the way. Thank goodness she'd had the sense to return to her family and her faith then, so Papa and Aunt Gerda had been raised in an Amish district.

"Surely our grandfather was not like these men." They arrived at the boardinghouse, and Emma helped her grandmother up the wooden steps and into the shade of the deep porch. "He didn't spend his time in saloons."

"Certainly not." *Maummi* sank into one of four rockers behind the railing and eyed Rebecca. "Most *Englisch* are rowdy in their ways, and to look on them overmuch will invite temptation. Remember your instruction, girl. 'Keep your eyes cast down until the Lord raises them. Then you will see only what He wants you to see.' " She quoted the oft-repeated proverb in the tone of one about to launch into a lesson on humility.

Though Emma might agree with the lesson when it came to her fanciful younger sister, she herself had no desire to hear it repeated. She hurried toward the door. "I'll speak to Mrs. Gorham. Rebecca, stay here with *Maummi*."

With a resentful stare, Rebecca sank into the second chair while Emma made a hasty retreat toward the boardinghouse door.

" 'Tis unfair." Rebecca's surly voice trailed after her.

"What?" *Maummi* asked absently.

"That the *Englisch* are so . . . charmingly rowdy."

FOUR

A few miles outside Gorham, Luke returned to a sluggish herd and seven even more lethargic men. Yesterday's stampede had sapped the energy out of them and run a few pounds of meat off the beef besides. He'd suffered some hard days in the saddle in the months since they started out from Texas, but yesterday's incident was the worst. And they were within a few days of their goal. He couldn't afford to let it happen again. The cattle had already lost weight on the long trail, and no time was left to fatten them up again before they were counted and loaded on the train in Hays.

When the two men approached the herd, the others greeted Jesse with sullen stares. His job had been to accompany the cook into Gorham to replenish supplies and escort him back. Unfortunately, while Mc-Cann arranged for the provisions, Jesse wandered into the saloon and then insisted he'd catch up later. The minute Luke saw the chuck wagon roll into sight without an escort, he knew what happened and headed in to town to fetch his employee. By then Jesse had seen the bottom of at least a dozen shot glasses.

Jesse passed Willie, jerked a nod, and continued on toward the chuck wagon. Following behind, Luke held Bo in check while he scanned the herd's condition. The cattle were spread out for almost a mile across the prairie, with the majority of them clustered in the center. Their heads hung down, and he saw a few gaping mouths, sure signs of fatigue and thirst. Still, they weren't looking too bad, considering the rough night they had.

He checked the position of his men. Willie and Charlie rode drag, following at the rear to keep the herd moving. Griff and Morris were flank riders, maintaining a position at either side to make sure the herd didn't spread out too far. Off to the left, directly behind the chuck wagon, Vic was the wrangler in charge of the forty-horse remuda.

Because Luke and Jesse had been gone for a few hours, Kirk, who normally rode flank, had taken the position of point rider. He appeared to be doing a fine job keeping an eye on the lead cows. A good point rider was critical, because if a lead went astray, the entire herd would follow.

Pa would be proud. This might be his first time to personally be responsible for the herd, but Luke planned to make it successful. Following in his father's footsteps wasn't easy, and he wasn't certain it was what he wanted, but for the time being he'd do what he'd done since he was a youth: herd cattle to market. Only this time he was trail boss, not Pa.

Luke overtook Willie, the youngest of his men. "How are they doing?"

This was only Willie's second cattle drive, but he'd done a good job on the trail. He made no secret of the fact that he intended to hire on as a flank rider on his next drive, now that he had some experience under his belt. Luke would recommend him without hesitation. The drag position was the least favorite on a drive, because the men at the rear rode in the dust and stench of the herd.

"Tired." Willie didn't bother to hide a big yawn and then an even bigger grin. "I'm not the only one either."

Luke gave the kid a sympathetic smile. "Hang on. I'm going to call it a day soon."

He kneed Bo into a gallop and caught up with Jesse as they neared Griff, who was riding flank on the left. An experienced cattle wrangler, Griff countered his grizzled experience with a rough manner that offered no quarter.

"Hold up a minute, Jesse," Luke called.

Jesse slowed. Griff gave him a narrow-eyed glare and spat into the dusty grass as they approached. "I see you found him."

"Yeah. He's not feeling too good at the moment, if it's any consolation."

As if to prove Luke's point, Jesse moaned and pushed his hat further down on his forehead.

Griff's glare deepened. "Nope. No consolation."

"Hey, you'd deny a fellow a couple hours' of fun because you can't join him?" Jesse shook his head and clucked as he fell into step beside them. "Selfish. That's what these men are."

"Selfish or not," Luke replied, "they have been working all afternoon while you've been throwing your money away on whiskey and women."

"No women." He heaved a dramatic sigh and pulled a mournful face. "I ran out of money."

Luke wasn't in the mood to humor him. He'd worked hard not to show favoritism during the past two months on this drive, and he couldn't ignore Jesse's infraction.

Everyone knew they had been friends for years, ever since they worked their first cattle drive together as boys. A good trail boss treated his men equally and made sure everyone was treated fairly. For this stunt, Luke was going to assign him a double watch tonight, and deliver an even more pointed message now.

He speared Jesse with a look. "Willie needs a change of scenery. Go relieve him, and tell him I said to move up to the right flank."

Jesse's jaw gaped. "Me? A drag rider? You're pulling my leg, right? I'm the best point rider on the Chisholm Trail."

Luke kept his face expressionless. "You are when you're sober." He poured an unspoken warning into an unblinking stare. For a moment he thought his friend would argue. Then Jesse snapped his jaw shut, jerked his horse's reins, and headed for the back. Griff guffawed and then sat a little straighter in the saddle.

"He's too cocky for his own good," the cowhand commented.

Luke nodded. "Problem is, he's right. He is the best."

Griff shrugged. "He's all right."

That was about as close to a compliment as Griff ever gave. Luke nodded and then kneed Bo into a gallop to join Kirk on point.

They hadn't made five miles that day when Luke thought it wise to call a halt. Dusk was setting in, and the cattle were dragging their hooves in the dust when they came to a wide, shallow river. A grassy plain on this side provided plenty of late summer grass for grazing, so the herd could fill their bellies and hopefully rest easier that night. He gave instructions to let the cattle have their fill while McCann set up camp and rounded up a hearty supper of beans and biscuits with thick pan gravy that the cook called Texas butter. Luke took the first watch alongside a sullen Jesse, and he encouraged the men to cut their tale-telling around the campfire short in favor of a good night's rest.

The next morning the sun rose in a clear blue sky. After a cup of strong coffee, Luke toed Jesse awake with the tip of his boot. Loud snores stopped abruptly as his buddy snorted to wakefulness.

"Wha's wrong?" His sober early morning voice was even more slurred than it had been the previous afternoon. He sat straight up on his bedroll, his spiky hair bearing witness to a rough night. "Stampede? Not again."

Grinning, Luke had to get his goat. He had one — no, ten times coming for the headaches he'd caused him. "Wrong? Why, not a thing. It's a grand morning, and time to get a'move on!"

Jesse groaned, settled back on his bedroll, and plopped his hat over his face. "A few more minutes, Ma."

Luke toed the hat off his face and hauled him up into a sitting position with one hand. Then he thrust a mug of hot coffee in Jesse's hands. "Drink this. McCann brewed up axle grease this morning, but it'll get your blood pumping. Then saddle up. I want you to scout upstream to see if there's a better place to cross the herd."

A low, miserable moan came from Jesse's throat. He sipped at the coffee and then gave his body a shake. "You're after me this morning, aren't you?"

Luke grinned again. "Yep."

With a sigh Jesse took another swig and then struggled to his feet. "Okay, okay. I'll do it, but only because I wouldn't put it past you to put me riding drag the rest of the way."

"I'm glad we understand each other." He slapped Jesse on the back with enough force that coffee sloshed out of the mug. "The next time I have to pull you out of a saloon or dance hall, you're gone, Jesse, quicker than you can spit and holler howdy."

Thirty minutes later the herd had roused and started to graze. Luke and McCann were eating biscuits slathered with apple butter when Jesse rode back into camp. He looked better today, his eyes clearer and his cheeks not so sunken. He dismounted, crossed to the campfire, and filled a mug.

"We're at the best crossing." He sipped the steaming brew and then pointed toward the river. "It's wide and shallow here. Up that way it gets deeper, and there's a muddy bank on the other side that will bog down the chuck wagon."

Luke tossed the final bite of biscuit in his mouth and chased it with the last of his coffee. "Sounds good." He raised his voice to address the rest of the drovers, who were in various stages of packing up camp. "We're crossing here. Let's get a move on."

Jesse squatted down beside the fire and grabbed a biscuit. "You won't believe what I found a half mile or so up the way." He tore the bread open and piled on a dollop of apple butter before McCann snatched the can away from his grasp with a grunt.

"What's that? Another herd?"

"Nah, better than that." Jesse popped half the biscuit in his mouth and spoke as he chewed. "I found those *Aim*-ish people's wagon. Looks like the thieves tried to take it across the river, got it stuck on the far bank, and then just left it there."

"Are you kidding? Was there anything left in it?"

"Oh, yeah. A monster piece of furniture, and what looks like a trunk in the wagon bed. Some empty crates and such lying around the ground. I didn't cross over to get a closer look."

The faces of the Switzers flashed in Luke's mind. Jonas with his trusting gaze, assuring him that the Amish paid their debts. And Emma, her eyes framed by those long, curling lashes, looking at him and saying in her low voice, *"If the Lord places it in your heart to help us, you will have our gratitude."*

They might never know that their wagon and at least some of their belongings were only a few miles away. Not unless someone told them.

"Aw, no." Jesse took a step forward and made a show of peering closely into his eyes. "I see the thoughts churning up a dust storm in that brain of yours."

Luke straightened and replied with an innocent arch of his eyebrows. "What are you talking about?"

"You're thinking about going back there

and fetching those *Aim*-ish people out here to their wagon, and I'm standing here telling you it's a bad idea."

"You're accusing me of bad judgment? And it's *Ah*-mish, not *Aim*-ish. What's so bad about the idea?"

Jesse jerked his head toward the herd that had spread out and started wandering as they grazed. Kirk was already on his horse and standing guard over a couple of the leads to make sure they didn't take off in the wrong direction. "You're the trail boss. Your responsibility is here."

A flash of irritation itched the hair on the back of Luke's scalp. He hated it when Jesse was right. Still, he wasn't about to just stand there and endure a lecture by a rowdy cowhand.

"You're a fine one to talk to me about responsibility." He scooped up his Stetson and set it low on his head. "How long could it take to ride back and let them know where their wagon is? You and the men can handle the crossing. I'll wager a steak dinner that Bo and I will be back before the herd's hooves are dry on the other side."

Jesse peered closely at him. "What's behind this, Luke? You don't owe those people anything."

As an answer, Luke set his jaw. No, he

didn't owe them a thing. Still, something had grabbed hold in his mind, and it had bothered him all night. He couldn't shake the thought. The Switzers believed the Lord had sent him to help. What if they were right?

"I won't be gone long."

Jesse put up his hands in surrender. "You're the boss, even if you are as stubborn as an old mule. But mark my words, Luke. This good deed of yours is going to end up costing us. You wait and see."

He shoved the last half of his biscuit in his mouth and tossed what was left of his coffee on the fire. The embers hissed and fragrant steam arose as Jesse strode toward his mount.

It won't take me any time at all to ride back to Gorham and let the Switzers know where their wagon is. Still, a small part of him worried over Jesse's words. He was the boss, and this was his official first cattle drive. True, they were on schedule to arrive a couple of days before the cattle train left Hays and an hour or so delay wouldn't affect the timing at all.

On the other hand, his pa used to say, "Better early than late. Those what miss a date shouldn't have started at all."

We won't be late. Bo and I'll run back there,

*tell Jonas Switzer where to find his wagon,
and be back here in two shakes of a steer's
tail.*

"Men," he called as he strode toward the
remuda where Bo had been corralled for
the night. "I'm heading back to Gorham on
a quick errand. Jesse's got the reins while
you get the herd across this river. It's slow
and shallow, so crossing won't be a problem.
I'll see you on the other side."

FIVE

Emma sat in one of the rockers on the porch of the boardinghouse and watched Papa pace in the dusty street. Beside her, *Maummi* and Rebecca rocked in silence, their gazes also fixed on Papa. The fourth rocker sat empty. A brilliant sun peeked above the general store at the far end of the settlement, and she squinted against the dazzling rays.

"We must move on to Troyer," Rebecca said for the fourth time. "Aunt Gerda is expecting us. She'll worry."

Frowning, Emma gave her a sideways look. Her sister's enthusiasm for the journey had more to do with getting out of Apple Grove and into the excitement of a bigger community than concern for Aunt Gerda. Troyer offered far more in the way of frolics and singings and, of course, men, than little Apple Grove could hope to match. From the time Papa had first announced his decision to send Emma to Aunt Gerda, Rebecca had wanted to join her, and not necessarily due to sibling affection.

" 'Hard it is to wait on the Lord,' " *Maummi* quoted from her immense store of Amish proverbs. " 'But worse to wish you had.' "

They rocked in silence for a moment.

" 'Tis the Lord's judgment, to my mind." *Maummi* gave a decisive nod. "He never wanted us in Troyer to begin with."

Rebecca responded with a pout and an increase in the speed of her rocking. Emma hid a smile. *Maummi* had not been in agreement with the move to Troyer since the beginning. If it weren't for the loss of her precious hutch, Emma would almost suspect her of arranging the disaster in hopes that Papa would forget the plan and return home.

Her gaze still fixed on Papa, Emma tried to comfort her sister. "If we go home now, Rebecca, maybe that will give you time to convince Papa to let you live with Aunt Gerda instead of me."

"If you're set on returning home, Emma, have you decided in favor of Amos Beiler, then?" *Maummi*'s voice, though carefully even, held a barely concealed laugh.

"No!" Emma replied, too quickly.

The laughter came out, and Rebecca joined in. Emma refused to respond. They would forever tease her about Amos. She sank further into the soft wolly covering of her chair and rocked in silence. It would serve *Maummi* right if she married Amos and filled the house with cross-eyed children for her to tend.

A movement down the street drew their attention. The doors of the saloon opened, and a woman stepped into the street. The morning sunshine caught in an untidy tangle of curls that hung down her back and brightened the abundant lace around the hem of her dress. Emma drew in a gasp when she realized the woman wore nothing but a thin chemise on top, right out in the open for the whole town to see. She raised bare arms and stretched in the sun, and then she called a cheery greeting to a man across the way, standing in the doorway of the general store.

Emma turned to see *Maummi*'s shocked eyes wide, her lips parted. On her left, Rebecca stared with undisguised delight.

"Look at the color of her hair," the girl whispered. "It's like a field of yellow buttercups."

"Don't stare." *Maummi* accompanied her sharp retort by snapping her fingers in front of Rebecca's eyes. "Where the eyes go, the mind follows."

After a moment of standing in the sun, the woman disappeared into the saloon again. With growing dismay, Emma saw that Rebecca watched the doors for another glimpse. Though it was natural to be curious about different lifestyles, Emma worried that her sister's interest in the *Englisch* they had encountered bordered on fascination. The sooner they left Gorham, the better.

The odor of freshly baked bread from the morning's breakfast clung to the air wafting through the boardinghouse's open window. From down the street, the metallic ring of a blacksmith's hammer echoed off the buildings. Papa paced away from them to the end of the street, leaned an arm against the sign that had welcomed them to Gorham, and bowed his head. From the porch, Emma watched him pray, and she formed an unspoken prayer of her own. *Lord, guide Papa in this decision.*

Though *Maummi* and Rebecca both held their own hopes for their destination, Emma wasn't sure what she thought anymore. She'd much rather stay in Apple Grove forever, but if Papa said the move to Troyer was God's will, then how could she disagree? In Troyer she might find love and her future. What girl didn't want to find a godly husband and start the process of building a home?

But what if *Maummi* was right? Was this disaster the Lord's way of changing their plans? Returning to the comfort and familiarity of home would be wonderful, and if the Lord wanted, He could send a husband to Apple Grove. God had a plan, she knew that for sure. All she must do was surrender to His will and submit to the authority He had placed over her. At the moment that authority was her father, and the decision on where she would go rested with him.

Papa lifted his head and strode toward the porch, his feet kicking up dust around the bottom of his trousers with every step. Had he reached a decision? Emma sat straight in her chair, her feet on the wooden planks beneath her, waiting for his approach. Beside her, Rebecca and *Maummi* did the same.

"Well?" *Maummi* demanded when he stood before them. "From which direction will we send for help?"

Papa straightened his shoulders and replied, "The decision is not yet made."

Emma clamped her teeth together and gripped the arms of the rocker. A whole night and part of a morning, and still he didn't know the Lord's direction? Was the Lord silent, or were Papa's ears stuffed too full of indecision to hear? He had ever been overly cautious and slow moving, like the time he took two weeks before deciding whether to hang her swing on the tree in front of the house or the one nearer the barn. Many times during those weeks of waiting she'd wanted to stomp her foot and shout that if he didn't decide, she would. She fought the same desire now.

Guilt flooded her mind at the uncharitable thought. She folded her hands in her lap and lowered her gaze to them so he couldn't see the irritation on her face. Papa was a good provider and she loved him. He did his best to follow the Lord's leading. Obviously she had not yet mastered the lesson she needed most to learn — patience.

Judging by *Maummi*'s tightly pressed lips, Emma wasn't the only one who hadn't learned tolerance. The old woman's jaws bulged with the effort of keeping her mouth closed as Papa mounted the two wooden stairs and sat in the unoccupied fourth rocker.

"We will continue to pray," he announced. "Soon we will have an answer."

Silence returned to the porch, broken only

by the quiet squeak of the chairs as they rocked back and forth on the wooden planks. Emma sent a new request heavenward.

Lord, we can't stay here forever, so please send Your answer soon. *You know how Papa is. You might need to do something obvious in order to get his attention.*

She opened her eyes to see a horse and rider enter the settlement on the far side of the street. The cowboy's lean body sat tall in the saddle, his shoulders broad beneath a leather vest. Though he was still too far away to be seen clearly, Emma's heart flipped inside her chest. Could this be the Lord's answer already?

When he neared enough to be recognized, her rocking chair came to an abrupt halt. What was that cowboy doing here again?

Lord, surely You didn't send him *again. What makes You think he'll be any more help this time than before?*

Luke nodded a greeting at the storekeeper as he passed. Though the morning was half over, there was very little activity on the street. A movement through the blacksmith's open doors caught his eye. Somebody was working, anyway. He spared a longing glance at the bath house. No time for that. At least he'd only have to make do with streams and rivers until they got the herd safely to Hays. That was just three days away.

He glanced ahead, toward the boarding-house, and almost lost his grip on the reins. In the shade of the porch the Switzers were all in a row. What were they doing just sitting there? Four pairs of eyes fixed on him as he rode up the street.

"Mr. Switzer?"

"Good morning, Mr. Carson." Jonas rose from his chair and stepped to the edge of the railing. "Your sleep was good, I hope?"

Luke didn't answer at first. The man didn't even sound surprised to see him. It kind of spooked him, the way they sat there, as though they had been waiting for him. From the look on Emma's face, she wasn't thrilled at his arrival. Not surprised, but not happy about it either.

Well, she'd change her attitude in a minute.

"I did, thanks." He dismounted and lashed Bo's reins over the post. "I have some good news for you folks. Jesse found your wagon this morning."

The women jumped out of their chairs and ran to the edge of the porch.

"My hutch is still there, yes?" Mrs. Switzer's eyes pleaded for him to agree.

"Yes, ma'am. I didn't see it myself, so I don't know what shape it's in, but Jesse said it was there." He glanced at Emma. Her rosy cheeks shone with health after a good night's sleep. "Said a chest was in there too."

Hope flared in her round eyes. She raised clasped hands beneath her chin. "Are our belongings inside?"

She must have something important packed in that chest. He would have loved to assure her that the contents were safe, to see a smile break out. Instead, he had to shake his head. "I don't know, but I wouldn't get my hopes up. Jesse mentioned some empty crates were scattered around." He looked away from her disappointed expression and spoke to Jonas. "He also said the wagon is mired down in a river about a half mile beyond where my herd camped for the night. Looked like the thieves looted whatever they could and deserted the heavy stuff."

"*Ja,* that makes sense." The round straw hat bobbed up and down with a nod. He turned to address his family. "This is why the Lord did not give an answer earlier. He knew we did not yet have all the information we needed. We will get our wagon, and then our destination will be made clear."

"We'll go to Troyer," Rebecca said.

Jonas cocked his head but didn't commit. "Perhaps."

A wide smile brightened the girl's face, and she clapped her hands. Mrs. Switzer regarded her son with a scowl but remained silent. Luke couldn't stop his eyes from straying to Emma. Her expression remained impassive, her lovely lips parted enough for him to glimpse a set of even white teeth. He found himself wondering what her hair looked like when she brushed it out at night.

With a jerk he realized he hadn't delivered all the news. He looked at Jonas. "I don't think that wagon is going anywhere unless you're planning on pulling it yourself. Your oxen are gone, along with all your provisions, probably."

Jonas seemed unconcerned. "We will buy more oxen."

Luke glanced down the lonely street. "Gorham's a pretty small settlement. There is a livery stable behind the blacksmith's shop, though. If you're lucky you might get ahold of a couple of mules."

He shook his head. "I use oxen for my farm. The Lord knows my need. He will provide."

The man seemed awfully confident. The chance of someone having a pair of oxen to sell in tiny little Gorham was slim, but Luke didn't want to argue. Besides, he didn't have time. "I expect you're right. Well, I'll leave you to it, then." He nodded toward Mrs. Switzer and Rebecca, and touched a finger to his hat brim when his gaze slid to Emma. "Ladies, it's been a pleasure."

He started to turn away, but Jonas stepped in front of him. "The Lord will bless you for the help you have given already." A flush rose on the man's face, above the point where the untrimmed beard gave way to tanned skin. "May I ask for your help one more time? We have no money to pay for the oxen the Lord will send, or for provisions to replace those taken from us."

Of course they didn't. Everything they owned had been stolen. Luke held back a sigh. It was short-sighted of him not to see this coming. He did have some U.S. notes in his wallet and a stash of gold pieces in his satchel, expenses for the trail. McCann's thriftiness when provisioning the chuck wagon along the way had left them in good shape. The men had each received advances when they camped near towns big enough to afford a man a decent time, but Luke had kept the advances small. Give a man a wad of money when there's a saloon nearby and he's been on the trail for a month, and the herd might not move for days. As a result of wise money management, he had some put aside. He could help the Switzers and replenish it from his own pocket when he got to Hays. Then he would pay a visit to that Amish bishop.

He eyed Jonas. "You're good for it?"

The man straightened. *"Ja."*

Luke believed him. What decided him, though, was the intent way Emma watched him, as though she wanted him to say yes but expected him to refuse. Something about the way that girl looked at him made him think she didn't trust him. That wasn't fair, because he'd gone out of his way to be nice since the moment he landed in the dirt at her feet. That expression on her face, the slightly narrowed eyes and the way she tilted her head a tad so her laces hung uneven from her *kapp,* stirred up a yearning in him to prove her wrong.

"I expect I can spare enough to buy a decent ox or two." He twisted his lips in a crooked grin and directed it toward Emma. "That is, if the Lord can manage to round up a pair out here in the middle of no-where."

The corners of her lips softened in an almost smile, and she gave a nearly imper-ceptible nod that made Luke stand a little taller in his boots. Whether she shared his skepticism about the oxen or she was grateful for his help, he wasn't sure. Either way, he'd never been more eager to hand over a stack of notes to a stranger.

When he extracted his leather wallet from his saddlebag and started to open it, Jonas put a hand out to stop him. "We are not worldly in the ways of bargaining with the *Englisch.* Best you come along to make sure we are good stewards of your generosity."

Luke arched an eyebrow. "Your English sounds pretty good to me."

Rebecca giggled and then rattled off something in another language to her grandmother, who clucked and shook her bonneted head.

Were they trying to confuse him? They talked about not speaking English *in* English and then spoke in a foreign tongue. Luke took off his hat and scratched his head. "Pardon?"

Emma explained in the low, melodic voice that made him realize he'd been itching to hear her speak again. "*'Englisch'* is the name we use for all who are not Amish."

Color crept up his neck as he smoothed his hair and put his hat back on. She must think he was a fool.

"I'm sorry, but I left my boys to handle a

water crossing, and I need to get back to them." From his wallet, he counted out a generous handful of notes and extended it to Jonas. The man made no move to take the money but simply stared at it.

Emma stepped up to stand beside her pa. "Mr. Carson, our people keep themselves separate from the world. This sometimes puts us at a disadvantage when dealing with the *Englisch.* If you could find it in yourself to help us once more, I know the Lord will bless you for it."

The plea in the beautiful blue eyes gazing up at him put him at far more of a disadvantage than they. How could he refuse a pretty girl's request, even if she was dressed in funny clothes?

Besides, she and Jonas were right. The Switzers would be suckers when it came to the ways in the world. The folks here in Gorham were decent people, but they would do whatever they could to strike a good deal, even at the expense of a family in trouble. That was the nature of a settlement like this, to make money off the few travelers who happened into town. He'd been dickering for deals in settlements like this for a dozen years, ever since his first trail ride at fourteen. Of course, it might take a while to convince Jonas to settle on a pair of mules when he had his heart set on oxen. Providing, of course, they were lucky enough to find even a mule for sale in this tiny, out-of-the-way settlement. More likely they would end up hiring a horse and cart. Still, how long could it take to inquire?

No need to mention it to Jesse, either. Everything will be fine as long as I get back in a decent time.

He slid the notes back in his wallet. "I guess I can spare a few more minutes."

The Switzers expelled a collective breath. He caught his first sight of a dimple in Emma's cheek when she tilted her head sideways and smiled her thanks up at him. Quite an improvement over the suspicious look she'd awarded him earlier. He couldn't help smiling back.

"Shall we go?" He gestured down the street toward the blacksmith shop.

Jonas and Emma both fell into step beside him, and Rebecca practically skipped off the bottom porch step in her hurry to catch up.

Mrs. Switzer halted them with a stern voice. "The girls will stay here and leave the bargaining to the men."

Both Emma and Rebecca came to a halt with a puff of dust at their feet. Rebecca let out a disappointed moan. "Papa, please," she pleaded.

Emma reached out and gave her sister's sleeve a warning shake. "If *Maummi* says to stay, here we will stay." The stern note in her voice brooked no argument, though she cast a quick longing glance of her own down the street.

Luke turned to face the old lady, who stood with her arms folded tightly across her chest. "Ma'am, that shady porch is pretty inviting, I'll give you that, but I'm thinking you might want to go into the store and start selecting some provisions while we check on transportation. That is, unless you're planning on going without food until you get wherever you're going."

The scowl on her face deepened, but the grip of her hands on her arms loosened as she considered his suggestion.

"Oh, I'm sure Papa can arrange for our provisions," Emma told him. "After all, whether we go on to Troyer or return to Apple Grove, we'll arrive in another three days . . . at least, as long as the weather stays good and we don't encounter even more trouble. Surely he can get everything we need for only three days."

Though she spoke in a tone free of guile, Luke noticed her eyes went a little rounder with what might be feigned innocence. The effect of her words on her grandmother was obvious. The woman straightened and her hands dropped to her sides. Her eyebrows drew together as she studied Jonas with obvious mistrust. Apparently, she didn't like the idea of leaving the responsibility of food shopping to her son.

After only a moment's hesitation, she marched down the steps and into the street. As she passed, she hooked arms with both girls and dragged them with her.

"We'll need two baskets," she announced. "One for each of you to carry."

If she knew she'd been manipulated by her eldest granddaughter, she didn't deign to show it. Jonas nodded, a smile twitching the corners of his clean-shaven mouth. He exchanged an amused glance with Luke and then started after them.

Luke followed, watching the three black-clad women stride down the street, arm-in-arm. There was nothing dull-witted about that Emma. She knew how to get what she wanted.

Six

Emma stood in the open doorway, a basket slung over her arm, while Rebecca followed *Maummi* around the small store. The shopkeeper sat on a stool behind a wide counter arranged with a variety of goods, puffing on a pipe. The tangy odor of vinegar from the pickle barrel mingled with the sweet-smelling smoke. Canned goods were stacked in crates along one side, and bins of beans and flour lined the rear wall. While *Maummi* inspected the store's assortment of pans and roasting spits, Emma leaned out of the doorway and strained to catch the sound of male voices coming from the nearby blacksmith's shop.

Luke had certainly surprised her with his news of their wagon, and especially with his generosity. She'd watched closely to see if he treated Papa with any hint of arrogance, and she could detect none. Perhaps she had judged him harshly yesterday.

The low drone of the men's conversation drifted to her. She was able to identify Papa's higher-pitched voice from Luke's low drawl, but she couldn't make out a single word.

Frustrated, she took a cautious step backward. Her grandmother was so engrossed in searching for bargains on the store's shelves that maybe she wouldn't notice if Emma edged away to see how the negotiation was progressing.

"Emma!"

She jerked upright. Though she hadn't appeared to be watching, *Maummi* turned a stern glance on her. Disapproval darkened her scowl. "Lift that pan down for me. The one on the hook." A gnarled finger pointed at a heavy iron skillet hanging perfectly within the old lady's reach.

Flushing damply beneath her high collar, Emma crossed the floor to comply. The shopkeeper hurried out from behind his counter, his pipe clutched in one hand, and arrived at *Maummi*'s side a step ahead of her.

"Allow me, ma'am. This here's a mite heavy for a little thing like you." He lifted the pan off the hook, and placed it in *Maummi*'s hands. "A fine piece of cookware. Of course, it needs seasoning, but I expect an experienced cook like yourself knows that."

"Hmm." *Maummi* gave Emma a final warning look and then turned her attention to examining the cookware. She weighed it in her hands. "Not as heavy as mine."

"Ah, but this one packs lighter for traveling. Besides, it's the skill of the cook that matters the most, not the weight of the skillet."

While the two discussed the various features of the frying pan, Rebecca sidestepped toward Emma and spoke in a whisper. "You think he's handsome, don't you? Mr. Carson, I mean." She cast a look toward the door with a grin.

Emma drew herself up. "Of course not. He's *Englisch.*"

"*Englischers* can be handsome too." She hooked the basket handle over one arm and covered a giggle with her free hand. "That one who rode away with him yesterday was most delightful to look upon. I wonder if he's married."

"You shouldn't say such things, Rebecca." Emma pitched her voice low and adopted a stern tone. "You shouldn't even think them. Only think such things about Amish boys."

Maummi turned her head to spear them with a look and then resumed her conversation with the shopkeeper. Emma sauntered over to the crates stacked on the floor and picked up a tin of peaches. A dent creased one side.

Rebecca followed, her basket clutched in front of her apron. "I'll bet neither of them are married. I've heard those cattle drives take the cowboys away from home for months and months. They would miss their families too much if they had them, so 'tis better not to marry until they are finished with life on the trail."

Emma was impressed in spite of herself. "Where did you learn that?"

Rebecca shrugged. "I heard Jakob Miller talking to Aaron Zook after church one Sunday."

Of course twelve-year-old boys would be full of thoughts of cowboys and cattle drives. And thirteen-year-old girls would be full of thoughts of marriage. Emma put the tin back in the crate and selected one without a dent. "I'm sure many cowboys are married."

Her sister swung the basket from her arm. "I don't think Mr. Carson is. Otherwise he wouldn't look at you the way he does."

Heat crept up Emma's neck and into her face. Yes, she'd seen the way his gaze strayed toward her. Seen and enjoyed it too, even though enjoying the attentions of an *En-*

glischer felt slightly naughty. If Rebecca had noticed, then of course *Maummi* had. No wonder she hadn't allowed them to go along with the men to the livery stable.

Emma replaced that can as well and moved toward a stack of tightly wrapped packages, with labels identifying them as dried apples. "I don't know what you mean."

Rebecca heaved a forlorn sigh. "Well, I wish his friend had noticed me like that."

"Rebecca!" She regarded her sister with a shocked stare. Dreams of marriage were one thing, but to voice such a wish about an *Englisch* man? One of *Maummi*'s proverbs leaped to mind, and she delivered it in a stern tone. " 'Think only pure thoughts, and purity will guide your life.' "

Rebecca's eyes rolled toward the ceiling, and she moved away from Emma's side.

Only pure thoughts? Emma glanced through the doorway in the direction of the blacksmith shop, where Luke Carson and Papa stood bargaining.

If enjoying the attentions of a handsome *Englisch* man wasn't pure thinking, perhaps she should heed her own advice.

"Nah, I don't have any oxen for sale here." The blacksmith, a huge man with thighs nearly as big around as Bo's neck, tossed his hammer into the loose sawdust that covered the floor. "I have one mule, but he ain't for sale."

Luke tried to keep an I-told-you-so look off his face, but he wasn't sure he succeeded. He felt bad when he watched Jonas's confident expression fade to one of dismay. Kind of a shame to see a man disappointed in his beliefs like that.

The smith dusted calloused hands on the thick apron tied around his middle. "But old Weaver has a team of oxen he's been talking about selling."

Luke felt his jaw go slack.

An oversized grin spread across Jonas's face. "The Lord provides for all our needs."

Had he just been fed a dish of roasted crow by an Amish man? Or did defeat come from a higher source? With a suspicious upward glance, Luke asked the smith, "Where can we find Weaver?"

"His place isn't far. About two miles south of here."

From the look on Jonas's face, Luke knew his next request without being asked. Would he go with Jonas to Weaver's place? The words were on his tongue to say sorry, but no. He couldn't keep the herd waiting any longer. Besides, Jesse would rib him for days.

But Jonas's faith was a lot stronger than his. What if the Lord did want him to help the Switzers, as they said? Who was he to turn away from that? Besides, he'd given his word to help with the bargaining for a pair of oxen if they could be found. A man who went back on his word wasn't worth steer's spit.

Resigned, he gestured toward the back of the shop, where he'd glimpsed the livery stable through the open door. "You got a horse we can hire for my friend? We shouldn't need it for more than a couple of hours."

"Sure do." The man untied his apron and hung it on a hook.

When the smith headed for the stable, Jonas placed a hand on his arm. "Thank you."

"Happy to do it."

As he spoke the words, Luke realized they weren't entirely untrue. These folks had a way about them, something appealing in their openness that made him want to help. Well, all except that old woman, but he had the idea she might be sour by nature and not only with him. Of course, being on the receiving end of Emma's grateful smile was something of a reward in itself.

That thought brought him around to the details of getting the Switzers and, perhaps, their new oxen, out to their wagon. They would need to hire a cart or something to carry the women. A driver would be necessary in order to return the cart and horse to Gorham. All this wouldn't be cheap. And then there were the provisions.

He hoped Jonas was true to his word about paying him back.

"Why don't you go on and see about that horse. I'll go check on how your ma's coming and let them know our plans."

The round-brimmed straw hat bobbed up and down as he nodded, and then Jonas followed the blacksmith out the back door in the direction of the stable.

When Luke entered the general store, he found Mrs. Switzer standing before a counter full of cans and packages, chatting with the storekeeper as though they were neighbors. Her pleasant expression took him by surprise. So, maybe it *was* him she didn't like.

Emma and Rebecca stood at the far wall, fingering a bolt of fabric. From a side view, he saw that those black dresses weren't really as shapeless as he'd first thought. True, the white apron added a layer of bulk, but at this angle he had a fine view of Emma's trim waist, and nothing could hide her soft, womanly curves. When she looked up and caught sight of him, a pretty blush rose on her high cheeks, and she quickly lowered her eyes.

The old woman, on the other hand, didn't bother to hide a scowl.

"I have good news," he announced. "The blacksmith told us of some oxen for sale not far from here. Jonas and I are heading over there to see them. We'll be back as soon as we can, and you should be on your way by early afternoon."

He sincerely hoped they would *all* be on their way by then.

"Papa was right!" Rebecca clapped her hands, her eyes dancing. Then she sobered. "I'm sorry, Mr. Carson. I didn't mean to point out your wrongfulness."

Emma gasped.

He grinned. "I know enough to admit defeat when I see it, little lady, and I won't doubt the Lord's provisions again, especially when claimed by a godly man. But please call me Luke." His gaze slid to Emma's. "All of you."

She turned her back on him to focus on the bolt of fabric again, but not before he caught a smile and the deepening of her blush.

Mrs. Switzer drew in a breath that seemed to inflate her body to double its height. She glanced toward Emma and then speared him with a sharp gaze. *"Danki* for your help. We're in your debt, *Mr. Carson."*

Her meaning was unmistakable. No familiarities would be welcome from this old woman. And she wouldn't tolerate any with her granddaughter either.

The shopkeeper, a jovial man with a girth almost as wide as the blacksmith's, though without the benefit of muscle, gestured toward the goods piled on the counter. "These ladies have made good use of the time and my inventory. Though this one drives a hard bargain, I can tell you that. She'll rob me of a profit today." His grin belied his words.

Though he'd like nothing better than to stay and try to tempt another smile from Emma, Luke felt a tug of impatience to get this goodwill task accomplished and get back to his herd. "Keep a careful record, if you will. I'll settle up when we return. And I'd appreciate it if you can have the goods packed and ready to load so we can be on our way quickly." Moved by a spontaneous thought, he strode forward and extracted three sticks of candy from a jar on the shelf. "Add these to the total."

When he handed Rebecca hers, she giggled and dipped in a quick curtsey. *"Danki."*

He ducked his head to catch Emma's eye and held out the treat. She kept her head bowed and partially turned away, but she gave him a brief glimpse of those lovely blue eyes. Her fingers brushed his as she took his offering. Was the contact an accident or on purpose? He decided to believe the latter when she replied with a quiet, *"Danki, Luke."*

Rebecca giggled again, and Mrs. Switzer's scowl gained new depths. When Luke offered her the third stick of candy, her lips pressed together and her nose wrinkled as though it smelled like stinky cheese gone bad.

With a shrug, he stuck the stick candy into his mouth, tipped his hat in her direction, and exited the store.

Seven

"Those two over there are a fine pair." Old man Weaver pointed a gnarled finger at a couple of oxen standing near the barn.

"They look good to me," Luke conceded. "What do you think, Jonas?"

They had found Weaver's place with no problem, though the trip had taken longer than he'd hoped. Though Jonas could keep his seat in the saddle, he wasn't the horseman Luke was. Apparently the Amish didn't ride much, though he mentioned owning a horse that pulled his family's buggy. Every time Luke glanced upward at the sun, it had crept up a little farther in the sky, and his sense of frustration mounted. His Triple Bar herd had certainly crossed the river by now. If he was lucky, the boys had taken the initiative to keep them moving instead of waiting around for him. The way things were going, this good deed was going to cost him one of the three spare days they had.

Jonas didn't answer for a long moment as he examined the animals. Finally, he shook his head slowly. "These are not for me. They are *eltlich*."

Eltlich? Luke studied the pair more closely. "They look like oxen to me."

A small smile curved Jonas's clean-shaven lips. "They are old."

Weaver didn't deny it. "This pair's seen some years come and go, but there's a lot of work in them yet. They'll do you fine."

Jonas's pleasant expression didn't fade as he eyed Weaver. "The animals taken from me were young and strong, and they worked hard on my farm. I will pay for new ones, but they must live a long time. I have not the money to replace my oxen again in two years, or even five."

A new respect for his Amish friend rose in Luke. He might not be accomplished when it came to negotiating a deal, but there was nothing wrong with his eye for farm animals. And judging by the glint of steel in those honest eyes, he wasn't about to settle for less than he wanted. So much for Luke's hope that this transaction would take no more than a few minutes.

He scanned the area around the barn. "What about those over there?" He pointed to four animals clustered around the feed trough.

Weaver lifted a shoulder. "Good animals, and younger. They'll cost you a bit more, though."

Of course they would. Luke clamped his jaw shut.

Jonas took off across the field, leaving Luke and Weaver to follow. When he drew near to the feeding animals, a couple skittered sideways a few steps. He spoke to them in a low, soothing voice in his own language, and when the oxen calmed, he walked in a full circle around them, his gaze traveling over every inch of their sturdy bodies. He squatted down on his haunches and inspected their underbellies, and spent a long time examining their strong legs.

When he approached Luke and Weaver, his expression was confident. "*Dat* one." He pointed. "And *dat* one."

Weaver dipped his head. "You have a good eye, mister."

"All right." Luke turned to face Weaver. Now it was his turn, and he intended to get them for the best price he could, and as quickly as he could. "So how much for the pair?"

Jonas held up a hand. "First, I must see them pull together."

Weaver's smile broke forth and he nodded approval. "Not only a good eye, but a good head for buying livestock. Never buy a team without seeing them work."

Luke stifled a groan. Next thing he knew, Jonas would insist on plowing a field to try them out.

Weaver clapped a friendly hand on the Amish man's back. "Come on and give me a hand with the yoke." They set off together for the barn.

Luke didn't bother hiding his sigh as he trudged after them.

With their purchases packaged and piled around them in front of the general store, Emma and Rebecca perched on crates and sipped a sweet drink, compliments of the storekeeper. The man had brought a straight chair outside for *Maummi,* who drank her soda pop with obvious pleasure. Emma savored the liquid on her tongue and tried to identify the source of flavor. Orange for certain, and bubbly stuff that backed up in her nose if she drank too quickly. Eyes watering, she took another delightful sip.

*Maummi'*s voice sliced into her analysis like a knife through a hot cake. "Emma, mind you your learning about Amish and *Englischers?*"

There was no question of the reason behind her comment. Emma sipped once again before answering with a lesson that had been quoted to her from infancy. "Amish live in the world but are not of the world. By staying separate, we are more able to honor Christ with lives of purity, humility, modesty, and peacefulness."

After studying her for a long moment, *Maummi* nodded. "See that you mind it well."

Rebecca lowered her bottle. "You didn't stay separate, *Maummi*. You married outside the church."

Maummi's back stiffened, and she fired another shot from her arsenal of sayings. " 'Young folks should use their ears and not their mouths.' "

Under the weight of her grandmother's disapproving glare, Rebecca fell silent. Emma considered the point well made, though she couldn't think of a way to voice her question without giving the impression she harbored feelings for Luke. Which she did not. Not serious feelings, anyway.

After a moment *Maummi* consented to answer the charge. "My Carl was a gentle man, with such humility that he might have been Amish himself." A faraway wistfulness gathered on her face. "Patient too, which trait he passed on. They are alike, my Carl and my Jonas." Then she shook herself. "When he died, *ach!* The pain. I thought I would die with him." She held Emma's gaze with hers. "Where must we go when we are hurt?"

Emma knew the answer as well as she knew the story. "We go home."

Maummi nodded. "Always home. To family, to community. My district made me a part of them, and my children with me. Without them the world would have swallowed us up." She cupped her soda pop in both hands and examined the contents. "I would spare you that pain."

"But surely pain comes to Amish and *Englisch* alike."

"*Ja,* but the *Englisch* way is lonely." She shook her head. "The Amish have each other."

Emma witnessed that truth every day. When the Yoders' barn burned at the beginning of the summer, the entire district helped raise a new one. Not a harvest or a planting passed without neighbors lending a hand, and not a person fell ill without receiving meals from dozens of kitchens in the community. Hadn't all the women of Apple Grove helped Amos Beiler care for his children since Lydia died giving birth to the last one? With a start, she realized *Maummi* and her two little ones had probably received the same care as Amos. Emma's own papa had been a fatherless child, and yet he had never lacked for attention or for strong examples to guide him into manhood.

These were reasons she loved her Amish life and never intended to leave it. When the instruction was offered again in a month or so, she would attend the classes and be baptized into the faith she loved come fall. Why bother with *rumspringa?* Let Rebecca have her time of running around, as most young people did before they were baptized. Emma saw no reason for it. Why sample the ways of the world when the way of happiness had surrounded her like a soft wool blanket all her life? No, her plans were set. She would enjoy the peaceful Amish lifestyle, commit to her faith through baptism, and then wait for the Lord to show her the husband He had selected for her, either in Troyer or back home in Apple Grove.

She leaned forward to cover one of *Maummi's* blue-veined hands. "Don't worry for me." With a sideways smirk at her sister, she added, "Save your worrying for the place it's needed."

Rebecca responded with a grin and a show

of her tongue. Then her face brightened as her gaze fixed on something behind Emma. "There's Papa, along with a new pair of oxen."

Emma turned to see a small parade approach the first of the buildings lining the main street of Gorham. Two sturdy-looking oxen walked side-by-side, with Papa riding horseback beside them. He looked stiff atop his horse, his arms locked at the elbow while he gripped the reins in front of him. But even from this distance she could see his triumphant grin.

Though she didn't wish it, her gaze was drawn to the man bringing up the rear. Far from stiff, Luke sat sure in his saddle, as though his horse was an extension of himself. Even more than his snug tan trousers and elongated hat, his relaxed posture made a striking contrast to Papa.

Emma forced herself to look away. There was no profit to be gained in staring.

Besides, *Maummi*'s watchful gaze burned into the back of her head like a branding iron.

EIGHT

By the time Luke and Bo led the procession
back to the herd, the sun had sunk midway
in the sky toward the western horizon. The
oxen proved to be a docile pair and followed
alongside the small cart they had hired
without much prodding. Jonas perched on
the narrow bench alongside the blacksmith's
son, who had been recruited to help unload
and then return the cart home. The female
Switzers perched in the back amid their
newly purchased provisions. Though he'd
tried to catch Emma's eye a couple of times,
she'd kept her focus on overseeing the loading and her head turned away from him
since they started.

All for the better, as far as Luke was
concerned. A whole day wasted on good
deeds was time enough. He'd been hired to
do a job, and he intended to see it done
sooner rather than later.

They arrived to find last night's campsite

deserted. Luke scanned the rolling hills on the far side of the wide river for signs of the herd and saw none. Good. Jesse had taken the initiative and led them on. But he didn't like the looks of a dark cluster of clouds gathering to the northwest.

"We'll need to cross here." He raised his voice to be heard over the sound of the running water. "Jesse scouted ahead this morning and said there's no good place to ford up ahead."

In fact, the water looked a bit deeper than it had earlier, and the current a touch stronger. That storm must be dumping a load of rain upstream.

"Is our wagon nearby?" Jonas asked.

Luke pointed. "About a half mile that way. Jesse said it was on the far bank." He'd also said it was mired to the axle, but Luke didn't see the need to remind Jonas of that at the moment. He'd see for himself soon enough.

Herding the oxen through the water proved to be an easy task. Luke rode around the cart and came up behind them, and with almost no effort they obediently splashed across with no problem and continued along the herd's trail as obediently as a couple of well-trained dogs.

Bo was a little more hesitant. He wasn't

overly fond of water. Luke had a swimming horse he used for deeper crossings, but of course the remuda was with the herd, with any luck miles away from here.

Bo stepped gingerly across the sandy river bottom, coaxed by Luke's gentle clucking. The kid driving the cart had obviously spent some time on the trail with this rig, because he urged his mule forward with an expert flick of the rope. When Luke reached the bank on the other side, he stopped on the grass and watched as the cart rocked on its way across. In the back, the girls pulled their feet up into the bed to keep from getting wet. Emma leaned over to look into the water, the laces from her cap dangling over the side. In only a few minutes, the cart was up the narrow bank and onto dry ground. All in all, it was one of the easier crossings he'd seen on this drive.

The signs of the herd's passing were impossible to overlook. The ground had been well grazed and trampled dry. Luke instructed the boy on the approximate location of the Switzers' wagon and then rode on. Bo stretched his legs, and the trampled trail sped by beneath them. Luke let him have his head, enjoying the steady pounding of hooves against dirt, accompanied by the sound of running water at their side.

A tickle of disquiet disturbed his solitude when the feel of the wind blowing in his face changed. The rich, wild scent of distant rain tinted the air. As long as the storm carried only rain, the herd wouldn't pose a problem. But all too often storms along the plains were accompanied by fierce lightning and thunder, and that's what startled the beef into a stampede two nights ago. Once a stampede occurred, cattle remained jittery and prone to stampede again for days or even weeks afterward. Another stampede would put them in risk of missing their deadline.

Bo galloped up over a swell in the land, and Luke's feelings of disquiet deepened. Not a mile ahead he caught sight of the tail end of a herd. He'd have to wait until he was closer to spot the Triple Bar brand, but he felt sure these were his cattle. Jesse and the others must have waited around for him after fording the river because they had only gained a few miles all day.

The numb wits! Why didn't they push on?

Immediately, his irritation fled. Luke had no one to blame but himself. The task of leading the herd didn't fall to Jesse. He was the trail boss. The decision of when to move and when to tarry fell on Luke's shoulders alone. And he hadn't been here to direct them.

He caught sight of a cluster of horses and riders at the river's edge up ahead. Hard to tell at this distance, but he thought they might be his men or it could be the location of Jonas's wagon. He urged Bo into a faster pace.

When he arrived he found Jesse, Willie, Charlie, and Griff wet to the skin and covered in mud. They stood on the shore staring down at the Switzers' wagon. Luke took in the problem in an instant. Two of the wagon's wheels had made it up to the bank after crossing the river, though one rested in a muddy low rut. The back wheels were still partly immersed in mucky water, one deeper than the other. In the back of the wagon rested the biggest piece of furniture he'd ever seen. His ma used to have a hutch similar to this one, but only about half this size. Mrs. Switzer's piece leaned at a precarious angle in the tilted wagon. A large trunk sat beside it, up toward the front of the wagon bed.

Jesse broke away from the others and approached when he rode up. Water plastered his shirt to his body, and his boots made an unpleasant squishing noise with each step. After a quick glance at the fury in his face,

Luke decided to keep his seat and speak to his friend from a safe distance on horseback.

"That . . . thing!" Jesse spouted, waving a finger behind him in the direction of the wagon. "It weighs a thousand pounds. There's *no* way that wagon's coming out of the river with that monstrous chunk of oak inside."

The others trailed over, looking as wet and bedraggled. Charlie affirmed Jesse's opinion. "The back wheels are mired pretty deep, boss, one worse than the other. I think the axle might have cracked too."

Luke looked past them, where the water lapped at the lowest boards at the rear of the wagon. Jesse might be exaggerating the weight of that hutch, but not by much if Luke was any judge. It looked to be solid oak, which meant the weight was probably close to six hundred pounds. If the wagon's axle was broken, Jonas would have a hard time fixing it with the hutch inside. No way would he be able to unload and reload it by himself, or even get it out of the river on his own.

A thought occurred to Luke. He glanced behind him. The Switzers were not yet in sight. What if he left now, before they arrived? He'd done all he promised. Getting their wagon unstuck wasn't his responsibility. When they got here they would find their hutch, and Luke would have done his duty.

Even as he considered giving his men the order to mount up and head out, he knew he couldn't do it.

The sooner I get them on their way, the sooner I can get on mine.

"Where have you been, anyway?" Griff squinted suspiciously up at him. "Back in Gorham all this time?"

"I'll tell you where he's been." Jesse unwrapped his bandana from his neck and made a show of squeezing out a stream of water. "He's spent the day playing guardian angel to a bunch of *Aim*-ish people."

He was standing beside Bo's withers. Luke considered taking his boot out of the stirrup and awarding him a well-placed kick for his ornery tone. Instead, he affirmed the words with a nod at Griff and the others. "A man and three women. Bandits stole their belongings early yesterday and left them without a thing. I'm trying to see that they get where they're going."

The old man studied him a moment and then said, "Never hurts to do a good turn." He gave Jesse a hard stare and then let his gaze sweep Charlie and Willie. "A man will never get anywhere in this world if he won't lend a hand now and then. See that you boys remember that."

Now it was Jesse's turn to scowl, and Luke had to bite back a smile when he slapped his wet bandana against his thigh and stomped away toward his horse.

Luke dismounted. "The family will be along in a few minutes with a pair of oxen and a fresh load of supplies. The way I see it, the faster we get this wagon pulled out, the sooner we'll be on our way." He glanced at the young drag rider. "Willie, ride on up ahead to the chuck wagon and tell McCann we need a couple of coils of that thick rope he's got. Maybe we can pull it out with horse power. Be quick, hear?"

Willie nodded and sprinted for his horse.

Jesse shouted toward Luke without bothering to look up from where he fiddled in his saddlebag. "That was my next suggestion!"

Luke exchanged a grin with Charlie and Griff. "I'm sure it was. If you're looking for dry clothes in there, don't bother. We're not done with this yet."

He watched Willie's horse skirt past a couple of dozen head of cattle and then gallop toward the main part of the herd. Stragglers, about a hundred or so, milled around the area, their pace slowed without drag riders nudging them ahead. They had spread out in search of fresh grass farther than he liked.

"Griff, would you and Charlie head over that way and round up those cattle?" He pointed toward the hill. "Bring them back this way in case we need your horses to help haul this thing out of here, and then we'll hurry them along toward the herd together."

When they had gone, Luke found a dry spot to sit and started tugging off his boots. Now that they were alone, Jesse joined him.

"I had a feeling you'd get held up back there this morning." He followed Luke's lead and tugged off first one already soggy boot and then the other. "I tried to warn you, but you wouldn't listen."

Luke pulled off his socks and stuffed them down in his boots. "You did. And I owe you a steak dinner when we get to Hays, like I promised." There. That was as close to *you were right* as he was willing to go.

He stripped off his shirt and spoke without looking at his friend. "Tell me something. Are you carrying a grudge against Amish people in general, or is it the Switzers in particular?"

The answer came immediately. "I got no problems with those folks. It's just that we've come a long way on this drive, and it's gone pretty well so far. You have a lot riding on this job, Luke, and I don't want to see you throw it away on a woman you can't have."

"What makes you think I'm going to throw anything away? Or that I want a woman? We're three days out of Hays, and the train pulls out of there in five." Jesse shot him a look, and he conceded the unspoken point with a nod. "Yeah, okay. I'd like to have a safer margin, but we'll make it. That's what counts." Stripped down to his breeches, Luke stood and folded his clothes into a neat bundle. When he'd placed them on the dry ground near his boots, he turned to give Jesse a hand up.

Jesse took it and held on for a minute, meeting his friend's eyes with a penetrating stare. "It's more than that, Luke. I've known you a long time, and I can tell something's been eating at you for the past few weeks."

Luke fought the urge to look away from his searching gaze. "You're always reading something into my actions. What am I guilty of now?"

"You're quieter than when we started. Moodier. The men have noticed it too. You don't talk much, and you haven't joined in on singing around the campfire at night like you used to. Mostly you sit off by yourself." He hefted himself to his feet.

Luke tried to shrug off the comment with a laugh. "Could be I've taken enough ribbing about my singing voice. A man can stand being likened to a bellowing calf only so long."

Jesse didn't laugh. "I'm trying to decide if you're sorry you took this job. Maybe you only did it because it pleased your pa. Or maybe you're fed up with trail life."

Were his inner struggles that apparent? Luke bent down to retrieve his hat from the ground. The burden of responsibility had weighed heavily on him lately. Things always got dodgy at the end of a drive, when the men had been in the saddle for months with few breaks. Squabbles broke out, complaints about the food increased, and heated arguments about poker hands around the evening campfire flared up. Because it fell to him to mediate, it was natural that he'd feel these more strongly as the trail boss than as a hired hand.

But Jesse's second guess hit close to home too. Luke's thoughts had gravitated more and more often toward life off the cattle trail. What would it be like, to leave work every day and rest your head in your own bed?

Trail Boss. The words still brought a surge of pride. Pa had spent his life taking beef to market, and Luke had ridden beside him on many of those drives, but this was his first time as boss, and it didn't feel as good as he thought it would. He wasn't sure he liked the responsibility of men, cattle, and what happened to both in bad weather. He was starting to think he preferred the smell of fresh hay waving in the fields and rich fertile earth turned beneath a plow. On the other hand, if he failed this drive, Pa would skin him alive. His laugh this time sounded a little forced even to him. "Can't see what that has to do with you not liking the Switzers."

Jesse stooped, grabbed his shirt by the shoulders, and shook it out. Droplets of water sprayed onto the grass. "I don't have anything against them personally. It just seems to me that when a man is struggling with something he can get distracted easier. And there's nothing more distracting than a couple of helpless women, even if they are dressed like nuns." He aimed a grin sideways. "I'd hate to see you quit and join up with the *Aim*-ish. You'd look stupid in the clothes."

The sudden image made Luke laugh. He threw back his head and let the sounds of his mirth flow downstream across the running river.

When the moment passed, he felt better. Hours and hours in the saddle gave a man a lot of time to worry things over in his mind. Sometimes that was good, but at other times the worries swelled like an old woman's ankles. Talking to a friend helped shrink them back down to size.

He clapped Jesse on the back. "You worry like a mother. My only thought right now is getting this herd to Hays on time. In order to do that, we need to haul this wagon out of the river."

Then with a clear conscience, he'd leave the Switzers behind and get back on the trail.

Still dressed in denims and a Stetson.

NINE

The young *Englisch* boy driving their cart was apparently in a hurry and not afraid to push his mule. Emma clutched the side rails and held on as they bumped over the rough terrain. The ground beneath their feet bore thousands of hoof-shaped pits and gouges.

"There it is! Oh, my."

Emma turned at Rebecca's words, and followed the line of the river in front of them. She spotted the wagon easily, half in the water and leaning at an awkward angle. *Maummi's* hutch was no longer covered but sat in the back, its polished finish gleaming warmly in the afternoon sunlight.

But the sun gleamed off more than the hutch. Three men stood on the shore, and two more in the water. The ones standing on the grass were dressed in vests and chaps and cowboy hats, but the two standing in waist-high water had stripped off their shirts. As they drew near, she recognized

Luke and his saloon-loving friend. Spray from the river had wet their skin, and for a moment she couldn't tear her gaze away from the sight of his glistening strong shoulders and broad chest.

"*Ach!*" *Maummi's* cry rang in the air over the sound of the rushing river.

With a stab of guilt, Emma jerked her gaze away from Luke and turned a warm face toward her grandmother. *Maummi's* mouth gaped, her lips moving soundlessly like a fish's, her eyes round as wagon wheels. *You'd think she never saw a bare-chested man before.*

"Oh, my," Rebecca's repeated. Her eyes were nearly as round as *Maummi's*, but the sudden flush that brightened her face bore the unmistakable stamp of delight.

"Rebecca." Emma spoke her warning low as she fixed her sister with a hard stare. Better that than turn around again, where her gaze would be drawn to the water.

Even before the cart stopped moving, *Maummi* leaped down to the ground. She ran toward the cluster of cowboys at an astonishing speed, her apron strings trailing behind her. Emma hurried after her, her cheeks burning. *Maummi* would humiliate them all by scolding a group of grown men as though they were small boys for running around without shirts. She'd probably even come up with a proverb about nakedness.

A large number of cows hovered near the water's edge, but *Maummi* ignored them. They skittered away when she ran by and came to a halt in front of the wagon. A stream of Pennsylvania Dutch words flew from her mouth, so quickly that even Emma had a hard time following. The cowboys nearby watched her, their expressions helpless.

Then *Maummi* found her *Englisch* tongue. "My hutch! Rescue for me my hutch, before the water takes it!"

For a moment Emma couldn't respond. Apparently she hadn't noticed the barely clothed men in the water. She had eyes only for her hutch. A nearly uncontrollable giggle tickled the back of Emma's throat. When she was as old as *Maummi,* maybe she would focus more on furniture than handsome men, but that certainly hadn't happened yet.

She snuck a quick glance, and the heat in her face intensified.

Her grandmother's moan distracted her. "Made with my dearly departed's own hands."

Emma placed an arm across her shoulders. Being so upset couldn't be good for her heart. "Calm down, *Maummi.* They will get the hutch."

"We're sure trying, ma'am." The oldest of the three cowboys dipped his head in her direction. "So far we haven't had much luck. The axle seems to be caught on a rock ledge or something down there."

Papa arrived with Rebecca and their hired driver. He stood on the riverbank with his thumbs hooked behind his suspenders and his head tilted sideways, studying the wagon.

"The hutch is safe, I think, unless the entire wagon is washed away," he told *Maummi.*

"Ach!" She raised a hand to cover her heart and wilted against Emma. "Forty years and not a scratch, only to lose it in the river."

A splashing sound alerted her to the fact that Luke and Jesse were exiting the water. Emma mostly kept her gaze averted, but she couldn't help another quick peek.

"Jonas, what say we put your new oxen to the test?"

A sloshing close by told her Luke had gained the shore. Oh, how she wanted to turn around and stare at him. *Maummi's* saying repeated in her mind like a mantra. " *'Keep your eyes cast down until the Lord raises them.'* " She knew for a fact that the Lord would not approve of her staring at Luke's half-clad body, so she kept her back turned, standing in front of *Maummi*. *Lord, lead me not into temptation.*

Rebecca, on the other hand, openly gawked. Emma grabbed her by the arm and jerked her around. "Go help the boy unload our provisions." She added an unmistakable command to her voice.

Her sister surprised her by obeying, though her gaze was so firmly fixed on Jesse and Luke as she wandered in the direction of the cart that she ran right into the hind end of a cow, which sent the poor beast into a sudden gallop.

Luke described his plan to Papa and the others. "There's a narrow rocky ledge all the way across, which I figure is what the bandits tried to cross. But this side of it, the bottom's nothing but sand and muck. That back wheel slipped off. We tried using a couple of horses to pull her free, but it's stuck fast. The best I can tell, the axle is wedged on a rock outcropping. Not by much, but enough. If we're lucky, it's not cracked."

"Please," *Maummi* intoned in a loud voice, "no cracks."

Emma placed a hand on each of her grandmother's upper arms and squeezed comfortingly. An odd pair they must have looked, she with her back to the river and

Maummi's gaze fixed over her shoulder on the hutch.

"What we need to do is roll the wagon backward a little. Not too much, because there's some pretty deep sand this side of that ledge, and if the wheel gets moored in that, she'll tip for sure."

Maummi moaned and clutched Emma's arms. Her fingers dug into the soft flesh, as if by holding more tightly to her granddaughter, she could keep the wagon upright.

"Once that axle is clear, we're going to have to pull it out at a sharp angle. It will take a mighty strong and steady hand leading those oxen."

From the corner of her eye, she saw Papa's shoulders straighten. "Amish hands are strong."

"Judging by your handshake, I'd have to agree." Emma heard the smile in Luke's voice and fought a powerful temptation to turn so she could see his expression. *Keep your eyes cast down . . .*

The older cowboy stepped up beside Emma and removed his hat. Though he looked to be around the same age as *Maummi,* deep lines crisscrossed the leathery skin of his face, which was shaved clean like an Amish youth. "Ladies, you might want to stand back a piece, out of the way."

Emma realized they were standing directly in the path the wagon would travel when it came out of the water. "Oh, of course. *Maummi,* we'll watch from over here."

She guided her reluctant grandmother to their hired cart, where the boy was busy unloading their purchases and piling them on the ground. Rebecca made a pretense of picking up a light crate, but she moved so slowly to place it near the others that it would have gotten there faster if it had grown legs and walked by itself. Emma could hardly blame her, and not because of the sight of men's chests. The fate of their wagon and belongings were at risk.

The boy placed the last sack on the ground and leaped back up onto the bench.

Emma went to stand beside the cart and looked up at him. "You'll wait a moment, please? To see everything's fit for our wagon to travel?"

He cast an anxious glance toward the darkening sky to the northwest but then gave her a reluctant nod.

"*Danki.*" She went to stand beside *Maummi* and Rebecca to watch Luke's plan unfold.

Luke helped Jonas and Griff hitch the new oxen to the stranded wagon.

"I hope this works." Jesse's tone an-

126

nounced his skepticism for all to hear.

A worry that he might be right niggled deep in Luke's mind as he double-checked the knots. The oxen's yoke wasn't usable because of the angle of the wagon on the bank, so they were forced to use rope. That back wheel was sunk pretty low, and when the wagon backed up, it was going to take brute strength in the water to keep it level enough to tip it up over the ledge so it could be pulled forward. There was no telling how heavy that hutch was, but no way could one man lift it on his own. He hoped he, Jesse, Willie, and Charlie could handle it between the four of them.

Even Jonas's confidence seemed uncertain. He left Griff holding the oxen steady long enough to follow Luke to the river's edge. "If the wagon turns over, mind you are not beneath it."

Luke grinned. "You worried about me, Jonas?"

His expression remained solemn. "Possessions are not worth a man's life." A pause, and then he smiled. "Not even an *Englisch* man's."

Luke laughed and slapped him on the shoulder. "Rest easy. I don't plan to be under that wagon when it breaks loose."

Jonas returned to the oxen's heads, while

Jesse, Charlie, and Willie splashed into the water to take their places around the rear of the rig. Over by the cart, the women stood side by side, the hems of their black skirts sweeping the grass. Luke gave a single wave intended to relay his confidence — a conviction he didn't feel. This thing could be in here forever.

Rebecca lifted an arm above her head and returned the gesture with enthusiasm, while Mrs. Switzer raised both hands in front of her mouth in a posture of prayer. Emma's only response was to loop an arm through her grandmother's elbow. Not even a smile for luck.

He plunged in and waded through the rising river toward the rear of the wagon. Water swirled around his waist as he took his place beside the others.

"Willie and Charlie, you two stand there." He pointed at a place along the wagon's back panel. "Stay as close to this end as you can. Jesse, you take the corner and hug up close to me."

Concern drew lines across Jesse's forehead. "That's a sandy bottom there, isn't it?"

"Mostly, but the rock is jagged so I can get a foothold."

"See that you keep it, boss," said Charlie.

"Don't worry. If I sink, Jesse will come after me."

Jesse aimed a glance at the hutch. "In your dreams."

Luke sized up the leaning piece of furniture. It towered over him like that big old oak tree in the backyard when he was a boy. He glanced over his shoulder, toward the place where Emma stood. His grandmother said she used to say a prayer for his safety every time he took a mind to climbing that thing. If Mrs. Switzer truly was praying, he hoped she'd send one up for him and not only for her precious possession.

With a hand on the wagon's side, Luke edged slowly around the corner, feeling his way with his boot. He hated soggy boots, but couldn't risk a cut that might fester, so he'd have to put up with wet leather till they dried. He located the stone he'd found before and fixed both his feet. Not six inches behind him, the rock's edge gave way to the riverbed. Not much maneuvering room, but it ought to be enough. Jesse and the boys slid into their places.

"Ready?"

They all bent their knees, grabbed the underside of the wagon bed, and nodded. He slid his fingers below the lower lip until the thick plank rested in his palms.

"Jonas, when I give the word, you back those oxen up one step. Only one. Then when I shout again, take them forward as quickly as you can. Got it?"

"*Ja.* I got it."

Luke firmed his grip, nodded at the three by his side, and shouted, "Go!"

On the shore Jonas uttered something to the oxen in his low, calm voice that was almost snatched away by the rush of the water. The wagon started to roll backward. Luke tightened his muscles and tried to lift a tad, enough to keep the wagon relatively steady as the wheel rolled from beneath the ledge. The weight of the thing was staggering. Beside him, Jesse grunted, and Willie's fair complexion purpled with the shared effort. Luke's bulging muscles trembled. He hadn't lifted anything this heavy since . . . well, ever. His eyes switched to Emma standing on the bank. Was her smile really pretty enough to break his fool back for?

He felt the wheel jerk upward when the axle slid loose from the outcropping. Only an inch or so, but the bed wavered at the sudden release. The strain in his muscles shifted, and Luke's balance tilted. Though his brain knew better, instinct kicked in. He staggered backward — and found no footing. "Ease up! Ease up!"

His shout rang out as he plunged into the water. The errant foot sank into the sandy muck and jerked his other boot off the rock. A dark object loomed above him. The hutch was tilting his way. He splashed and kicked backward, but the muck held fast.

"Luke!"

Jesse's yell mingled with a woman's scream. A tiny, detached part of his brain wondered which one. Probably the old woman, worried about her hutch. Kicking harder, he threw his arms over his head, trying to move backward through the water with a powerful stroke.

Not enough.

Above him Jesse edged around the corner of the wagon and slid into the place he'd vacated. With a shout that was half-grunt, he strained against the weight of the wagon as Jonas coaxed the oxen ahead at a trot.

In the chaotic seconds that followed, everything happened at once.

The wagon rolled forward, out of the water and onto the shore.

The alarming sound of hooves thundered against the grass behind him. A stampede?

He turned his head and caught sight of a black dress and white cap racing across the grass. Emma. Startled cows scattered before her.

The water behind him splashed and churned as cattle plunged into the river, running blind to get away from the unknown black-clad figure racing toward them.

A hard object slammed into his body as Jesse lost his footing on the narrow rock and fell backward. The force of a cowhand's backside hit him square in the face.

In the second before the river closed over him and sucked him under, he heard Mrs. Switzer's cutting voice echo across the water.

"Dopplich Englischer."

He had no idea what it meant, but he was fairly sure he'd just been insulted.

TEN

Emma sat on the empty trunk beneath a tall tree on the riverbank and tried not to look anyone in the eye. She hadn't *meant* to cause a stampede. Granted, she didn't know cattle would startle so easily. And she certainly didn't mean for *so many* to run straight into the river. After the first two sank belly-deep in the mud, couldn't the rest of them see the predicament and stop?

And after all that, their trunk was empty. All her belongings, along with Mama's quilt, had been removed. Luke had barely spoken a word since his men fished him out of the river, half drowned. And he certainly couldn't be pleased right now. Once again he was waist deep in the rushing water trying to haul his cattle out. She kept her gaze to the ground lest he looked up and saw her misery.

"Jonas, pull her out," Luke called from the middle of the river.

She raised her eyes to watch without lifting her head. Papa had one end of a length of rope around an ox's neck, the other end secured around a steer in the river. Jesse stood on one side of the frightened animal, and Luke on the other. Papa led the ox, pulling the bellowing steer forward. Its head disappeared under the water, cutting off the sound with a gurgle, and then it resurfaced a moment later, still bawling. The steer was dragged onto the shore, where it wallowed on the grass, loudly voicing its displeasure.

Luke cut the knot from around its middle while Jesse loosened the second rope with which they had tied the rear legs together to stop the steer from struggling. They both jumped back when the animal broke loose. It scrambled to its feet and trotted off down the trail toward the main herd.

The cow's rescue set the rest of them to hollering. Emma's gaze swept over the last six bovine bodies mired fast in the muddy riverbed bottom. With only the top of their backs and their heads sticking up out of the water, they were like a logjam of frightened roasts. The sound of their bawls filled the air, accompanied by the shouts of cowboys who hollered instructions to each other about how to safely maneuver them out.

It was all her fault.

Emma's chin drooped lower on her chest.

Up in the wagon, *Maummi* straightened from a crouched position, a hand pressed against the small of her back. She'd inspected every square inch of her hutch, and judging by her fierce expression, she wasn't happy with the condition. She stepped to the wagon's rear edge and sat, preparing to drop to the ground. Griff hurried to help her.

"Here you go, ma'am." With strong arms, he lifted her down and set her on the grass as gently as if handling a baby.

Maummi brushed her apron and looked sideways up at him. *"Danki."* Then she switched her gaze to Emma. *"Dopplich Englischers.* A scratch, on the far side. Forty years and no scratches. Now?" She sliced through the air with a vicious gesture. "A scratch."

"I saw that, ma'am." Griff hooked a thumb in his belt. "More a scrape than a scratch. You might be able to buff it out when you get to where you're going."

She pursed her lips but acknowledged the suggestion with the faintest of nods.

The old cowboy turned a kind gaze toward Emma. "Don't feel too bad, miss. The sight of that wagon tipping would have stampeded me too. Nothing but plain bad luck that the cattle spooked in the direction of the river. Since we didn't lose a single head, there's no cause to fret. There's not a man here who hasn't seen worse than this."

For some reason, his kindness only made Emma's misery worse. Swallowing against a lump in her throat, she managed a weak smile of gratitude.

Even *Maummi* spoke in a voice without its usual sharp edge. "Did any of our things in the trunk survive?"

Emma drew in a shuddering breath. "Nothing."

"I'm guessing when that wagon got mired down, the thieves packed up whatever they could carry and chucked the rest in the river." Griff turned to look upstream. "All except that stuff over there."

Emma jerked upright. He pointed to a small cluster of trees behind them.

"Not much left, and some of it took a beating, but we moved it out of the way so the herd wouldn't trample it any further."

"Rebecca," *Maummi* called as she headed toward the trees. "Lend a hand, girl."

Rebecca turned from her vantage point on the bank and followed. With a quick "Thank you" to Griff, Emma hurried after them.

Stuff was an appropriate description for

the mound of clutter piled on a grassless embankment inside a small copse of trees. Emma stood, speechless, and stared at the havoc that had been made of their belongings. Everything had been uncrated, and the few breakable dishes *Maummi* had carefully wrapped for the journey lay in shards. A couple of the crates had been splintered.

Maummi crossed to the other side of the jumble to where her rocking chair lay on its side. She stood over it and peered downward. "Broken."

Emma knelt and grasped the corner of a bed sheet between a thumb and forefinger. When she lifted it up, she spied several slashes in the fabric, as though it had been purposefully cut with a knife.

"Why are they so mean?" Rebecca tugged a black garment free of the rubble, and then another. Dresses. They had been similarly destroyed.

A frantic flutter began behind Emma's breastbone. Had the thieves slashed Mama's quilt to pieces? She bent over and began tossing things out of the way, searching for a glimpse of bright color or the thick bag in which she'd wrapped it. Nothing.

"Here's something, anyway." Rebecca lifted a heavy black skillet out of the wreckage and held it up for *Maummi*'s inspection.

The old lady's scowl deepened. "Why could we not find it before we paid good money for a new one?"

Behind them, the volume of the cattle's frightened mooing diminished, and Emma peeked through the trees. Another cow had been rescued and galloped after the other.

While *Maummi* began the task of separating the few usable items from the debris, Rebecca sidled over to her.

"Why did you run toward the wagon, Emma?" She spoke low enough that *Maummi* wouldn't make out the words while her attention was elsewhere. "Did you think to hold it upright yourself when four men could not?"

Emma kept her eyes averted under the pretense of picking up a sadly bedraggled prayer *kapp.* "I didn't think anything. I ran because . . ." She shrugged. "I don't know."

In the silence that followed, she formed an unspoken prayer of forgiveness for the blatant lie.

And for the alarming reason behind her foolish action.

When the last steer had been hauled out of the river, Luke climbed the bank and collapsed beside his men lying on the grass. The work had been exhausting, and as he

138

lay beside Jesse, his muscles protested. Judging by the sounds of the moans coming from the others, his weren't the only ones.

Jesse spoke without opening his eyes. "She's staring at me."

Luke turned his head to eye his friend. "Who?"

"The younger one. Been staring at me all afternoon. It's starting to make me edgy."

A glance toward the Switzers' wagon revealed Rebecca standing by the bench, her face turned their way. "How do you know she's not staring at me?"

"First of all, because I'm better lookin' than you." A weak chuckle rumbled in his chest. "Second of all, watch."

Jesse rolled onto his side and propped up on one arm to look the girl in the face. Startled, she swung around and became suddenly busy fiddling with something on the wagon bench. Her shoulders shook with a girlish giggle.

"See? She's spooking me."

"Since when did a girl's attention spook you?"

"Since the girl isn't older than thirteen or fourteen. Add another five years and it would be a different story." He drew in a sharp breath with a hiss when he rolled back around to face Luke. "I think I busted a gut on that dad gum wagon. Thing's as heavy as a full-grown steer."

"That reminds me." Luke sat up and rested his arms on his knees. "I haven't thanked you for saving my hide back there."

"You're welcome." Wincing, Jesse rose to sit beside him. "So now I figure you owe me a steak dinner *and* a bottle of whiskey when we get to Hays."

He chuckled. "You know I won't buy your whiskey, but I'll buy you a bath and a shave. How's that?"

"That's all your life's worth? A bath and a shave?"

"Nope. I'm worth a five-dollar steak, not one of those cheap things you'd try and force on me." He grinned sideways. "But you *need* a bath. You're starting to smell so bad you're scaring the herd."

Jesse pointed at the river. "I had my bath, thank you. And washed my long johns at the same time."

Speaking of which, Luke would welcome some dry clothes. He climbed to his feet and scanned the sky. The storm had skirted around them to the north. He glanced toward the herd. From this vantage point he could see the chuck wagon in the distance on the far side. When the cattle had mired in the muck, he'd sent word to halt

140

and let the herd graze. Kirk, Morris, and Vic kept guard while the rest had helped out with the rescue. Judging by the position of the sun, they only had a couple of hours of travel time left before they would need to find a good place to bed down for the night. He searched his memory of his last drive on the Chisholm Trail. As far as he could remember, there wasn't another appropriate place within four hours of here. This would have to be it. What was a couple more hours when they had lost a full day?

He spoke to the men lying in the grass around him. "We'll graze the herd a little longer and then settle them here for the night." Jesse drew breath for an accusation, but Luke held up a hand to stop him. "It's my fault. You men did a good job today. Let's get those cattle taken care of and then get some extra shut-eye ourselves. Tomorrow we'll get an early start."

There was less grumbling than expected when the men rose and started gathering their belongings.

"I hope the cook ain't serving beans again tonight," Charlie said to no one in particular. He winked. "Been noisy enough around here today."

Griff scooped his hat off the ground. "Some of those molasses cakes he whips up sure would go down good. Got an ache in my sweet tooth tonight."

"I'll see what I can do," Luke promised. "You fellows go on ahead. I'll be along in a minute."

They mounted their horses, and when the rest headed in the direction of the herd, Jesse paused to look down at him. "She's doing it again."

Luke glanced toward the Switzers' wagon, where Rebecca stood openly staring in Jesse's direction. When he looked her way, she giggled and turned away, more slowly this time.

Jesse shook his head, disgusted. "Can't say I'm sorry to see the last of those *Aim-ish*." He kicked his horse into a start and galloped off.

When he'd gone, Luke headed toward Jonas, who was inspecting the yoke still attached to his wagon. Mrs. Switzer was up in the back, sorting through a crate, while Rebecca stood watching Jesse ride away. He didn't trust himself to look beyond the wagon, where Emma knelt in the grass beside the big trunk. Every time he remembered the sight of her running toward those cattle, spooking them into the river, anger heated the blood in his veins. No one had been harmed today, but wrestling a frightened steer mired in river muck had killed more than one cowhand in the past. She'd endangered the lives of his men and delayed his herd's progress by several hours. No amount of sweet smiles could make up for that.

"Everything look okay?" he asked Jonas when he approached.

"*Ja.*" The man stood. "I can work around the missing pins. I feared for the bows, but thank the Lord they suffered no damage."

"That's good." He glanced toward the oxen grazing nearby. "They are going to make you a fine team. They pulled hard and steady today. Made the job of getting the cattle out of the river easier and quicker than trying to use horses. Thanks for lending us a hand."

A smile turned the corners of his shaved lips upward. "It is what friends do."

Friends. Yes, he could honestly say he had made an Amish friend in Jonas. "You'd better get a move on if you want to make good time tonight."

He shook his head. "Like you, we will stop here and start fresh tomorrow."

"You need me to give you a hand with anything?"

"You have done much. Truly, you have been the Lord's blessing to us. Our debt goes far beyond the money you have spent."

Luke smiled and cocked his hat. "Which you'll pay back, right?"

Solemn-faced, Jonas raised a hand, palm out. "You have my word."

That his word was good, Luke had no doubt. He extended his hand, and Jonas took it in his strong, calloused grip.

"Good luck to you," Luke said.

"The Lord bless your journey," Jonas responded.

When he turned, Rebecca had fetched Bo and handed him the reins with a smile. "Thank you for the oxen and the candy and . . . everything. You will be in my prayers, Mr. Carson."

In the back of the wagon, old Mrs. Switzer rose to tower over him. Was that disapproving stare of hers slightly less stern than before? Probably only because she was about to see the last of him. She straightened and lifted her chin as though about to impart a particularly important piece of wisdom.

"Danki." That said, her lips snapped shut and she returned to her work.

"You're most welcome. God go with you, ma'am." Chuckling, Luke started to climb up into the saddle. A movement in the corner of his eye caught his attention, and he paused with his boot in the stirrup. Emma approached, her head downcast, her hands folded in front of her apron.

"I am sorry I almost drowned your cows."

Her voice was so low he had to bend down to catch the words. Something inside him stirred with compassion, but he squashed it. This girl could have cost the lives of a dozen cattle, not to mention his men.

He kept his voice cool. "I accept your apology."

A moment's hesitation, and then a nod. She started to turn away.

Luke took his foot out of the stirrup. A wet slosh when he set it on the ground served as an unpleasant and unnecessary reminder of this afternoon's near disaster. He stopped her with a question.

"What were you doing, anyway? Screaming and running as though you were chasing hens in a chicken yard?"

"I . . ." A blush stained the curved cheek half turned away from him. "I was worried about *Maummi*'s hutch."

For some reason her answer whipped up his anger the way wind whips up a bonfire. Why, when that was exactly the explanation he'd expected? He set his teeth together to keep from snapping a response and swung up into the saddle. When he was looking

145

down at the top of her *kapp,* which was no longer blindingly white and sat cockeyed on her head, words ground out between his teeth.

"Have a nice life, Miss Switzer."

With a kick from soggy boots, he urged Bo into a gallop toward the herd, glad to have his duty over.

ELEVEN

The gathering around the campfire ended early. McCann usually kept the men entertained with stories and singing, but tonight they were too tired to do much more than shovel fried beef, beans, and molasses cakes into their mouths.

Those who had the first guard of the night retrieved their night horses from the remuda and rode off to stand watch over the sleeping herd. The others slipped away one by one to their bedrolls. Soon only Griff and Luke were left seated around the banked fire, while McCann banged around in the chuck wagon, lining up breakfast.

A log collapsed in the fire pit, and sparks shot upward to disappear into the dark sky. The wood snapped and crackled as fresh flame engulfed it. From the direction of the river, a chorus of tree frogs serenaded sleeping men and cattle.

"Sure was a full day in the saddle, eh?"

"Wasn't much of it spent in the saddle." Luke winced at the note of self-recrimination in his voice.

"Quit beating yourself up, son. Everything turned out okay. We did some folks a good turn and lost nothing but a few hours. We'll make it up tomorrow."

The man was being kind. Luke appreciated it, but he refused to accept the grace offered. "We lost more than a few hours, Griff. We lost a whole day, thanks to me." He picked up a piece of dry bark off the ground and tossed it into the fire. "A day we can't afford to lose."

"We'll get to Hays on time." The firelight cast an orange glow over his creased features. "You got any idea what that little gal was running after?"

A humorless laugh rumbled from Luke's chest. "Yeah. That monster of a hutch. Like she could have done anything to stop that wagon from tipping over."

"Ain't that the truth?" From the confidence in the man's tone, it almost sounded as though Griff were goading him. "You're sure that was her worry? To save that hutch?"

"She told me so herself."

"Doesn't matter what she told you." He leaned back on one elbow and looked up at the night sky. "I know different."

His manner was one of a man who knew something and was purposefully holding it back. Luke got hold of his temper before he spoke again "What do you know, Griff? Or think you know?"

"You heard her scream when that wagon started to tip?"

"Yeah." He remembered wondering who had screamed after he'd stepped back into the muck.

"Well, you probably didn't hear what she said after that as she was running to help. I did, because I was standing closer than anyone else, watching out in case Jonas needed a quick hand with those oxen." Griff studied him with a sharp eye. "She was crying out your name."

Luke jerked upright. The man couldn't have surprised him more if he'd slapped him awake with a wet towel to the face. "Mine?"

"Yep. Like this." Griff lifted a hand to flutter over his heart dramatically, and swept his eyes upward. He affected a high, feminine voice. *Luke! Oh, no. Luke!*

Griff started to laugh, and a flush crept into Luke's face at the ribbing. He picked up a green branch the width of his thumb and used it as a poker to stir the fire. The old man's deep guffaws gave way to a cough, and the hacking doubled him over for a minute. When he caught his breath, he was still chuckling.

"At least one of us finds your joke funny," Luke said in a voice as dry as a Texas plain.

"Oh, it's funny, all right, but I'm not joking. That little slip of a girl was running to rescue you, calling out your name."

Disbelief stole over Luke. Emma was coming to his rescue? Not that she could have done a thing. And her *help* caused far more harm than good, but knowing why she acted as she did started a warm glow simmering in the pit of his belly.

He turned around and strained through the darkness, looking over the sleeping herd. There, in the distance, a campfire flickered in the area where he'd left the Switzers and their wagon. The memory of Emma as he left her, her head downcast, wrenched something in his chest. He'd responded coldly to her apology. There'd been no cause for that. Especially when she'd only been trying to help.

With a rattle and a grunt, McCann climbed down out of the chuck wagon. Luke turned back to see him bend over and pick up the metal dishpan by the handle. "I aim to give these dishes a good scrub in the river, and then I'm hitting the sack."

He crossed to the campfire and hooked the arm of his cook pot off the tripod with a towel.

An idea formed in Luke's mind. "What are you going to do with the rest of those beans?"

"Throw them out, unless you boys want them." He looked from Luke to Griff.

"Not me." Griff patted a rounded belly. "I ate my fill."

"Rather than throw them out, do you have a crock or a smaller pot I can put them in?" Luke cleared his throat and cast a warning glance at Griff to keep his silence. "Those folks back behind us might appreciate a sample from the best cook on the Chisholm Trail."

McCann looked at the pot in his hand and shrugged. "I got a couple of empty cans I can put them in."

He headed back to the chuck wagon. The axle creaked when he climbed up inside, while Luke carefully avoided eye contact with Griff.

The old man rose to his feet and stood in front of Luke. "You and I have guard duty together in a couple of hours. You'll be back by then, won't you?"

Luke cleared his throat. "Of course. I'm

151

only going to drop in on them for a minute and check to make sure they don't need anything."

"Uh-huh."

When Griff turned away and headed toward the front of the chuck wagon, Luke glimpsed a grin deepening the creases around the edges of his mouth.

Emma sat beside the campfire and gritted her teeth against the tug of the comb through her hair. *Maummi's* hand had never been gentle with this nightly task. When she was little, Mama used to comb her hair with such care that Emma hardly knew the task was being accomplished.

Thoughts of Mama turned her mind to the lost quilt, and the sting of tears prickled her eyes.

Stop it! There is no sense in being silly over a piece of fabric.

She blinked hard and managed to banish the tears before they filled her eyes. It wasn't only the quilt bothering her tonight. The blundering dash that caused the incident with the cows, followed by Luke's chilly farewell, lay heavy on her heart. But what weighed her spirits down most was the underlying cause for her action. Hours before, she'd determined to stay true to her faith and her community and reject thoughts of the handsome *Englisch* man. But what happened when she saw that hutch tilting toward him in the water? An emotional wave unlike anything she'd ever felt washed over her, and her feet carried her toward him at a run.

This doesn't mean I care for him. I'd feel the same no matter who was in danger.

Would she? Oh, how she hoped that were true.

"There." *Maummi* finished weaving her hair into a tight braid and tied off the end with a strip of leather.

"Finished in good time," Papa said from the other side of the fire. He stood and lifted the rocking chair he'd been working on. "Good thing you are light, *Mader,* else this might dump you on the ground. When we arrive home, I will do a proper repair."

"Home?" Rebecca, seated beside Papa, started to attention. "Not to Troyer?"

Papa placed the chair on the hard-packed dirt near the fire. "The Lord has restored a portion of what the enemy took from us, and I am grateful. But He has seen fit to put us in debt to an *Englisch* man."

Maummi quoted a proverb. " 'The debt that is paid is best.' "

He smiled. "*Ja.* I cannot ask Bishop Mil-

153

ler to repay the large debt I owe Luke Carson. We must return home, so I can repay my own debt as soon as needs be." He turned a tender smile Emma's way. "It appears the Lord has granted me more time with my daughter."

Warmth flooded Emma at the love she saw in her papa's face. Rarely did he display emotion, and even more rarely did he speak of it. Instead, he showed his love every day through hard work and dedication to his family's well-being. Tonight, when her feelings were so near the surface, his unexpected words moved her nearly to tears.

A satisfied grunt that was almost a purr came from low in *Maummi*'s throat, though the news that they weren't going to Troyer hit Rebecca hard. Her mouth turned downward in a pout. "But I thought the Lord told you to send Emma to Troyer in the first place. Did He change His mind, then?"

Emma held her breath, shocked at her sister's question. Such disrespect as to question both the Lord and Papa in the same breath. Rebecca must be extremely disappointed in the decision to voice such a rebellious thought.

Papa turned a thoughtful expression her way. "Would you have me question the reason for the Lord's directives like Job of old?"

The mild rebuke was as harsh as Papa ever gave, and Rebecca snapped her mouth shut. He stared at her a moment and then put a hand on the top of her bowed head. "The Lord's reasons are unknowable, daughter, but we must trust that He has them."

When she nodded, Emma released the breath she'd been holding. Papa was right. Though returning home might look contradictory to the Lord's initial direction, who knew but that He sent them on this disastrous journey in order to accomplish His unfathomable will? What that might be, involving the theft and destruction of their belongings, she could not imagine, unless it was to emphasize the truth of His sufficiency and their dependency on His daily provision for their needs.

Or perhaps He wanted us to meet someone along the way.

She shoved a sudden thought of Luke out of her mind.

Papa gave the chair a gentle push that set it to rocking, and then he stood back and spoke to *Maummi.* "Come and try out my work."

Emma rose and helped her grandmother stand. The broken pieces of the chair leg had been fitted together and secured with sturdy slats from the useless crates and bound with rope like a splint on a broken leg. Two spindles in the back had to be removed, but they were not side-by-side, so the resulting gaps weren't big enough for a body to slip through.

When she'd seated herself gingerly and gave a trial rock or two, she nodded. "A fine job. *Danki,* Jonas."

At the sound of approaching hooves, Emma's muscles tensed. Had the thieves returned to steal Papa's new oxen? A quick glance at Papa's face confirmed the idea had occurred to him too, though the only sign that he anticipated trouble was a tightening of his lips as he straightened and faced the approaching stranger. She couldn't make out details, but she relaxed a fraction when she saw the silhouette of a lone man on horseback. A moment later he rode into view, and her muscles tensed again.

Luke.

Papa's posture relaxed when he identified their visitor. Rebecca jumped to her feet, smiling broadly, but *Maummi* stopped her from running toward the horse with a hand on her arm. Emma remained where she was beside the fire, her legs drawn up beneath her dress, arms wrapped around them. Had he come back to chastise her for her foolish behavior? If she could slink off into the darkness and hide, she would. Instead, she hugged her legs closer and rested her chin on her knees.

"Evening, folks." Luke dismounted, looped his horse's reins around a nearby tree branch, and strode into the circle of firelight cradling a bundle in one hand. "I'm on guard duty soon, but I thought I'd check to see if everything's going okay here first."

"You are welcome to share our fire." Papa gestured for him to be seated.

"Thank you."

Instead of sitting on the opposite side, near Papa, he came around the campfire and dropped to the ground between Emma and *Maummi*. Surprised, Emma drew her feet up closer to her body and hugged her legs even more tightly.

He set his bundle between them and unwrapped the thick cloth covering two large cans and a smaller cloth-wrapped package. A savory odor arose from the open cans. "My cook thought you might be able to make use of these beans for your supper, ma'am, or maybe your breakfast." He offered them to *Maummi*.

Maummi regarded the cans with obvious suspicion. "You have given us much already,

157

Mr. Carson. We would not like to be a burden and take your food as well."

"Ah, don't worry about that." Luke turned an endearing smile up at her. "We ate well, and these were the leavings. If you don't want them, the cook will throw them out."

Her eyebrows arched and her lips pursed. Emma knew her grandmother well, so she had no difficulty following her thoughts. Hadn't she heard the lesson often enough? *Waste is ungratefulness for God's bounty.* *Maummi* rose from her chair and took the cans from his hands, and then she inclined her head. "*Danki* to your cook." She headed toward the wagon, a can in each hand.

"I snagged these too." He picked up the smaller bundle and folded back the cloth to reveal a pile of flat little cakes.

He reached around the empty rocking chair and handed two to Rebecca, indicating with a nod for her to pass one to Papa. Then he turned and extended one toward Emma. Turmoil churned her insides. Why was he being so nice? By all rights he should have ridden off and counted himself lucky to be rid of her. That's what she thought he'd done a few hours ago.

When she reached for the cake, his fingers curled around it to prevent her from taking it. Startled, she raised her gaze to his.

158

"I wanted to apologize for being short with you earlier." A softness crept into his voice. "You had no way of knowing that these cattle were prone to run after their stampede the other night. I shouldn't have taken my temper out on you. Will you forgive me?"

A note of tenderness softened the gaze that held hers. She could push no words past the lump that wedged in her throat. When she nodded, he opened his fingers to release the cake.

"Ahem."

Emma tore her gaze away and fixed it on her grandmother, who was standing at the back of the wagon with a fork in one hand and a can of beans in the other. Her direct stare and crooked eyebrows spoke her disapproval louder than words could. Emma returned the stare without blinking. Would *Maummi* have her be rude and ignore his apology? Or did she worry that Luke intended more by his words and gesture than mere regret for a hasty reaction? The thought sent a happy thrill through her. On the other side of the empty rocking chair, Rebecca chewed a mouthful of cake, her round eyes fixed on Emma. Papa's calm countenance had not changed as he relished his treat with obvious enjoyment.

Luke spoke to *Maummi* in an easy tone. "How do those beans taste, ma'am?"

After a moment, and a weighty glance at Emma, her glower faded. She made a show of dipping the fork in the can and extracting a small sample. Her gaze became distant as she chewed, and then she gave an approving nod.

"Good." She tested another sample. "He cooks like a man, with no touch for seasoning. But good."

A relieved sigh seeped out of Emma's lungs. If *Maummi* complimented a man's cooking, that meant she was prepared to be nice. Either Luke was beginning to win her over with his kind ways, or she had decided that there was no cause to be cross because in the morning he would be on his way and out of her hair.

Luke laughed. "I'll relay the message."

He settled himself on the ground with his feet toward the fire and his hat resting on the ground behind him. The knots in Emma's stomach loosened as she bit into the cake. A good flavor but a little crunchy. Nothing near as good as *Maummi*'s, or even her own since she learned cooking skills at first her mother's and then *Maummi*'s hands. She took it as a sign of the elderly woman's determination to be nice when she settled back into the rocker, bit into her own cake, and said, "As well, good. A handful of chopped nuts wouldn't hurt them any."

"They are a favorite of the boys on the trail." Luke popped the last of his cake in his mouth and leaned back, his manner easy. "Were you able to recover many of your things from the mess those marauders left?"

"They ripped up all our linens, and even our dresses and Papa's breeches." Rebecca pulled a face. "And everything they didn't rip, they smashed."

"Not everything." Emma worked hard to keep the bitterness from her voice, but the probable fate of Mama's quilt weighed heavily on her mind. "What they didn't destroy, they stole."

Luke turned his head to look her way. "You had something in that trunk, didn't you? Something special."

Tears sprang to her eyes at the sympathy in his tone. She nodded. "A quilt made by my mother."

Papa's gentle voice admonished her. "But we have forgiven them, haven't we, daughters?"

Rebecca lowered her head, and Emma avoided the searching gaze that sought hers from across the fire. Times like these made her wonder if she would ever be ready to take the training and receive baptism. Surely forgiveness was the hardest teaching in all of *Die Bibel.* Forgiving Rebecca for a hasty word, or her friend Katie for slighting her at a Sunday night singing, was hard enough. But to forgive lawless men who had stolen one of the few precious ties she had to her mother? It would take her a lifetime to learn how to do that.

Luke might have been hearing her thoughts. "If you can forgive those no-good thieves, you're a better man than I am, Jonas. You know if they cross your path again they'll do the same thing."

Papa nodded. "In all likelihood."

Maummi rocked back in her chair and quoted, *"Und vergib uns unsre Sünden, denn auch wir vergeben allen, die uns schuldig sind."*

"Pardon me, ma'am?"

"It is from *Die Bibel,*" Papa explained. " 'We forgive, even as we are forgiven.' " He shrugged. "It is our way."

Maummi nodded, as if that explained everything. Luke's expression betrayed his struggle to understand, but he remained silent, probably out of respect for their beliefs. The thought warmed Emma. A man who respected others deserved respect

162

himself. Did he know *Die Bibel*? A person didn't have to be Amish to love the Word of God.

Curiosity pushed a question out of her mouth before she could stop it. "Do you have faith of your own, Luke?"

A smile crooked his lips. "I used to think so until I met you folks. When I was a boy, my grandma read to me from the Bible at night." His gaze slid upward to *Maummi*. "Only hers was in English. I loved the stories about David and the Philistine, and Noah, and so on. I learned my letters reading about the Lord's life and death. She and Ma took me to preaching every time the preacher came to town, and when I was nine I was baptized in a river." He glanced behind his back, where the waters of the river reflected a soft moonlight. "Kind of like this one, only without the muck."

Maummi's rocking stopped abruptly. "You are Christian, then?"

"Yes, ma'am." He ducked his head. "I do a lot of thinking and praying during long days in the saddle. I admit, though, it's been a number of years since I read the Bible on my own."

"Your grandmother lived with you?" Rebecca grinned up at *Maummi*. "Like ours?"

"That's right. Pa was a farmer early on,

like you, Jonas." He nodded across the fire. "But then he got a chance to ride along on a cattle drive back when I was seven or eight. He took to the trail and wasn't home much after that. Grandma helped Ma raise me and my brothers. We worked hard on that farm."

While he talked, he picked up a stick and scratched absently in the dirt they had cleared around their campfire. Emma watched his profile. His eyes grew distant with memories, and the hint of a smile played around his lips.

"Do you miss farm life?" she asked.

Her question jerked him out of his reverie. He gave a quick shrug. "Sometimes."

"What happened to your farm?" Papa asked.

"The bank took it." The words were clipped through tight lips. "That's when I joined up with my pa on my first cattle drive. I've been riding the beef ever since." He tossed the stick into the fire.

An ache tugged at Emma's heart at the idea of losing his family's farm. When he stopped being a cowboy, where would he go if he had no home? Her gaze was drawn to the drawing he'd etched in the dirt. At the top, a half circle pointing downward with lines radiating from the outside. Below, a smaller half circle faced up.

"What is this?" she asked.

He looked at the drawing as though startled to see it there. "A silly sketch. When I was younger I had plans to buy a farm one day and raise my own herd. You've seen the Triple Bar brand on the cattle in my herd?" Emma nodded. "That's Mr. Hancock's brand, and it's pretty plain. I always wanted something different. I wasted hours designing a brand for my cattle." He pointed to the top circle. "That's a sun, and that," his finger indicated the smaller inside circle, "is a *C* on its back, called a lazy *C*. My grandma used to tease me when I was a boy." He stiffened his back and adopted a high-pitched tone. " *'Luke Carson, the sun done risen over your head, you lazy boy. Git up outta that bed.'* " He laughed. "She knew I used to stay in bed on purpose to rile her."

Everyone joined in with a chuckle, even *Maummi*. A glance at her face revealed a softer expression than Emma had seen her display for Luke yet. The comment sounded so much like something *Maummi* would say, full of honeyed vinegar. Sharp, but with the sweetness of love to tone down the bitter taste.

Luke picked up his hat and climbed to his feet. When he stood, he swept his boot in

165

the dirt and blotted out the sketch. Emma wasn't sure anyone had noticed except her. Something about the finality of the unobtrusive motion saddened her.

"I need to get back. I don't want Griff thinking I've left him to stand guard alone." He set the hat on his head, and nodded toward Rebecca. "It's been a pleasure meeting you."

She climbed to her feet and dipped into a polite curtsey. "Thank you for the cakes."

"Glad you liked them." He offered a hand to *Maummi.* "I enjoyed meeting you, ma'am. I hope you get those scratches out of your hutch."

"*Danki,* Mr. Carson. The Lord keep you safe on your travels."

When Emma pulled her feet beneath her to rise, Luke turned to help her stand. She stared at the hand he extended. A strong hand, well shaped. She laid her hand inside his, and his fingers wrapped around hers, cradling them like tender arms around a newborn. Throat constricted, she allowed him to pull her to her feet.

"Have a nice life, Miss Switzer."

The same farewell he'd spoken earlier, only this time the words were gentle, almost whispered. His gaze searched her face, as though memorizing her features, until she felt heat rise up her neck and threaten to flood her cheeks. Thank goodness for the dim orange glow of the firelight that might hide an embarrassing blush.

"You too, Luke." Gently, she extracted her hand from his and swept it behind her back to clutch it in the other.

He shook hands with Papa. "Safe travels, Jonas. I hope you get to Troyer without any more trouble."

"We have decided to return home," Papa told him. "Will you stay in Hays until Wednesday? I will bring your money there."

At the mention of Luke staying in Hays, a few miles from Apple Grove, Emma's hopes rose, only to be dashed at Papa's arrangement to pay back his debt. On the occasions when Papa and the other men of Apple Grove ventured into the infamously wild town, the women rarely joined them. If Luke didn't come to the farm to collect his debt, she would not see him again.

Luke's head cocked in surprise, but he made no comment on the change in their plans. "I'll be staying over a few days to take care of some business and arrange for my next cattle drive. You can find me at the Howell House."

His farewells made, he mounted his horse and turned it toward his camp. For a moment he paused outside the ring of firelight, a tall figure silhouetted by a narrow sliver of moon. Then he turned Bo toward the herd of cattle and galloped away. Emma fought a lingering sense of loss as she watched his shadow melt into the darkness.

It was a very good thing this *Englisch* man was gone from her life.

A very sad but good thing.

TWELVE

Morning saw the herd up and ready to move early. Luke's sleep had been fitful after his watch, plagued by dreams of his boyhood farm and working alongside his ma, back before she died of consumption. The morning sun burned his tired eyes, and it was a good thing McCann's coffee was strong enough to raise the dead this morning. As he filled his mug for the second time, he scanned the landscape behind them. A thin line of smoke rising into the sky told him the Switzers were up early. Today was Thursday, and the herd had lost yesterday. They had to cover considerable ground today. If they did, they would still arrive in Hays with a day to spare before the cattle train left on Monday.

After a hearty breakfast of biscuits and gravy, Luke took his place in the lead with Jesse and Kirk riding point. He pointed Bo toward the herd and watched his boys take up their positions. Griff, Kirk, and Morris stood ready at the flank positions. Vic whistled and clucked to his charges in the remuda, and they were ready to go. Charlie and Willie galloped toward the back of the herd, and as Luke watched, he couldn't help taking a final glance toward the Switzers' campsite. The smoke from their campfire had ceased, and that big hutch was an unmistakable landmark in the back of that wagon. The reddish hair of the oxen was also visible, yoked at the front of the wagon. The Switzers had broken camp and were on the move.

Right behind his herd.

"All right." He whistled. "Move 'em out."

The call went down the line, Griff shouting back toward Charlie and Willie. Full bellies, plenty of water, and an easy day had rendered the cattle cooperative. The lead cows surged ahead without much prodding, and the rest followed. In a short time, they had spread out wide on the prairie and settled into a comfortable gait. The day promised to be hot, with few clouds in the sky to break the sun's heat. Luke decided not to push too hard, but set an easy pace.

A few hours into the day's journey they left the river behind and headed northwest across a wide plain. Easy travel, because the only interruption to the landscape were stands of flowering persimmon, bittersweet berries that by fall would be a deep red, and tall black walnut trees. According to Luke's map, by early evening they should be able to make up the ground lost by the stampede and pick up their previous route, the western variation of the Chisholm Trail that headed toward Hays. At that point the Switzers would veer off to the west and head home. He turned in the saddle to check their location.

Still there.

All morning they had kept up, and now it looked as though the wagon had gained a little on the herd.

Jesse rode up beside him, his expression dark. "What in tarnation is going on?"

"What?"

He jerked his head backward. "That *Aim*-ish bunch is following us."

Rather than give his friend anything to harp about, he glanced over his shoulder and adopted an air of innocence. "They are? Well, I'll be a monkey's uncle."

"You are a monkey's uncle. You've been watching them all morning. Besides, Griff told me that you took supper to them last night." His scowl deepened. "My pa always warned if you feed a stray, you've got him for life."

Lifting an indifferent shoulder, Luke faced forward. "I figure tomorrow morning they'll break off and head for home."

"You figure, do you?" Jesse studied Luke through narrowed eyes, their horses keeping step with each other. "You don't suppose they'll trail us all the way to Hays, do you? Especially one of the females, for instance. Last thing I need is an adolescent runaway trailing after me."

Luke shook his head. "Not a chance. Where one goes the others follow. Relax. You're English and —"

"You're a monkey's uncle," Jesse finished. "Why aren't they going east? I thought they were visiting family out there or something."

He shrugged. "I guess they changed their minds." The less knowledge he claimed of the Switzers and their plans, the less likely he would get ribbed or lectured. The weight of Jesse's accusing stare stepped on a nerve. "Haven't you got work to do?"

"You know, we're moving pretty slow today." Jesse's statement held a note of suspicion.

Luke slowly turned to face him. Now he was stepping on his *last* nerve. "We're making good progress."

"Could be making better." Jesse held his

gaze. "You're not purposefully holding the herd back so that wagon can keep up, are you?"

The accusation sent an irritated flash through Luke like a lightning strike. Who was the trail boss on this drive, anyway? Friend or no friend, Jesse needed to learn how to keep to his proper place.

Luke turned and focused on the herd. "I'm not going to answer that. I don't have to explain my decisions to anybody. If you don't like the way I lead this cattle drive, then don't sign on for my next one."

Jesse must have heard the anger in his tone, or maybe he saw it in his face, because instead of flaring up, he jerked a nod. With a tug on the reins, he galloped back to his point position without another word.

Luke let his anger simmer a while. This was the problem with hiring friends. Jesse took liberties and the other men saw it. The result was a lack of respect for his position as trail boss. They talked too familiarly about him. One example was Griff telling Jesse about his visit to the Switzers' campsite last night.

As soon as the thought entered his head, he knew it was unfair. How many cattle drives had he ridden? Plenty. And he couldn't remember a single one where the men didn't speculate over the boss's actions and decisions. Even when he'd ridden under Pa's leadership, the boys didn't curb their talk because the boss's son was sitting around the campfire. Days were long and lonely, and nights were for talking — about the boss, and each other, and any other subject that came up.

He turned and glanced behind him to the right, where Jesse rode. Luke had hired him partly because he was a good point rider, but mostly because he was a friend. He could be counted on to speak his mind, and if his opinions weren't always impartial, at least they were thoughtful. Which meant he'd been thinking about Luke and the Switzers — or, more likely, Luke and Emma — and wouldn't have made that accusation if he didn't think there was a possibility that Luke was getting in deep water.

A bad joke, considering yesterday, but he laughed anyway. Then he sobered. Was that a possibility? Luke's hand tightened on the reins as he searched his motives. Had he purposefully set a slower pace than he could have in order to keep that wagon in view? The reasons he'd come up with were true — the herd had run a few pounds off during that stampede, and he didn't want to risk them losing any more weight. It also wasn't wise to push a herd that had stampeded recently because of the risk of causing another blind run. He glanced backward and watched the lead cattle's pace, which was nowhere near a run. It could even be called leisurely. Maybe even slow.

His gaze was drawn to the wagon behind them. Jonas had maintained his position, easily keeping up with the herd. Though they were too far away for him to see their faces, he clearly picked out Emma on her father's right, for she sat taller than her sister on the other side. From this angle, he could see a flash of white from Mrs. Switzer's *kapp* where she sat in her rocking chair in the back of the wagon.

Is Jesse right? Am I setting an easy pace so they can keep up?

He shrugged off guilt. He was doing what any man would do in his place. Any Christian man. After all he'd done to help them, he'd hate to see those outlaws come back and take what little remained. On the other hand, he had no intentions of letting the Amish follow the herd. They were grown folk; they could do for themselves. He straightened and pulled a kerchief up over his nose. In spite of the rains, dust was kicking up. All he needed was a nice, blinding dust storm.

But Luke knew there was a reason why his eyes strayed to the back of the herd more than usual. He had no doubt he would see Jonas in Hays on Wednesday, money in hand to repay him.

Jonas. Not Emma.

When that wagon drops out of sight, I won't ever see her again.

He turned back in the saddle, the sudden knowledge burning in his mind. Jesse's accusation was true. His attraction for Emma really was at the root of the day's slow pace. Part of him wanted to make sure she was safe, but the biggest part of him wanted to keep her in sight. Stupid, because after tomorrow they would return to their very different lifestyles — hers as an Amish woman and his as a cowboy. Those two were about as compatible as cougars and kittens. Throw them together, and somebody was going to get hurt.

My responsibility is to get this herd to the railhead in Hays on time. Early is better.

They could safely pick up the pace with no danger to the cattle. And putting some distance between him and Emma suddenly seemed like a good idea.

He shifted his weight in the saddle, ready to urge Bo to a faster pace. Hooves pounding the ground beside him drew his attention to Kirk, who drew up to his side.

"You see that?" He pointed to something in the distance.

Luke looked. The ground up ahead was littered with debris, as though someone had broken camp and left some of their belongings scattered on the ground. The sunlight reflected off a white surface. Had they found more of the Switzers' belongings?

"I'll check it out."

He urged Bo into a gallop. As he neared the area, the white object took shape. His pulse surged when he identified it.

A quilt.

He dismounted and picked up the thick blanket. Pieces of brightly colored fabric had been assembled into an intricate pattern and stitched in place with small, even stitches. On the ground around the quilt lay a few pieces of clothing and some pottery containers. Some were empty and one was smashed, but several were still sealed with canvas and secured with twine.

Jesse galloped up beside him as he was scooping up the pieces and piling them in the center of the quilt.

"What's going on?"

Luke continued his work. "I have a hunch this is part of the Switzers' personal things. They're going to get trampled when we bring the herd through."

"Hmm." Jesse dismounted and bent over to snatch up a garment. "You're going to put these things off to the side in plain sight, so that wagon will come across them, right?" He held up the garment. "Or are you planning on wearing these?"

Luke turned and saw that he held up a pair of ladies' bloomers, a smirk touching the corners of his mouth. Heat crept up the back of Luke's neck. He snatched the garment out of Jesse's hands and tossed it on the accumulating pile.

"The herd's running wide," he said. "There's no place to put this stuff where it'll be safe. Somebody will have to take it back to them."

The last of it landed on the quilt, and he grabbed the corners to gather them up into a bundle. Though Jesse didn't say anything, Luke felt his stare.

"Look, I've been thinking about what you said." He wrapped a piece of rope around the bundle to close it, his gaze fixed on his hands. "We're picking up the pace. We can cover at least another five miles before we have to stop for the night."

He looked Jesse in the eye and let him see the apology there. Then he held out the bundle. "You want to run this back to them for me?"

Jesse held his gaze, and then his lips curved into a smile. Luke returned it, and an uncomfortable knot unraveled in his gut. Friendship was restored with few words, the same as when he was a boy growing up with his brothers.

Jesse held up his hands to refuse the bundle. "I wouldn't go near that wagon if you paid me extra. The old woman doesn't like me, and that younger girl bugs me. You take it. I think Bo needs to stretch his legs a bit."

The herd had nearly caught up with them. With a grin, they climbed back into their saddles.

"Jesse's got lead," Luke told Kirk when he rode past. "I'll be back shortly."

"Sure you will!" Jesse called. "Just like all the other times!"

"*Ach,* a dozen washes and this stink will never scrub from our clothes."

Maummi's complaint gave voice to the misery they all felt. Emma had tried breathing through her mouth to avoid the terrible smell, until her tongue dried out and her lips became chapped. Seated on the bench beside Papa, she'd dozed off once and dreamt that a herd of rotting skunks had taken up residence beneath her bed.

Rebecca lowered the scant protection of her apron from her face. "I worry that the stink won't scrub from our bodies."

She immediately clapped the fabric back over her mouth and nose, though what good it did to breathe through an apron Emma couldn't imagine. Perhaps if they came across some lilacs or roses they could rub the blossoms into the fabric. Even that wouldn't kill the stench, though surely rose-scented manure smelled better than the fresh variety.

"A few more hours only," Papa said. "Then the cows will continue north, and we will point our wagon toward home."

If his words were meant to be comforting, they missed the mark with Emma. By tomorrow morning Luke and his herd would be out of sight. No longer would she be able to strain her eyes ahead to catch a glimpse of him overtop this sea of cattle. Not that she could see many details from this distance, but she could easily pick him out far ahead in the lead. Her gaze was drawn there now, and she scanned the distance for a broad-shouldered figure wearing a familiar hat.

When she failed to locate him in his usual place, she sat upright on the bench. Had he gone on ahead? An unusual movement drew her attention to the east, where a cowboy on horseback traveled around the edge of the herd. Her pulse stuttered when she recognized Luke. He was heading this way.

"Papa, look." She managed to keep her voice at a normal level. "Luke is coming here. I wonder why?"

Perhaps they had angered him by following too closely.

The wagon rolled to a halt as Luke approached. Emma watched his face, squinting, until his features came into view. When she realized his gaze was locked onto her and a smile curved his lips, her heartbeat fluttered. He drew near and halted his horse on her side of the wagon.

"You folks are making good time today."

Though he spoke to all of them, he did not look away from her. Emma returned his gaze, stomach quivering as though she'd swallowed a bird.

"We are eager to get home, now we've decided to return."

Papa sounded distracted, and Emma became aware that he was watching her closely. She tore her gaze away from Luke and lowered her eyes to the hands clasped in her lap. Though she didn't turn her head, she felt *Maummi's* scrutiny like a coal applied to the back of her prayer *kapp.*

"Well, I won't keep you long," Luke said. "We found more of your things up ahead, so I thought I'd return them before you turned away."

Emma couldn't help looking up then. Her hopes rose when she saw the smile Luke fixed on her. He pulled a bundle from the other side of his saddle and edged his horse close to the wagon to lay it on her lap. Tears sprang instantaneously into her eyes, and she didn't try to stop them when she spotted the familiar, brightly colored pattern.

Mama's quilt!

"Oh, Luke." The words came out on a breath that placed them somewhere between a sigh and a sob. "You found it."

"Kirk spotted it first." His voice softened. "It's so beautiful, I knew as soon as I saw it that it had to be yours."

In a moment that pierced straight through to her heart, Emma knew he wasn't only referring to the beauty of the quilt. His features blurred behind a veil of tears. She couldn't see her fingers fumbling with the knot in the rope that secured the precious quilt around the other belongings inside. *Maummi* climbed out of her rocking chair and stepped forward to peer over her shoulder. On the other side of Papa, Rebecca rose and stood on the floorboard, one hand resting on Papa's shoulder for balance while she watched Emma untie the knot.

"What else is there?" her sister asked.

Emma laid back the folds to reveal a jumble of items, mostly clothing.

"Not much, I'm afraid. The way I figure it, they must have bundled a bunch of things inside the quilt back at the river and rode ahead a ways before stopping to sort out their takings. They threw out the things they had no need of."

Maummi leaned over the backrest and gathered up three small crocks. "Spices they left. Tomatoes they took."

"Men must eat," Papa said. "Even thieves."

In the pile in her lap, Emma spied a piece of fabric she recognized, and picked up the white canvas bag with Katie Beachy's gift inside. The warmth in her chest expanded as she clutched the small piece of home in her hand.

"Well, I'll leave you folks to sort those things out. I'll see you in Hays, Jonas." Luke held the reins in his left hand, and touched the brim of his hat with his right. "Afternoon, ladies."

With one long searching glance at Emma, during which heat rushed into her face and she could not meet his gaze, he turned his horse and galloped away. Aware that Papa studied her from the side, she purposefully did not look up to follow his progress.

"Of all the things the thieves could have left behind, why didn't they leave us something useful, like bed linens to protect us from the ground at night?" Rebecca leaned across Papa's lap and snatched up a piece of clothing. "Instead, they leave this."

She held the garment up. Horrified, Emma recognized her own set of underclothes. Luke had handled her bloomers! Her face burning, if she could have sunk to the floorboard and covered herself up with the quilt, she would have.

Papa stood. His expression, ever unreadable, was even more blank than usual. Never a good sign, in Emma's experience.

"I will walk beside the oxen for a while," he announced.

Emma drew her knees up to let him edge around and hop to the ground. Her face still aflame, she set about folding the miscellaneous clothing piled inside the quilt while Papa urged the oxen into movement, and the wagon lurched forward.

THIRTEEN

Emma hefted her skirt and watched where she placed each foot. Following in the trail of a herd of cattle not only smelled terrible, it made walking a straight path impossible. Her gait resembled that of Mrs. Eicher at a frolic last year before anyone realized the cider had turned hard.

Still, picking a clean path was not a problem when traveling at the painfully slow pace Papa set. The wagon crept along behind her, every creak and crack magnified in the silence that surrounded them. When Emma had climbed down to walk beside Papa an hour back, Rebecca stretched out on the hard bench and drifted off to sleep. *Maummi* sat in her chair, her head bent over the mending in her lap, her body swaying with the movement of the wagon as the oxen plodded ahead.

Emma was careful to keep any hint of frustration from her tone. "I think the oxen could move a bit faster, Papa." She glanced sideways, disappointed to see no reaction whatsoever on her father's face. "At this rate, I fear we won't see Apple Grove before August."

"We are not expected before then." He didn't turn his head to speak, keeping his eyes fixed forward. "The Millers will mind the farm until our return."

Emma drew a slow breath into her lungs and willed the anxious knots in her stomach to loosen. Up ahead, Luke's cattle had dwindled to bug-sized spots of brown on the horizon. If she strained her eyes, she occasionally caught a glimpse of a cowboy or two, riding back and forth across the rear of the herd, but the men in the lead had disappeared behind a swell in the land far beyond. She had lost sight of Luke.

When she could once again trust her voice, she said in a pleasant tone, "If we delay, you'll miss your meeting with Luke on Wednesday."

Papa gave no reply but simply continued walking at the frustratingly slow saunter he'd maintained all afternoon.

Maybe she could push him a little. Gathering her skirts a touch higher, she stretched her stride a tiny bit. Not enough to draw comment, but enough that Papa would be forced to speed up in order to keep pace with her, perhaps without noticing.

Within a few minutes, she had pulled ahead of him like a sprinter outpacing a child. A backward glance revealed the same patient, unreadable expression on his face. Her teeth ground against each other. Was he doing this on purpose?

"A rest we are due, I think. This place is good."

Emma came to a halt so quickly a cloud of dust swirled around her feet. "A rest? Rebecca has been resting for the past hour, and I'm not walking fast enough to need a rest."

His tone held the tiniest touch of reprimand. "I need a rest, daughter."

Her lips snapped together. He *was* slowing them down on purpose. A strong man like Papa would not need to rest after the leisurely stroll they had taken since Luke returned Mama's quilt. She glanced over her shoulder at the quickly dwindling herd. Papa was trying to put distance between Luke and them. Between Luke and her.

Still perched in the back of the wagon, *Maummi* stopped work on the shirt she was mending and folded the garment. "A light meal we'll have to keep up our strength."

Emma worked hard to keep her frustration in check. They had no need for strength if they were going to inch across the Kansas prairie like turtles.

When Papa stopped the oxen in the shade of a cluster of trees, Rebecca stirred awake and sat up on the wagon bench. She stretched her arms high in the air and arched her back. "Are we there yet?"

"We have barely gone twenty yards all afternoon," Emma shot back too quickly.

She ducked her head away from Papa's look and went to the back of the wagon to help *Maummi* down to the ground.

"Reach that crate for me, Emma."

Maummi pointed to indicate the one she meant, and Emma climbed up into the wagon to retrieve it. When she'd slid it over to the edge so her grandmother could rummage inside, she spoke in a low voice that could not be overheard.

"Why is Papa going so slowly, *Maummi?*"

The elderly woman didn't bother to look up. "Why ask a question when you already know the answer?"

With a grim nod, Emma acknowledged her suspicions. "He is trying to put a distance between Luke and me."

" '*Höret, meine Kinder, die Zucht eures Vaters; market auf, daß ihr lernt und klug Werd!*' " The biblical proverb was one

188

Maummi had often repeated when Emma was younger. *Hear, ye children, the instruction of a father, and attend to know understanding.*

She didn't bother to hide an audible sigh as *Maummi* selected four plump apples from the crate. "I know Papa is wise and I must learn from him. It's just that . . ."

That what? That she wanted to moon after Luke even though she knew there was no possibility for a future between them?

She picked up one of the apples and returned it to the crate before she slid the box back to its storage position. She couldn't force a bite down her throat. When she turned, she caught *Maummi*'s sympathetic eyes fixed on her.

" 'Young birds must learn the paths of the sky from older ones. Else they lose themselves in the joy of soaring.' "

Emma made no response to the proverb as she hopped down from the wagon and trudged a little distance away. She knew *Maummi* meant the lesson kindly, but she was not a brainless young bird. Had she not always been obedient to Papa, as was proper? Did he think her incapable of making wise choices on her own?

While her family gathered in the cooling shade of the sparse trees, Emma climbed a short swell in the land where she could watch the cattle dwindle in the distance. When the last cow disappeared over the hill where Luke had vanished earlier, her frustration turned to heavy sorrow that dragged at her heart. She truly had seen the last of Luke Carson.

Well, and what of it? If she was as level-headed as she professed to be, why was she acting as if she'd lost a beau? He was not her beau and never would be. Too much separated them, not the least of which was their faith. She did not want a husband who stayed gone for months at a time on the cattle trail. When she found the man she wanted to spend her life with, he would attend Sunday meetings with her, and singings, and drive her to town in a proper buggy. He would raise barns with the other men in Apple Grove while she cooked noodle casseroles to serve him when his work was done. He would read *Die Bibel* in German, and train their children using proverbs. He would . . .

She blinked back the traitorous tears that threatened, suddenly impatient with them. He would not be Luke.

Loneliness rose up inside her. Whom, then would she marry? Though she had not relished the thought of Aunt Gerda parading her in front of every eligible man in Troyer, she'd been fairly certain she would find her future husband there. Now that she was going back home to Apple Grove, was Amos Beiler to be her only option? Her gaze strayed once again to the horizon.

Lord, has that been Your intention all along? Did You send me out on this ill-fated journey simply to make me agreeable to a future with Amos? She kicked a dried clot of dirt and watched it roll down the hill. *If so, You could have saved me a lot of trouble by saying so.*

Enough moping. Such dour thoughts were unbecoming to an Amish woman. She left the hilltop and headed toward the wagon. Rebecca had wandered off to the east and stood a distance away, her back bent as she inspected something in the grass. *Maummi* and Papa were out of sight, but as Emma approached the wagon she heard the low murmur of their voices. They had seated themselves in the shade, leaning against the wheels on the far side of the wagon.

Emma started toward the rear to get the apple she'd refused earlier, but *Maummi's* words stopped her.

"I like the *Englisch* man. He makes for me a warm feeling in my heart."

"The trouble is not in liking him," Papa's gentle voice answered. "He is not Amish."

They were discussing Luke. Emma hesitated. She should make a noise to announce her presence. Instead, she ignored a warm rush of guilt and remained still.

"He is Christian." From *Maummi's* decisive tone, Emma could almost see her firm nod. "Like my Carl."

"I fear you see in him too much of my *fader.* You would push our Emma to him."

"Not so. But neither can you build a wall to trap her inside your backyard. She is a good girl and loves the Amish way. You must let her choose for herself."

"*Ja.* I know. I have raised both my daughters to serve the Lord and obey the *Ordnung.* If she chooses to leave the Plain way, as is her right, I can do nothing." A long sigh sounded. "If the Lord had left my Hannah here, she would know what to do. Her desire matched mine, that our daughters choose baptism and the church. I fear I will fail her, and my Emma, and my Lord all at once."

Maummi's voice held a note of gentleness Emma rarely heard. "You have not failed, Jonas."

Emma could listen no longer. She crept away without a sound and went back up the low hill, where she dropped down to sit in the grass. Hot guilt churned in her stomach,

leaving her faintly sick. The guilt of eaves-
dropping was one thing, but the sorrow and
self-accusation she'd heard in Papa's voice
was enough to make her sob. How could he
consider himself a failure when he had surrounded her with love and guidance her
whole life? What an ungrateful daughter she
had become.

A breeze stirred the golden grass around
her and she welcomed it, drawing it deep
into her lungs. When she exhaled, she blew
all her foolish feelings for Luke out with it.
Her future was in the Lord's hands, not her
own. If He wanted her married to Amos
Beiler in Apple Grove, so be it. She would
not disappoint her Lord or her papa.

Luke awoke to the smell of coffee and
bacon, one of the best combination of odors
God ever concocted. Today it failed to rouse
him. His eyes protested when he tried to
pry them open, and grogginess hugged his
brain like fog hugs a Texas river on a cool
morning. He knew he'd be tired today when
he had taken both the first and second
watch last night, but he'd rather be in the
saddle doing something productive than
tossing on his bedroll, his brain too full to
sleep.

The Switzers' wagon had dropped out of

sight yesterday, and the empty stretch of land behind the herd had pestered him like a bothersome horsefly. He couldn't stop turning around and stretching his sight, trying to catch a glimpse of white from a bonnet. He'd even welcome the sight of that doggone hutch. But the prairie to the south of them remained empty.

He rolled off his pallet and stood to stretch while he scanned his surroundings. The cattle had stirred, and more than half were already up and grazing. Behind them, the prairie was still empty.

I hope the family isn't in trouble.

With a final mental shake, he rejected the worrisome thought. He wasn't their hired hand. He'd done his Christian duty, and now they were on their own. Emma was on her own.

As he shook out his bedroll, Luke surveyed the camp. Griff, Charlie, and Jesse were the only ones still buried in their blankets. Everybody else was out of sight, probably milling around the breakfast fire or getting their gear stowed for the day.

"Morning, boss." Willie rounded the chuck wagon with a tin mug of coffee in each hand. "Thanks for taking the extra watch last night. I slept great."

Luke took the mug he offered as he

brushed off the thanks. "No problem. You'll burn some added energy today. I intend to push this herd halfway to Hays before nightfall."

He took a swig of coffee and nudged Jesse's slumbering form with his foot. "Up and at 'em, cowboy. We have a lot of ground to cover today."

Jesse stirred but didn't sit up. "It's early yet. Sun's not even up."

Laughing, Luke kicked the hat off his friend's face. "Now it is. Come on, sluggard. Last one out of the sack gets to ride drag today."

The threat got him moving. Groaning, Jesse sat and squinted upward, his eyes unfocused and bleary. "There. You happy?"

Luke didn't have time to answer. A gunshot cracked nearby, answered by another from a short distance away. The shouts of men filled the air — wild, high-pitched cries from unknown voices, and answering cries of dismay from his own men.

Jesse lunged to his feet. "What in tarnation —"

Luke didn't bother answering. A sick certainty settled in his stomach as the shouts continued and more shots disrupted the peaceful morning. Startled cattle answered with distressed bawls and danced on nervous hooves. He leaped for the pile of gear near the head of his pallet and the rifle secured on the side of his saddle, while around him men scrambled to their feet. Griff's harsh growl answered Jesse's question.

"Rustlers."

The word sent a bolt of hot, sticky fear straight into Luke's gut.

FOURTEEN

Papa seemed in no more hurry this morning than he had yesterday, but Emma didn't mind so much now. During much of the night she had begged the Lord to make her more compliant, more obedient, more willing to accept the life He had planned for her. Long after midnight she finally fell into the peaceful sleep of one submitted to the will of the Father, who knew her heart's desire.

She awoke to the sun rising into a clear blue sky over the wide Kansas plain. A persistent wind had blown all night and swept away much of the stench of the cattle herd. Instead, the sweet smell of prairie grass and the fresh scent of water filled the air.

After breakfast Emma and Rebecca collected the dishes — plain metal ones purchased back in Gorham — and took them to a nearby stream to scrub them clean.

Sunlight danced on the moving surface of the narrow creek that had carved a deep swath through the land. When their chore was complete, Emma took the opportunity to wash the dust from her neck and face, while Rebecca wandered upstream.

"Emma, look here. I found a school of tiny fish. How colorful they are, like bits of rainbows playing about the rocks."

Emma glanced at her little sister, who was bent over the stream's edge and staring intently into the water. Delight made the girl's tone light, and Emma couldn't help a smile in response. Not so many years had passed since Rebecca was a child, tromping off to school swinging a book strap in one hand and her lunch pail in the other. How proud Mama would have been had she lived to see what a lively young woman her baby had become.

A movement in the distance drew her attention. Something was heading their way from the north and kicking up a lot of dust as it came. She caught a glimpse of brown hides. Alarm pricked her nerves to attention. Horses, maybe? Had the thieves returned?

"Papa!"

When he looked up from his inspection of the oxen's legs, she pointed. His head turned as he followed the direction of her hand. Staring at the quickly approaching objects, Emma noticed that these animals were riderless. As they drew near, she also realized they were not horses but cattle.

They slowed on their approach, and the dust began to settle. Perhaps the wagon with the towering hutch in the middle of the trail looked like a barrier, or maybe they were tired from running. Regardless of the reason, their pace dwindled from a run to a trot, and then to a walk. One of them left the trampled trail and stood in the tall prairie grass. It inspected Emma and her family with a solemn, dark-eyed stare, its sides heaving from exertion. When it had caught its breath, the horned head casually lowered and the steer began tearing up mouthfuls of grass. Soon the others followed suit.

Where had they come from? A note of concern worried her thoughts as she counted them. Eleven cows did not just appear from nowhere. Either a ranch was nearby, or they came from a herd traveling in the area. And there was only one herd she knew of that had been through here recently.

With a determined step she strode toward them.

"Emma!" *Maummi's* sharp tone sliced through the distance. "Take care."

She waved a hand in answer but didn't slow until she drew near enough to see the brand seared into the rump of the nearest steer. Three bars, two vertical and one horizontal, stood out clearly on the brown hide.

She turned and found Papa's eyes on her. "It's the Triple Bar brand. These are from Luke's herd."

Though his expression remained impassive, she saw acknowledgment in his eyes and his slight nod.

How did Luke lose almost a dozen cattle? Perhaps they had wandered off while one of the cowboys wasn't looking. Surely in a herd of two thousand it wasn't uncommon to lose a few along the way, but if that were the case, why had they been running?

Several possibilities presented themselves. Something had happened to frighten them. She herself knew how easily the silly things became startled. A prairie dog, maybe, or a snake in the grass. But then surely one of the riders would have noticed, wouldn't he? Wouldn't someone have come after them?

She scanned the horizon, but no cowboy on horseback appeared. At the sight of the wide open plain, the muscles in her stomach drew tight. What if something had happened to the riders? Or — she swallowed against a mouth gone suddenly dry — to their leader?

She ran toward her father, who stood watching the grazing cattle, lines heavy on his brow. "Something must have happened to frighten them away from the herd."

He didn't answer, but his lips tightened.

"We have to help them."

His calm gaze slid to hers. "There is nothing we can do."

The words pulled the knots in her belly tighter. "We can gather them up and return them."

"Emma." A soft smile curved his lips. "We have no horses, no way to move cattle forward."

"We have our feet." With an enormous effort, she stopped herself from stomping one of hers out of sheer frustration.

Rebecca ran up to join them. "She's right, Papa. Emma knows how to make cattle move. We all saw her do it yesterday."

Had the situation not been so dire, Emma would have pinched her sister for her smug grin.

"We can all do it," Emma insisted. "The four of us, along with two oxen, can certainly push a few cows down a trail. Especially if they belong to the man who has helped us over and over."

A struggle clear on his features, Papa's eyes moved as he studied her. What was he looking for? Did he suspect her of concocting a ploy to see Luke again? With a flash of guilt, she could not deny that she found the idea appealing. And yet what else could they do? Leave his cows grazing on the side of the trail and continue on their way? How could they live with their consciences after all he had done to help them?

Emma returned Papa's gaze without flinching. After a moment, he turned away.

"I will pray on the matter."

A low groan threatened to rumble from deep in her throat. And how long would that take? They could be here for days while Papa waited to hear from the Lord, and all the while Luke could be in trouble. In fact, with every moment that passed she became more certain that he *was* in trouble. He might even be hurt and waiting for someone to come to his aid.

Lord, please don't take long to get through to Papa.

She'd barely had time to pace once from the stream to the wagon and back again before Papa turned to face his family. Whether the Lord heard her prayer, or Papa's own sense of responsibility toward

202

their rescuer convinced him, Emma couldn't be sure.

"We will gather these cows and take them with us," he announced. "If we find the herd along the way, we will return them. Otherwise we will take them home to Apple Grove, and I will send word to Hays for Luke to come and get them."

Relief swept over Emma at the words. She lowered her head demurely to hide a smile she could not prevent.

One way or another, she would see Luke again when he reclaimed his cattle.

Luke squatted on his haunches in the grass, his gut churning as he inspected Jesse's leg.

"It's not that bad, Luke. If we splint it and wrap it tight, I can still ride." Regardless of his brave words, pain pinched white creases at the corners of Jesse's eyes, and he spoke in a clipped manner, as though every word was a struggle.

"Don't be an idiot." Luke didn't mean to snap the words, but at the moment he couldn't muster the effort to comfort his friend. "I can see your bone sticking through your pants. You aren't riding anything but a wagon to the closest doctor."

To take the sting out of his words, he gently clapped Jesse on the shoulder before he rose to his feet. Even that light movement caused the tough cowboy to hiss in pain.

Luke's gaze strayed beyond the chuck wagon to a somber place in the prairie grass. Grief filled him at the sight of a pair of bodies, cocooned in blankets. Kirk would have made a fine trail boss one day soon. Luke would have recommended him without hesitation. And Willie —

A knot of sorrow threatened to choke off his breath. He cleared his throat, fighting against the sting of tears. That boy wasn't but fifteen years old, on his second cattle drive and young enough to still be in love with the idea of life on the trail. At home he had a ma and a houseful of younger sisters and brothers. Around the nightly campfires he'd told how he aimed to send most of his pay back home to help out.

Jesse followed his gaze and spoke in a soft voice. "They died well, Luke."

A sarcastic blast exploded from Luke's mouth. "Yeah? I don't see how any fifteen-year-old can die *well*. Or twenty-five-year-old, either. They are dead, same as those rustlers lying over yonder."

His gaze switched to the second line of bodies, set off a little ways outside the campsite. His men had taken out four of the rustlers during the skirmish. Luke was fairly sure his rifle had not fired a fatal shot because he'd aimed over the bandits' heads hoping to scare them off. He'd watched Griff charge at a pair of men as they galloped through the herd to scatter it, and the old cowhand had taken them both out. In the ensuing confusion of gunshots and shouts and stampeding cattle, Luke didn't see the other two fall. He and his men found the bodies when their compadres high-tailed out of there in a cloud of dust.

A retching sound from nearby drew his attention to Charlie, who stood at the back of the chuck wagon, his waist bent as he vomited on the ground in front of his boots. Luke exchanged a sympathetic glance with Jesse, and then he went to put a steadying hand on the boy's back.

"It's all right, son." He set his voice in a soothing tone. "You made it. You're going to be fine."

Charlie straightened and wiped the back of his hand across his mouth. "It ain't that, boss." His gaze strayed toward the rustlers' bodies, and his skin took on a green tint. "I ain't never shot nobody before."

The agony in the young man's voice twisted something inside Luke's chest. How could he answer the soul-sick grief of someone who had taken a life, however justified? His hand still on Charlie's back, he pulled the young man into an awkward embrace. "Don't let guilt eat you up. You did what you had to do."

"Does that make it okay?" Charlie's voice sounded tortured. "I'll never get used to this feeling. Never."

Luke thumped his back before releasing him. "I pray you don't."

At the sound of hoofbeats, Luke turned to find Griff and Morris riding toward them. They stopped as McCann exited the chuck wagon with a pail of clean water and some strips of cloth to bind Jesse's wound.

"Looks like we've lost about five hundred head," Griff reported as they reined their mounts to a stop. "The remuda scattered too, but Vic took off after them. He'll bring 'em back."

From his place on the grass, Jesse looked up at Luke. "Not as bad as it could be."

"Bad enough," Luke replied, his voice grim. How could he show up in Hays having lost a quarter of the herd and two men? "Anybody get a count of the rustlers?"

"Eight." Morris's gaze strayed to the line of bodies. "That means four escaped. I saw two riding off together to the west, one northeast, and one due east. They'll meet up with each other again soon enough."

"The cattle went in every direction." Griff raised a hand above his head and made a circling motion. "Those rustlers were high-tailing it away without thought for the herd they tried so hard to get. The way they were going, the cattle are miles from here by now."

Charlie found his voice. "We can hunt down the strays, boss. We'll get 'em back."

Nods all the way around. Luke forced a smile of appreciation for the men's attitudes, but his heart plummeted toward his boots. They had started out with a minimum crew to begin with — nine men to drive a herd of two thousand head plus a forty-horse remuda — and now they were down by three. Despite Jesse's brave words, he couldn't ride with that leg. In fact, he'd be lucky if infection didn't set in before they got to Hays. McCann, who knelt over the injury, cleaning it and then binding it with clean cloth, looked pretty grim. Jesse might end up losing his leg, and whoever heard of a peg-legged cowboy?

Morris's voice cut through Luke's worries. "What in tarnation is that?"

They all looked toward the south. An unusual sight on the horizon sent Luke's jaw dangling.

"Well, I'll be a cross-eyed mule." Jesse shook his head in disbelief. "It's those *Aim-ish* folks."

Sure enough, the sight of that ridiculously huge hutch in the back of an ox-drawn wagon was unmistakable. Even more amazing was the small herd of cattle being driven in front of the cart. Leading this bizarre parade was Jonas on foot, his round-brimmed straw hat and black suspenders unmistakable at any distance. And on either side of the cattle, Emma and Rebecca trotted along in flank positions, long sticks in their hands and black skirts trailing in the high grass.

A sudden lightness lifted his spirits and a slow grin spread across his face. It looked as though the Lord had sent him help this time. His gaze focused on Emma.

And He chose a mighty pretty delivery method.

Fifteen

Emma and her family stood in the shade of the chuck wagon and spoke with the somber men. Though Luke had greeted their arrival with true gratitude, sadness hung over the cowboys like a low-riding cloud. They had lost two of their own, and Emma's heart grieved at the pain she saw in each face. Especially Luke's.

Their little group of eleven stray cows had swelled to almost forty by the time they caught up with the main herd. The Switzers had encountered clusters of wandering steer along the way, and the poor things needed almost no prodding to join them, as though they had been lost and looking for someone to lead the way home. Since their arrival, they had melted seamlessly into the herd, which hung closely together as they grazed, as though drawing strength from each other. It was almost as if they sensed their handlers' grief at the loss of their friends.

Emma had not met Kirk, but the thought of the smiling young Willie going to his premature grave was enough to make her weep.

"The first order of business is to bury our friends," Luke told Papa, though his glance kept stealing toward her, which kept a perpetual flow of heat rising into her cheeks.

"What about them?" Rebecca, who had dropped to her knees beside Jesse to watch a grim-faced McCann clean the nastiest wound Emma had ever seen, pointed toward the bodies of the four cattle rustlers. "Will you leave them in the open?"

Luke shook his head. "That might be what they would do with our dead, but we won't stoop to their depths. We'll give them a proper burial and take their belongings with us to Hays. Maybe the sheriff there can identify them and notify their next of kin."

The gesture warmed Emma's heart toward him even more. He was too kindhearted, too upright, to leave the bodies of even dishonest men without proper handling.

"Eight, you say?" *Maummi* stood behind Rebecca, watching the ministrations to Jesse's wound from over her shoulder. "Eight there were who robbed us."

Papa looked at her for a moment, and then without a word he strode away toward

210

the corpses. When he approached, he removed his straw hat and held it in two hands in front of him while he inspected the bodies. After a moment, he replaced his hat and returned.

"Their faces are familiar." His expression was troubled as he glanced at *Maummi* and then at Luke. "Those men took our belongings. The man who showed us mercy, the leader of the others, is there." He bowed his head and closed his eyes in a moment of silent prayer.

"And what of the man with the black teeth?" Emma asked. Lester, his boss had called him. That man had frightened her more than any of the others. Something about the way he looked at her, the disrespectful way he sneered at *Maummi,* disturbed her far more than the mere act of taking their possessions.

Papa shook his head. "That one is not here."

So. Emma lifted her gaze to a swell in the land that bordered this plain to the west. The man with the black teeth was still out there.

"Wrong!" *Maummi's* sharp reprimand startled all of them. She glared down at the cook. "Not clean enough is that wound. And set it before it is wrapped, else you'll lame him for life."

McCann bristled. He drew himself upright and glared at her. "I've been dressing cowboys' wounds for more'n twenty years."

Maummi didn't back down one inch but returned his glare full measure. "A slow learner you must be, then."

The man's bushy eyebrows dropped lower over his eyes. "If you think you can do better, ma'am, then have at it."

Maummi had been waiting for the invitation. She dropped to the ground and quickly unwrapped the strips of cloth. "Fresh water," she barked toward the cook. "And alcohol for cleaning."

"The only alcohol we have is the drinkin' kind," he said. "Whiskey —"

He shrank before the glare she turned on him. "Bring it."

Emma almost felt sorry for him as he struggled to his feet and slunk away toward his wagon. When he passed Luke, he muttered sideways, "I can't abide no *woman* taking over. No good will come of this, mark my words." His glance slid to Emma, and he ducked his head. "Sorry, ma'am."

Beside her Luke nodded absently, his gaze fixed on a faraway point. Emma drank in the sight of his rugged profile, the fresh lines of stress around his tight lips. The burden he must feel! If only she could help him.

"We have to round up strays. The fact that you found so many, Jonas, is encouraging. Maybe they're too tired from the last stampede to run far." He shook his head. "I can't spend much time looking, though, nor can I spare men for the hunt. We're running way too lean now."

The older man, Griff, had been standing quietly off to one side. "We have four able-bodied men here, Luke. You, me, Morris, and Charlie. That's got the compass points covered. We'll cross our fingers that Vic will be back soon with the rest of the horses."

Luke shook his head. "I can't send you out alone, Griff. You know that. There are four rustlers still out there, and for all we know they're lying in wait for us."

"I'll go," Jesse put in from his position on the ground. "I'm feeling better already. Put a tight binding on this leg and heft me into my saddle."

Maummi's jaw dropped open and she gave him a stern stare. "Unless you want to lose your leg, you will stay here."

A stubborn look came over his face, but Luke stopped any argument. "Forget it, buddy. The only place you're going is into a wagon." His voice softened as he looked around the circle. Emma's heart ached at the tone of his voice when he next spoke. "Maybe we ought to cut our losses. Hit the trail and push hard. We might still make the train if we run them on the hoof. After all, it's better to arrive in Hays with three-quarters of a herd than to not arrive in time."

Concern deepened the creases on Griff's weathered face. "That'll do you in, Luke. Your first cattle drive, and you show up that light of beef?" He shook his head. "You won't work as a trail boss ever again."

He lifted a shoulder. "Probably not."

Something inside Emma's rib cage twisted at the resigned look on his face. Words flew out of her mouth before she could check them. "We can help. Papa and Rebecca and I brought those cows here. We can help you find the others."

Rebecca leaped to her feet, a delighted smile on her face, while *Maummi* drew in an audible shocked breath. Papa's normally impassive face held a myriad of emotions, disapproval primary among them.

Luke turned an indulgent smile her way. "You did me a great service. But you're not equipped to scout strays and ride herd over a long trail. You can't do that on foot, Emma."

A rod of steel seemed to slide through her

spine. "Give me a horse, then. I know about horses. We have Big Ed to pull our buggy at home. I care for him every day."

Beside her, Charlie hid a snicker behind his hand, while Griff snorted out loud.

"Emma." Luke's soft voice reached inside her with a warm touch. "Driving a horse is different than riding. I appreciate your offer to help, though."

Rebecca stepped forward. "It's not so different." She cast a glance toward Papa and then continued in defiance of his stare. "Emma and I can both ride. We've ridden Big Ed before. Many times."

Emma swallowed a groan. Leave it to Rebecca to confess their sins in front of *Englischers.* The Amish respected their horses for the important role they played in the household, but they rarely rode, and the one time she and Rebecca had asked, Papa had forbidden them to ride Big Ed. *Maummi* looked scandalized, while Papa's expression settled into resignation.

She locked eyes with her father and loaded an unspoken plea into her gaze. Later she would suffer any penance he deemed appropriate, but for now these men needed their help. At first his lips tightened, but she didn't blink, didn't look away. Finally, his chest expanded in a sigh.

"We will help, my girls and I."

At his words, Luke's head lifted higher. Hope lightened the darkness in his eyes. He took a step forward, his hand outstretched toward Papa.

"Thank you, Jonas. You are an answer to prayer."

As he clasped Luke's hand, Papa's reluctant smile broke free. "As you have been for us, my *Englisch* friend."

Emma exchanged a triumphant glance with Rebecca. Finally, they would be able to assist Luke as he had assisted them. And yet . . .

She glanced toward the west, where two of the bad men who robbed her family and killed Luke's friends had escaped. The man with the black teeth was out there somewhere.

This horse was taller than Big Ed back home. Emma stood beside the black mare and tried to still her trembling limbs as she looked at what seemed an immense height from the ground to the saddle.

Luke stood next to her, ready to give her, Rebecca, and Papa their first cowboy lesson.

"All right. Put your left foot in my hands and grab hold of Sugarfoot's mane. When I lift you up, swing your right leg over the saddle." He cupped his hands and extended them, ready to receive her foot.

What? He wanted her to *straddle* the horse? Emma's mouth dropped open. "I can't do that!"

Confusion crossed Luke's features. "Why not?"

How could he even ask? She spread her feet apart and planted her hands on her hips. "Because I'm a girl."

"I know that." A faint pink tint colored his cheeks. "But you said you'd ridden before."

"Yes, but we didn't . . ." She stumbled to a stop. How could she say this in a delicate way? Her glance slid to Papa and then to Rebecca. She avoided *Maummi's* gaze completely, though her grandmother's disapproving glare from a few feet away weighed her down like a full sack of wheat across her shoulders. "We climbed up onto Big Ed from the fence rail and sat sideways."

Luke stared at her a moment, and then he raked fingers through his hair. "We don't have a sidesaddle, Emma."

"Neither did we," Rebecca volunteered. "We held on to Ed's mane."

Behind her, *Maummi* looked ready to explode. Papa's lips drew into a tight line,

217

as though he was guarding his tongue with a monumental effort.

"You can't do that on a trail horse," Luke explained in a patient voice. "They're not used to bareback riders, and especially not women riding sidesaddle. You're going to have to straddle the horse like a man."

"Impossible!" *Maummi's* outraged shout echoed back to them from a distant hillside. A few cattle grazing nearby lifted their heads and glanced in her direction. She stepped up and grabbed Papa's arm. "Jonas, it is unseemly for girls to ride like men." She lowered her voice and spoke in a shocked whisper heard by everyone. "Their legs will show up to their knees, and even beyond!"

"Not if we wear trousers," Emma put in quickly.

Maummi's mouth fell open, and her chest heaved with her effort to reply. Even Papa had lost his impassive expression, and he stared at his older daughter with disbelieving wide eyes.

"Beneath our dresses," Emma hurried to add. "Black trousers that will preserve our modesty. Trousers like yours, Papa. *Maummi* has mended the damaged ones. Rebecca and I can wear those."

While *Maummi* sputtered with outrage, Papa closed his eyes and bowed his head.

Emma exchanged a glance with Luke, who had taken a subtle step backward, thereby removing himself from the family discussion. He lifted an eyebrow in her direction before turning to scan the horizon with feigned nonchalance.

After a long, silent moment, Papa lifted his head and opened his eyes. "In service to our Lord, the apostle Paul contended with strange customs in pagan lands. Yet the Lord sanctified him and kept him pure. I believe that will happen here, that my girls will be sanctified in this offering of assistance and kept pure." He turned toward Rebecca. "Bring two pairs of mended trousers."

Rebecca cast a triumphant grin toward Emma before turning and running for their wagon.

Maummi battled an obvious struggle, and then she stomped over to thrust her face a few inches from Emma's. "Some things the bishop does not need to know." Her sparse eyebrows lowered. "Mind that well, girl."

Emma kept her expression carefully clear as she nodded. When Rebecca returned, *Maummi* stomped off in the direction of the chuck wagon to check on her patient, as though she couldn't bear to witness the disgrace of her granddaughters donning men's trousers.

The men politely turned their backs while Emma and Rebecca slipped Papa's trousers over their legs. Papa's girth was much wider than Emma's. She grabbed a double handful of excess fabric at her waist. Giggling, Rebecca whispered, "We shall need suspenders to keep them on."

Should they ask to borrow Papa's spare suspenders as well? Emma glanced over her shoulder at her father's stiff back. No, they shouldn't push him any further.

"Tuck the excess into your bloomers, and be sure to hold them up when you mount the horse," she whispered back.

Rebecca's peals of laughter were contagious, and both girls were giggling uncontrollably when they finally turned to the men, their hands holding bunched fabric at their waists.

With an effort she regained control and announced, "We are ready."

Luke and Papa turned toward them. Papa kept his eyes averted, but Luke's gaze dropped immediately to her feet. Grinning, he caught her gaze and winked a private message for her alone. Her stomach fluttered in response.

"All right," he said, much louder than necessary, "back to the lesson." He stepped close to Sugarfoot's side, cupped his hands, and stooped low to the ground. "Miss Switzer, if you're ready."

With a grin for Rebecca, Emma approached. Placing a hand on Luke's shoulder to steady herself proved to be distracting. She was aware of the firm muscles beneath the rough fabric of his shirt, and the warmth of his skin. Her face was inches from his when he paused for a moment, her foot in his hands, his eyes searching hers with an intensity that she felt all the way to her core. His breath warmed her cheek and snatched her own breath from paralyzed lungs with an intense feeling she'd never experienced before.

And then he broke the moment with a deepened grin. "Up you go."

Her fingers wrapped themselves in Sugarfoot's coarse mane, and she pulled herself upward at the same time Luke raised his hands. Almost on instinct, her right leg swung over the horse's back, and in the next moment she sat high in the saddle, the faces of those gathered around turned up to look at her.

Luke awarded her with a huge smile. He lifted his hand to pat her leg but then stopped before he touched her. A tickle erupted in her stomach. He brought his hand back to his side with an embarrassed expression and turned away. "Rebecca, you're next."

Riding the horse wasn't nearly as difficult as Emma feared. In fact, straddling Sugarfoot was much easier than clinging to Big Ed's mane, trying to keep her balance with both legs on one side of the horse's barrel chest. Rebecca whooped with delight when she successfully mounted her own horse, and Emma didn't bother to control a grin that seemed insistent on plastering itself on her face.

Even Papa seemed to enjoy his cowboy lesson. He sat astride his horse, a chestnut belonging to the recently deceased Willie, with an erect posture and a wide grin of his own.

"You're doing great, Jonas." Mounted on Bo, Luke urged his horse to the front of his small cluster of students. "Okay, now I want you to let the reins lay loose in your hands while you grip the horse tightly with your knees. That's how you will communicate, through the pressure of your legs."

Papa's horse surged ahead of Emma's to follow Luke. Emma admired the way he sat tall in the saddle, his posture straight and at the same time relaxed. While she clutched the reins with a death grip, Papa let the leather straps slide freely in his grip.

Even Luke noticed the ease with which Papa rode. "You're not a bad rider, Jonas."

The grin on Papa's face tickled an answering grin from Emma.

"I may be Plain," Papa replied with dignity, "but I'm tough."

Emma laughed and then tightened her legs around Sugarfoot's chest. Her heart thrilled when the mare surged forward in response.

She urged the horse to Luke's side. "When will we learn to lasso a cow?"

Luke threw his head back and laughed, his expression the lightest she had seen it since they had caught up with him.

"I'll be happy if you can manage to keep yourself in the saddle," he replied. "Leave the roping to us."

"Hmm." Emma gave him a tight-lipped reply, and then she urged Sugarfoot forward with a tightening of her knees. Yes, the situation was serious, but before this herd was delivered in Hays, she intended to prove to Luke she could do more than keep her seat on a horse.

SIXTEEN

Six graves took a while to dig with only two shovels. While Luke taught the Switzers how to ride and move the herd, he assigned Mc-Cann and Charlie to dig and sent Griff and Morris riding off toward the southeast where Luke had seen a large number of cattle run during the earlier skirmish. The pair had instructions to ride hard for thirty minutes, gathering strays along the way, and then head back. Vic returned to camp shortly, having caught up with the scattered remuda a short distance away. He corralled his charges, and then he relieved McCann from digging duty so he could get a start on supper.

The sun had started to sink in the western sky by the time Griff and Morris returned, driving a hundred and fifty head before them. The strays approached camp almost gratefully and quickly lost themselves in the anonymity of their herd.

Griff's horse galloped to the campfire, and the man dismounted near Luke. "We caught up with them not more than five miles from here, standing around like they were waiting for us to come and get them."

"They're tired." Luke examined the cattle closest to him, noting the way their heads drooped on their necks and the halfhearted way they grazed. "It's been a long trail since El Paso, and I think that stampede the other night exhausted them. They don't have another one in them."

"Which is why those rustlers chose this place." Griff's eyes hardened. "Right at the end of the Chisholm Trail within a few days of the railhead. That sure wasn't an accident."

Luke felt certain the man was right. "Did you see any sign of them?"

Griff shook his head. "Not a one." His gaze shifted to the four fresh graves set off a distance from the other two, their occupants already in place and dirt mounded overtop. "They're shorthanded now. Probably take a while for them to regroup."

"Yeah." Luke heaved a bitter laugh. "But they have four men to run three hundred head of my cattle, which means they're not nearly as shorthanded as we are."

The grizzled cowboy looked over Luke's

shoulder. "How are the replacements coming along?"

Luke turned to where the Switzers sat near their wagon. Mrs. Switzer had requested that her rocking chair be set near the cook's campfire, where she watched over a sleeping Jesse stretched out on a pallet in front of her. He'd pitched a fit when she insisted on using perfectly good whiskey to clean his wound, and when she ignored him, howled like a wounded coyote when she poured it over the gash in his leg. Under her instructions, McCann and Charlie set the bone, and Jesse had screamed until he passed out. She seemed unconcerned. At the moment she rocked in her chair as though she were in front of her own hearth at home. Emma and Rebecca sat on the ground nearby, Emma stitching on her own sewing project while Rebecca stared at the unconscious Jesse like a starved barn cat yearning for a bowl of cream set just out of reach.

Good thing Jesse was out cold, or he'd be fit to be tied.

"They did okay," Luke told Griff. "They're not going to be competing in any rodeos, that's for sure, but as long as the herd stays docile they won't have a problem riding flank from here to Hays."

226

Griff nodded and then jerked his head toward the two empty graves. "Looks like they're ready for us."

Inside the second hole, Charlie tossed his shovel out onto the nearby ground and then Vic reached a hand down to pull him out. Luke shut his eyes and was swamped beneath a wave of sorrow. His first cattle drive as trail boss, and he was about to say a final farewell to two good men. Yes, Willie and Kirk had known the risks when they signed on, as every trail rider did, but that made no difference now. Not to them, and not to him either.

When he opened his eyes, he found Emma watching him. Their gazes met and held. He saw compassion on her face, and understanding lay heavy in her kind eyes. A sad smile softened those lovely lips. She knew his pain. She understood. Though she didn't speak a word, he somehow drew strength from their silent conversation.

He squared his shoulders. "I guess they are," he told Griff. He lifted his head and called in a voice loud enough to reach the entire camp, "It's time to say goodbye to our friends."

Griff clapped him on the back as they headed toward the graves.

■ ■ ■ ■

Emma listened to the music echoing back to her from a rise in the land north of them. Luke's voice, deep and vibrant, seemed to form a foundation for the others. It rumbled in her ears and in her heart. The tune of the song was unfamiliar, but the words were so touching that the sight of Charlie and Morris shoveling earth into the graves blurred behind a curtain of tears.

Amazing grace, how sweet the sound
That saved a wretch like me.
I once was lost, but now am found.
Was blind, but now I see.

The words reached into her soul with gentle fingers and tapped on a door to her inmost being. At times she felt as lost as a blind woman, stumbling around with her arms outstretched, searching for a safe path to travel. Did the song refer to the sight of those who have passed from this life to the next, when the veil would be torn away and the faithful would encounter the Savior face-to-face? Or did it mean something more imminent?

I once was lost, but now *am found, was blind but* now *I see.*

228

Emma glanced sideways at Papa, who stood with his head bowed, his hat in his hand. Her gaze switched to *Maummi,* who clutched her hands before her with a white-knuckled grip, eyes and lips tightly shut. Did they see, really *see,* right now? Did they ever feel lost, as she did, wandering through life, looking for the place where they would encounter grace and happiness?

This funeral service was so different from anything she had ever encountered before. The one seared into her memory was Mama's. When Mama breathed her last breath, the Amish community had converged around Papa and Emma and the infant Rebecca. Though Emma had been only seven years old at the time, she remembered the sight of the plain wooden coffin being lowered into the ground with ropes. The memory was as vivid as if the funeral had happened this morning. Bishop Miller, who had been a figure of authority even though at that time he had not yet been called to serve the Apple Grove district as a bishop, held one end of the rope. Emma still remembered his tender smile toward her across the grave as he let out the line. No graveside words then, no songs. A sermon and Scripture and lots of talking by various ministers in the community, followed by mountains of food on miles of tabletops. And the soul-searing ache that accompanied the knowledge that her beloved mother lay inside that simple wooden box being covered up with dirt.

I want songs at my funeral.

The thought startled Emma. The only music in any Amish service was plain German hymns whispered in monotone voices. But this music, though offered by the rough voices of trail-weary men, refreshed her soul in a way the chants of her Amish brothers and sisters did not.

"Amen." Luke's deep voice at the end of the song concluded the service.

Emma looped arms with Rebecca, who was curiously subdued, and headed back toward the campfire with the rest of the funeral-goers.

"After Mama's funeral," Emma whispered to her sister, "there was a big meal. That was the first time you tasted Mrs. Beachy's apple pie. Though only a babe, you ate it as though you'd been starved for weeks."

Rebecca smiled up at her and hugged her arm close. "I liked the music at this one," she whispered.

"Me too," Emma confessed, her voice low so as not to be overheard by *Maummi* or Papa. "And I like the way they spoke of

230

Willie's life. I feel as though I knew him and Kirk now."

"Me too."

They arrived at the campfire to find an argument in progress between *Maummi* and McCann.

"Spice!" *Maummi's* voice rang out over the prairie. " 'Tis the difference between a plain cook and a good one." She raised her finger and pointed in the cook's face. "Merely plain you are, and not in the Amish way."

McCann drew himself up, his face a mottled purple, and stared her down with bulging eyes. "I'll have you know I've been feeding cowpokes on the trail for more than twenty years and never had a single complaint. I'm the best trail cook west of the Mississippi!"

"Starving men, their tongues dulled from dust and numb from cow stink." *Maummi* stiffened her spine. "Little skill it takes to satisfy them."

McCann looked apoplectic. He cast around wildly for support from his fellow cowboys, but no man would meet his eye. Emma turned her head to hide a grin. She would not like to confront *Maummi* over the craft of cooking.

She sucked in a gasp when the cook lifted a hand and shook a finger in *Maummi's* face.

"Leave me to do my job, madam. Stay away from my beans."

If Emma had dared to shake a finger at *Maummi,* no doubt she would have lost it within three seconds. McCann, however, escaped with all ten digits intact when he turned and glared at Luke. "Keep that woman away from me," he shouted before stomping away to disappear within the confines of his chuck wagon.

Luke spared a respectful glance toward Emma before escaping toward his horse.

The moment McCann was out of sight and Luke's back was turned, *Maummi* whipped a jar of spice out of her apron pocket. She rushed to the pot of beans simmering over the campfire and dumped the contents in. Then she picked up the long iron spoon and gave the contents a quick stir. By the time McCann reappeared, banging pans and glaring all around, *Maummi* was seated once again in her rocking chair, her hands busy with a mending project.

Emma turned away again so the cook wouldn't see her smile.

"We'll form up in two groups of three," Luke told his strange little group of riders. "Nobody goes off alone, understand? Four of those rustlers are still out there somewhere, and a single man on horseback is an easy target."

"Or woman," Rebecca added from the opposite end of the loose circle they had formed between the cook's wagon and the Switzers'.

The truth of her words brought grim concern to the face of every man. Luke glanced at Emma, who stood nearby, watching him. If anything happened to her, he'd never forgive himself. For that reason, he didn't intend to let her out of his sight. Nor would he leave Rebecca's safety to chance, either.

"Or woman," he agreed, solemn. "I'm counting on the fact that those surviving rustlers scattered nearly as widely as our cattle. It'll take them a while to regroup and even longer to round up the strays, but if those strays are as tired as the bunch Griff and Morris brought in earlier, they won't have run far. We might find a good number of them nearby."

Morris nodded, and Griff's expression settled into one of agreement. Jonas's eyes fixed on him with an unblinking stare, his expression as unreadable as ever. At least it was obvious where Emma inherited her intent focus.

"Regardless, even if you don't find a single

steer, you get back here before nightfall. Come daybreak, we're breaking camp with whatever herd we have. Griff, you, Charlie, and Jonas head north. We still have a couple of hours of daylight, so ride out for thirty minutes, then swing around to the west. Vic, Emma, and I will ride the other way and swing up to meet you, and then we'll head back in."

"That means I'm going east?" Rebecca asked, her gaze straying in that direction behind Luke's shoulder.

"No, we've already covered the east. You're staying here to guard the main herd."

Rebecca's mouth pursed, her displeasure apparent in the angry eyes she fixed on him.

"It's the most important job we have," Luke explained to the girl in a patient voice. "We have seventeen hundred head of beef left, and we can't afford to lose a single one. You, Morris, and McCann will watch over them."

Morris nodded.

A voice behind him joined the conversation. "I'll stand guard too."

Surprised, Luke whirled around to find that Jesse had awoken and was struggling to lift himself up on one elbow, pain etched on every inch of his puckered brow.

Mrs. Switzer sprang out of her rocking

chair and sprinted to his side to stand towering over him, her hands on her hips. "Stand you will not!"

Either he didn't have the will to oppose his formidable nurse, or the pain of struggling to a sitting position convinced him "Yeah, so I'll *sit* guard." With much wincing, he leaned sideways, grabbed his rifle out of his pack, and laid it across his lap. "Somebody help get me up in that wagon so I can see, and I'll help keep watch."

Relieved to have an extra pair of eyes, Luke nodded toward Morris and Charlie to help Jesse. These cattle were his responsibility. He'd contracted with Mr. Hancock to deliver them to Hays, and he didn't intend to sit idly by and watch those rustlers take a single one.

When Jesse had been seated as comfortably as possible in the Switzers' wagon, his back resting against the hutch and his rifle in his lap, Luke gave the order to mount up. He was walking toward Bo when Jonas caught up with him.

"A word, please."

It didn't take a genius to know what was on the man's mind. Though he addressed Luke, he focused across the camp toward the place where Emma and Rebecca were being helped onto their mounts. Worried crevices were carved into Jonas's brow, and his clean-shaven lips were tight.

"You will watch after my girls." Though he voiced a statement, Luke detected a tacit plea for reassurance in the man's voice.

Luke matched his quiet volume so they couldn't be overheard. "Jonas, the rustlers won't return, not this soon. And besides, with Morris and McCann and Jesse, Rebecca and Mrs. Switzer are safer here than they have been since the day you left home."

"And my Emma?"

Luke turned to look toward Emma. She sat atop Sugarfoot, her legs swathed in her father's black trousers, and the bunched fabric of her wide skirt was settled into a modest yet comfortable position around her thighs. As though she felt his regard, she lifted her head. A smile lit her features when she saw him watching her, and a fierce protectiveness overtook him in response.

"I will protect her with my life." He looked Jonas in the eye. "You have my word."

Jonas held his gaze for a long moment, as if weighing the value of the word of an *Englisch* cowboy. Then he nodded and walked toward the horse he'd been assigned.

Luke continued on to the corralled remuda, where Bo stood already saddled and ready to ride. His promise to Jonas resonated in his soul, the words somehow more real and weightier for having been spoken.

He *would* protect Emma with his life, without a moment's hesitation.

Of course, that didn't mean she was anything special. He'd do the same for any woman, or man, even, especially one who was helping out at a time when he needed all the help he could get. Right?

He placed his foot in the stirrup and swung his other leg over Bo's back. As soon as he was secure in the saddle, Emma nudged Sugarfoot alongside him.

"I'm glad I am assigned to ride south." Her head dropped demurely, but after a moment her eyes cut up sideways to lock with his. "With you."

Luke had seen a rodeo show once. He had watched, fascinated, while a man did tricks and flips on the back of a charging stallion. As a boy he'd been amazed, exhilarated, and inspired to do those and even greater feats of daring and courage.

That was exactly the way he felt right now.

SEVENTEEN

Emma squeezed her legs tight around Sugarfoot, her muscles protesting the abuse of an extended period in an unfamiliar position. Herding the cows on foot this morning was far easier than this. How did Luke stand this day in and day out for months at a time? She shifted and squirmed, trying to find a more comfortable position, to no avail. Carefully, she set her feet securely in the stirrups, grabbed hold of the pommel, and rose ever so slightly out of the saddle. Blood rushed into her uncomfortably numb backside, bringing simultaneous rushes of pain and relief.

Sugarfoot veered sideways during her canter, and Emma nearly lost her balance. She dropped back into the saddle, and almost cried out at the impact.

Though ahead of her, Luke must have sensed her distress. He turned his head, slowed his horse, and fell alongside her. Vic, a quiet man with swarthy skin and intense dark eyes, kept up the pace and soon pulled ahead of them.

"You need to take a break?" Luke asked, his gaze searching her face.

"I'm fine." She forced a brave smile. "We haven't found any cows yet."

"We're getting close. This trail is fairly fresh."

Trail? For the first time, Emma observed the ground beneath her horse's hooves. She'd been so focused on her discomfort, and on staying near Luke, that she had missed the obvious signs of the recent passing of cattle. A fair number of them, judging by the wide swath of trampled grass.

Up ahead, Vic slowed when he approached a swell in the land. His horse climbed toward the crest of the hill, but before he reached the top, Vic's arm shot high into the air, his fingers splayed. With a jerk on the reins, he whirled the horse around and galloped back toward them. Luke and Emma slowed to a halt when he approached.

"We found them." The man's voice held a barely checked excitement, his eyes alight as he jerked his head backward, toward the hill. "Their camp's over yonder."

"The rustlers?" Luke asked.

"And our cattle." Vic's voice went hard. "Plus some."

Emma rose in her saddle again, straining her eyes toward the hill.

"Let me take a look." Luke swung his leg over Bo and hopped to the ground. Tossing the reins toward Vic, he strode forward.

The men who had stolen their things and scattered Luke's herd were right on the other side of that hill? Emma wanted to see. She mimicked Luke and swung her leg over Sugarfoot's back. But her stiff muscles protested the sudden movement, and the distance between the stirrup and the ground was greater than she thought. A moment later she found herself on her backside, staring up at a purple-streaked sky.

"Emma!" Luke doubled back to her as Vic jumped out of his saddle to rush to her side.

Heat rose from her collarbone up her neck, and she was sure her burning face shone bright enough to rival the late afternoon sun.

"I'm fine," she mumbled, but she couldn't meet Luke's gaze. What a clumsy oaf. What must he think of someone who couldn't even get off a horse by herself?

"Here, let us help you up."

Luke slipped a hand beneath one arm, and Vic did the same on her other side. The men lifted her to a standing position. Her feet felt unsteady, her legs trembled beneath the weight of her body, and she couldn't even enjoy the feel of Luke's steadying hand holding tightly to her arm. She clutched at him, afraid that if she tried to take a step she'd find herself back on the ground.

"The saddle can be hard on the legs when you're not used to it." Vic's voice held a wagonload of sympathy.

Miserably embarrassed, she nodded and concentrated on forcing her legs to support her weight. Setting her teeth together, she managed a step away from Luke.

"Good. You'll be fine. Stay here while I take a look over that hill," he said.

"I'm going with you. I want to see too." Though it was hard to sound firm and unyielding while hobbling like a babe taking her first steps, Emma tilted her chin in the air and hardened her jaw.

After studying her a second, Luke shrugged. "Keep quiet, that's all."

He held out his crooked arm as though offering to escort her to a fancy dinner. Emma took it gratefully, not at all confident that she could walk the short distance on her own, though the feeling was starting to creep back into her legs.

When they neared the crest of the hill, he

crouched and then dropped to his knees to crawl the last few feet. Emma followed suit, and side by side they climbed the rise and peeked over the top.

Before them lay a small valley, ringed on three sides by swells in the land such as the one they knelt upon. Cattle filled the bowl, their number impossible to count but probably close to half the size of Luke's herd.

"That's them, all right." Luke spoke quietly, his gaze fixed on the northeast corner of the valley, where a break in the hills formed a wide opening in the natural barrier.

She strained to see across the distance. "How can you be sure? I can't see their brands from here."

"First off, there are half a dozen different breeds down there. A cattle drive can take more than one breed from more than one owner, but there would be a bigger number of each. Second, there's no chuck wagon. Just them."

Luke jerked his head toward the open valley to the northeast. Emma caught sight of a trio of men, dismounted and talking to each other. It was impossible to identify them at this distance. They were nothing more than featureless figures.

"And third, don't you recognize the oxen?"

She looked where he pointed, and sure enough, a pair of oxen milled with the cattle nearest to their position. Though one ox looked the same as another to her, they were probably Papa's stolen animals.

"My guess is this crew have been rustling cattle for some time, a few here and there, trying to build up a decent-sized herd. They must have a buyer somewhere."

"Where's the fourth one?"

Luke studied them as he answered. "Probably hasn't caught up with them yet. He's around, though."

The words sent a chill sliding down Emma's spine.

After another long moment, Luke whispered, "Come on."

They crawled backward to the bottom of the hill, and then Luke helped her to her feet. She was glad to be able to cover the distance to where Vic waited with a more-or-less normal gait.

"What are we going to do, boss?" Vic asked when they approached.

"We're heading back to camp." Luke went to Sugarfoot's side and entwined his fingers to form a step for Emma's foot.

Rather than mounting, Emma stared at

him. "We aren't going to get our cows back?"

Another blush threatened at her subconscious use of the pronoun. She meant *his* cows, of course, but after rescuing forty of them this morning and learning to herd them this afternoon, she'd begun to feel a personal stake in their well-being.

"No, we're not." Luke's tone offered no room for argument. "We're going to Hays as planned, and we'll report this to the sheriff. They'll send a posse to find the rustlers and recover the cattle."

"Hays is a good day and a half away if we run 'em on the hoof," Vic said, swinging up into his saddle. "The rustlers might move out before the law makes it back."

"If they do, they do. There's nothing we can do about it shorthanded." He held his joined hands toward Emma again in a silent invitation that was more like a command.

She didn't move at first. Griff had said earlier that if Luke showed up in Hays missing so many of his cows, he would never get a job as a trail boss again. They might be shorthanded, but the men in Luke's command still outnumbered the cattle rustlers two-to-one, even without Papa and Jesse. No, the real reason he was willing to leave his stolen cows went unspoken, but she knew it anyway. She'd seen his pain clearly on his face during the funeral, and his determination afterward, when he looked toward her as he spoke with Papa. He wasn't willing to put anyone else in danger — not his remaining men, and especially not her and her family. He was willing to leave the stolen cattle behind in order to keep them all safe.

Though he may not realize it, his was an extremely Amish approach to the situation.

The mood around the campfire that night was somber. Even Rebecca had lost her bubbly enthusiasm, and Emma understood why. After hours in the saddle, the ground seemed far harder and more unyielding tonight than ever before. They both preferred to stand as they ate their supper.

"I think we could take 'em, boss," Charlie said between mouthfuls of beans. "We can turn their own stunt back on them and surprise them at daybreak when the cattle are starting to stir."

"Maybe." Luke didn't look up from his tin plate. "Maybe not. I'm not willing to risk it."

Jesse, whose injured leg had swollen despite the tight binding, picked at his food and grumbled loud enough to be heard by everyone, "A week ago we wouldn't have let a handful of desperados get away with rustling our herd."

Though he didn't look in Emma's direction, she felt the weight of his unspoken accusation. Jesse knew, like everyone else, that the Switzers — primarily she — were the reason behind Luke's decision.

Maummi got up out of her chair and crossed to Jesse's pallet to inspect his plate. She pointed an accusing finger at his huge portion of beans. "Eat! A foolish man refuses food, and wastes his doctor's skills."

Jesse's grumble became a grunt. With an upward glare, he took a huge bite and chewed with determined purpose.

"You'd better eat what she gave you, son." Griff climbed to his feet and grabbed the ladle from the pot of beans hanging over the campfire. "There aren't going to be any left tonight. Best beans I've ever eaten."

"Ain't that the truth?" Vic joined him at the pot and refilled his own plate. "What'd you do different, McCann?"

"Same beans as always," the cook insisted as he scraped the last of the thick soup into his mouth with a piece of flatbread.

"Well, they're the best you ever made," Charlie agreed.

McCann froze in the act of popping the

246

bread in his mouth. He turned a suspicious glare toward *Maummi*, who had returned to her rocking chair and picked up her sewing. "Did you do something to my beans?"

There was no hesitation in her rocking or a pause in her mending as she answered. "Such a fuss over a pinch of salt."

"You salted my beans?" McCann jumped to his feet, looking ready to explode. "Salt in my wounds, madam, that's what you are. Salt in my wounds!" He stomped off and disappeared into the chuck wagon.

Emma exchanged a quiet grin with Rebecca while *Maummi* continued to rock, unconcerned.

When Luke had finished his supper, he set his plate in the grass and spoke to those gathered around the campfire. "Everybody needs to get some shut-eye tonight. I plan to leave at daybreak, and we're going to push this herd harder than we have since we left El Paso. That means I'll be pushing *you* harder too." The stare that circled the campfire was grim. "We may show up in Hays light, but we're *not* going to show up late. Griff, you and Vic take first watch, McCann and I will take second, and Charlie and Morris can pick up the third." He turned his head and shouted over his shoulder. "You hear that, McCann?"

McCann's voice growled from within the chuck wagon. "I hear you. I'll be with you right after I hide the salt."

Papa, who had been even quieter than usual this evening, spoke up. "I will take a watch too."

Luke shook his head. "I'm sure you would, Jonas, but not tonight. You and Emma and Rebecca have worked hard today, and I know how difficult it is to spend a day in the saddle when you're not used to it. You get some sleep so you're fresh in the morning." He smiled toward *Maummi*. "You too, ma'am. You've had the hardest job of all, I think, riding herd over that mule-headed cowboy over there."

Jesse scowled but didn't answer. *Maummi* simply nodded and continued to rock and sew.

When supper was over the men wandered away, either to their pallets or to the remuda to retrieve their night horses. McCann emerged from his wagon, grabbed the dishpan, and, with a scowl in *Maummi*'s direction, headed for a nearby stream to wash up the supper dishes.

"I'll bet there's not a speck of salt to be found," Emma whispered to Rebecca, and the young girl grinned.

Emma decided to join the cook. There

were hard feelings to soothe. She caught up with him at the stream's edge and knelt by the bank beside him. Together they plunged their hands into the cold water.

"That grandma of yours is a piece of work." The man didn't look at her but focused on his chore.

Emma scrubbed at a stubborn speck of food. "She means well. She sees us helping and wants to do her part." Beneath the gruff exterior, Emma was fairly certain that was the reason for *Maummi's* meddling, though she did tend to take uninvited charge of all community meals back in Apple Grove. "She would not be much good on a horse."

His shoulders heaved in a laugh. "I'd pay good money to see her give it a try." When his chuckle ended, he lowered his voice. "Those were the best beans I ever ate, and it wasn't because of a little salt. I'd give a month's pay to know what she put in them."

"She loves to cook. She'll tell you if you ask her nicely." Emma set the clean dish on the stack beside her and reached for another dirty one.

"Hmm."

They finished their chore in companionable silence and then headed back for camp. Rebecca and *Maummi* had already disappeared behind their wagon, where they had set up their sleep pallets. Papa sat by the fire alone, his hat resting on the ground beside him. He looked up when Emma approached, a faint smile inviting her to sit with him.

Emma retrieved her sewing bag from the back of the wagon. She'd decided what to do with Katie Beachy's gift. She'd considered making something for Katie's wedding, but yesterday she had changed her mind. The fire was starting to burn low, but there was enough light left to select thread and begin.

Papa watched her silently for a moment, and then he cleared his throat. "Think you, daughter, that you could be happy with Amos Beiler?"

The question so startled her that she almost dropped her needle. "Papa, I —" The words stuck in her throat. Never had the topic of marriage come up between her and Papa. *Maummi,* yes. Rebecca, all the time. But Papa? He could be counted on to answer questions about anything from Christian beliefs to understanding the signs of the seasons in order to ascertain the best time for planting, but about marriage he had always remained mute. Emma assumed the subject was painful for him because he had loved Mama so dearly.

She made three stitches before answering. "No, Papa. Amos is a fine man, but he is not for me."

He nodded slowly, his gaze fixed on the flames. "I thought so."

Emma waited for him to go on, to offer an explanation for his question. The overheard conversation between him and *Maummi* replayed itself in her mind. Would he mention Luke's name to her? And if he did, how would she answer? Could she truthfully assure him that she felt no attraction for the handsome trail boss? Of course not. Her resolve to forget him had gone by the wayside the moment she saw those cows running toward them this morning.

Her fingers stitched almost of their own accord while Emma formed her thoughts into words, waiting to answer Papa's next question. Would she leave her church in order to chase after an *Englisch* cowboy? No, but maybe she didn't have to. Luke was a man of faith. Why could he not become Amish?

Finally, when the idea was about to burst from her mouth, Papa broke the silence with a loud sigh. He climbed to his feet and stooped to pick up his hat.

"Good night, daughter."

Emma sat beside the fire, her sewing

forgotten in her lap as she watched him disappear in the direction of the row of men's bedrolls.

Eighteen

Luke had managed to fall into a dreamless sleep when Vic nudged him awake with a rough hand on his shoulder.

"You're up for watch." Exhaustion dragged at the man's voice.

Luke stirred and saw that Griff had already roused McCann, who stumbled toward the remuda with an unsteady step.

"I'm up," he said. "Go to bed."

"G'night, boss." Vic stumbled off and collapsed, clothes and all, onto his bedroll.

Luke tried to shake off sleep, and when he failed, walked on unsteady feet toward the campfire. McCann had left a row of clean tin mugs on the grass outside the fire ring, and the coffee pot rested on a flat rock set near enough to keep the contents warm. He poured himself a generous swig and downed it. The heat scalded his throat, and he took in draughts of cool air as he awaited the caffeine jolt.

Night lay quiet over the herd. He scanned the sleeping cattle for any signs of restless movement and found none. They had drawn close together before bedding down for the night, which would make his job easier in the morning. They would rise as one and be ready to hit the trail probably sooner than his tired men wanted.

Men and women. Luke glanced toward the Switzers' wagon, where the women lay bedded down beyond. Emma had not been far from his thoughts tonight, even in sleep. The sight of her last evening, stumbling on legs numb from hours in the saddle with a determined set to her jaw, stirred emotions deep inside him. He was right to give the order to move forward without recovering the rustled strays from his herd. Her safety, and the safety of her family, were far more important than a few hundred head of cattle or any future job he may or may not land.

The horses in the remuda pranced nervously when he ducked under the rope Vic had strung to keep them contained.

"Whoa, there you go. It's all right."

He pitched his voice low as he made his way toward his favorite night horse. Bo had worked hard the past few days, and he deserved a full night's rest as much as the men. With an outstretched hand Luke approached Whitey, whose name described him perfectly, murmuring words of comfort. Whitey was fresh, fully rested, and eager to escape the confines of the corral. Luke swung the saddle over his back and cinched the girth snugly.

"There we go, boy." He lifted the rope barrier over the horse's head, and led him out to the other side. The sight of his white hide circling the perimeter in the night had served to calm a restless herd before, though this one slept soundly enough that Luke doubted his choice of mount would make a difference.

He swung himself up into the saddle and started his circuit. At the south end of the herd, he met up with McCann, who had swung around to the east. The man nodded and waved a hand in silent greeting, then turned and headed back in the direction he had come. They would pass their two-hour watch repeating the same path, on the lookout for invaders or restless cattle.

After a few uneventful passes, Luke's attention was drawn to the southwest. The moon lay veiled in clouds, but the sky painted a lighter picture than the blackness of the earth. Strain though he might, he could not make out the ridge of a hill in the distance, though he knew the land swelled high, like the waves of a restless sea. Beyond that the rest of his herd lay sleeping. As did the marauders who had stolen them.

Jesse was right. It would be ridiculously easy to surprise the rustlers and take back his cattle. Well, not *easy,* because there was always the danger they would put up a fight, and whenever a man drew a gun the possibility of injury or even death existed. Pa always used to tell him, "If you draw a gun against a man, you'd better intend to use it." Luke had drawn his gun many times during his life on the trail, but never with the intention to shoot another man. Even this morning he hadn't been able to bring himself to aim for the rustlers.

If I kill them, that makes me no better than they are.

He glanced beyond the camp, where six fresh graves bore witness to the morning's violence. The loss of life — even those of the marauders — sickened him to the point of nausea. If he'd pulled the trigger that resulted in one of those deaths, he was certain he'd be in the same shape Charlie had been after shooting that rustler, unable to hold anything in his stomach besides guilt.

He slapped a hand against Whitey's neck. "I'm not much of a trail boss, am I, boy?

My pa wouldn't waste a second thought about defending his herd."

Or about taking back his charges. Luke looked again in the direction of the rustlers' camp. The night was so peaceful.

On impulse, he whistled for McCann's attention. When the man looked up, Luke swept a hand over the sleeping herd and then pointed at him. He understood the message, that he was to keep an eye on the cattle for a minute, and nodded.

Luke turned Whitey southwest with a gentle tug on the reins and galloped off. He wouldn't be gone long, just long enough for one last look at those stolen cattle.

Emma lay awake on her pallet beneath the wagon, watching Luke's white horse pace around this side of the sleeping cows. Beside her, Rebecca's quiet breath was nearly drowned out by *Maummi*'s robust snores. Though she'd been tired when she left the campfire to find her bedroll, Emma's sleep had been fitful. When Vic roused Luke to take the watch, she had woken as well. Now sleep eluded her the way wild jackrabbits avoided the snares in Papa's vegetable garden.

A single question revolved in her mind. Why couldn't Luke become Amish? Since the thought had occurred to her, she could think of nothing else. It was the perfect solution. He could move to Apple Grove and go through the baptism classes with her. They could be baptized at the same service in the fall. And then . . .

A tickle in her belly accompanied a myriad of tantalizing thoughts. Luke working alongside Papa on the farm. A wedding. Eventually, Papa would move into the *dawdi haus,* leaving her and Luke to live in the home where she'd been raised. And soon after, babies to cuddle and teach to love the Plain life, as she had been taught.

Beautiful images crowded her mind and drove the last possibility of sleep away. She raised up on her pallet and scooted out from beneath the wagon, careful not to wake Rebecca or *Maummi.* Perhaps a breath of night air and a view of the stars overhead would calm her enough to sleep.

When she stood, her gaze was drawn inevitably to Luke. Would he do that? Would he give up his cowboy life and embrace the life of a farmer?

Surely he would at least consider the possibility. That is, if he felt the same attraction, and she was pretty sure he did. She'd felt the weight of the looks he fixed on her, the way he leaped to her aid this afternoon when she fell from her horse. A blush threatened, hidden in the dark night. Not her finest moment, to be sure, but he had responded with chivalry and concern. Surely he cared for her as she had come to care for him. But what if the idea of living a Plain life had not occurred to him?

There was one way to find out. Emma snatched her *kapp* off the wagon and twisted her hair up as she crept quietly away from her sleeping family. She headed into the darkness, intending to make a wide arc around the herd and come up on Luke's other side. The cows were sleeping, so they probably wouldn't be startled, but she didn't particularly want McCann or anyone else who happened to be awake to witness her approaching Luke.

With a guilty glance in the direction where Papa's bedroll lay, she walked with quiet caution. His earlier question proved that he trusted her to make her own decision about the man she would marry. Amish parents were usually not privy to the romantic interests of their children. Often they were not informed of the intent to marry until a few weeks before the wedding. Of course, in a district as small as Apple Grove there were few secrets. Everyone knew of the attraction between Katie Beachy and Samuel Miller.

As Papa was aware of the attraction between her and Luke.

And Papa liked Luke, she could tell. Wouldn't he be thrilled to have Luke as a son-in-law, an *Amish* son-in-law?

When Emma was far enough from camp that her footsteps could not be overheard, she blew out a pent-up breath. A cluster of trees formed the perfect barrier where she could stand and not be easily overseen by anyone who happened to awaken and look around. Luke's sentry path had reached the rear of the herd, a couple of hundred yards away. He would turn and head back this way, and she would be waiting for him. A nervous tickle erupted in her stomach. What would she say? She had no more than a few minutes to plan her speech.

But as she watched his hands rose to cup his mouth. A low whistle rode to her ears on the cool night air. He gestured, and then in another moment he turned and galloped away. Emma straightened and stepped away from the tree trunk, watching as the white hide of his horse diminished in the distance. Where was he going?

Something fell over her head and brushed her arms. She started to raise her hands to slap away whatever had fallen on her, but in the next instant she was jerked off her feet.

She hit the ground with a thud that knocked the breath from her lungs. Stars exploded in the night, and it took a moment to realize they were not in the sky but inside her head.

When her vision cleared, she looked up into the face of a man on horseback, towering over her. He held a rope in his hand, the lariat at the other end pulled tight around her arms and across her chest.

A low, dreadfully familiar voice whispered in the night. "Well, well, what do we have here?"

The man's lips parted in an unpleasant smile, revealing a set of rotted black teeth.

NINETEEN

Luke slid out of the saddle and draped Whitey's reins loosely around the gnarled stump of a scrub bush. Ahead of him lay the uneven ridge of land that sheltered the rustlers' stolen herd. To his right the ridge ended in a narrow flat pass. Moving with caution, he started up the hill.

What am I doing here? I can't recover the cattle by myself.

But that wasn't his purpose, and he knew it. No, he was here to give himself a mental beating. Three hundred of his cattle, his responsibility, lay right on the other side of that ridge, and he couldn't get them. No . . . not couldn't. Wouldn't.

What if the Switzers' presence is an excuse? Would I give the order to go after them if I didn't have the responsibility of protecting Emma and her family?

A Bible story his grandma used to tell replayed itself in his memory. He could see her sitting near the hearth, rocking in her chair the same way Mrs. Switzer did.

"The Lord understood raising livestock, He did," she told her audience of three little boys. "He knew that every sheep matters. He said if there were a hunnert sheep but only one got lost, the shepherd ought to go find it. And that's why he comes after you time and agin, no matter how often you go off."

She'd looked right at Luke when she said that. Being the oldest and most adventurous of the brothers, he'd had his hind end warmed more than once for wandering off without permission.

He shook off the memory. The point, of course, was about the Lord pursuing His children. But the story was based on a premise, that the shepherd of a flock valued each and every sheep enough to go after them when they were lost. And what was the difference between sheep and cattle? Especially cattle that belonged to someone else, cattle he'd been give charge of.

The fact was, Luke wasn't sure he would go after those rustled cattle even if the Switzers weren't around. The shoot-out this morning had shaken him badly. He wasn't afraid of dying, but he didn't intend to lose another one of his men.

I really am a lousy trail boss. Pa would go after what he wanted no matter who was standing in his way, no matter the risk.

The realization lay heavy on him as he dropped to his belly and crawled the rest of the way up the hill to get a final look at the proof of his failure, his stolen cattle.

Like the herd a few miles behind him, this one rested peacefully. They huddled close together in the center of the bowl, from this vantage point like a solid rug of multicolored cowhide. It was impossible to count them by starlight, but judging by the size of the area they occupied, there were upwards of seven hundred head. He glanced toward the camp. A fire burned bright, which meant the men had posted a guard, but they weren't circling the herd on horseback. Instead, they were probably counting on the ridge to form a natural corral which the cattle would not cross in the dark.

Luke considered creeping down the hill to get a closer look at the nearest steers. No doubt the Triple Bar brand could still be identified because the thieves hadn't had time to slice it off and rebrand them, but he'd love to know if a fake brand appeared on the hides of the others.

A movement east of the camp halted him. A horse galloped through the narrow break in the ridge. The sound of hooves pounding the ground echoed around the bowl and stirred the men who sat near the campfire. Luke counted three figures as they climbed to their feet and greeted the rider. So, the fourth rustler had finally returned to his desperado partners.

The ever-present Kansas wind blew wispy clouds across the night sky. A break in the coverage revealed a half moon, and white light painted the dark landscape with luminescence as the fourth man's horse came to a stop. He dismounted and then dragged something off of the saddle. He tossed his burden to the ground, where it rolled away.

As Luke watched, the dark shape moved, stood upright, and then crouched on the ground.

It was a person.

Luke froze, his eyes fixed on that dark, huddled figure. Moonlight shone clearly off a white *kapp.* Blood drained from his brain, and the world spun in an eerie, sickening dance. An Amish head covering. And the darkness in which the figure was swathed was an Amish dress.

Emma. That person was Emma.

And she was in the hands of murderous cattle rustlers.

TWENTY

For one agonizing moment, Luke was paralyzed with indecision.

What should I do?

He lay flat on the hillside, his head peeking up over the ridge, and watched the distant scene with increasing horror. The newcomer talked to his partners, his arms gesturing. And then he threw back his head and laughed. The sound echoed around the bowl and stirred up fear in Luke's gut. Though he could not see her face, Emma's figure on the ground seemed to draw more tightly into itself. Her posture indicated her terror.

The sight decided him. If he left, galloped back to camp to rouse the men and return with greater numbers, he would be leaving Emma alone in the hands of ruthless, vicious men. There was no telling what they would do to her before he returned. Correction. He had a couple of very good guesses about what they would do. Possibilities formed in his mind like bullets striking a target. Acid roiled in his stomach. No. He couldn't leave her with them, not even for a moment.

Moving as cautiously as possible while his insides screamed at him to hurry, he crept backward down the hill. When he was sure his silhouette could not be spotted, he rose and sprinted toward Whitey. He grabbed his rifle, a Winchester Model 1873, and checked to be sure the magazine was full of cartridges. Twelve shots. Plus his six-shooter in his holster. Surely that would be enough to take care of four mangy kidnappers.

A thought struck him in the instant before he leaped into the saddle. He'd answered his question of a moment before. No, he wasn't willing to risk killing another human being for a herd of cattle, but he would blow those rustlers' heads off before he'd let them harm Emma.

At the back of his mind, a nagging worry pounded its way to the front. What could he, a lone cowboy, do against four murdering thieves? If he went charging into their camp, no doubt he'd have the element of surprise, but it wouldn't last long. He'd probably get himself killed and Emma along with him. He needed a plan.

Lord, I'm fresh out of ideas. Help me. No. Help Emma!

The silent plea rose as he pointed Whitey in the direction of the pass into the bowl and dug in his heels. Surely the Lord wouldn't leave this one special sheep all alone with no one to rescue her but a cowboy who couldn't even manage to get his herd to the railhead intact.

The last jagged ridge loomed ahead on his left when he spotted movement off to his right. Four horses charged across the plain in his direction. A wave of relief hit him so hard he almost lost his seat. The riders were coming from the direction of his camp. In fact, he could make out a few identifying details. Jonas's round straw hat glowed in the cold white moonlight as though he'd set it afire.

Taking in their location at a glance, Luke judged they were not in sight of the rustlers' camp, but if they kept galloping ahead at that pace, they would round the shelter of the ridge in a matter of minutes. He jerked Whitey's reins and raced across the plain to cut them off.

"My Emma," Jonas shouted as soon as he neared. "Where is my Emma?"

"Shhh." Luke held up a hand as he closed the final few yards. "Keep your voice down or you'll give us away." His gaze slid from Jonas to Griff. "I don't know why you're here, but I've never been so glad to see anyone in my life."

"Jonas roused us," he answered in a voice lower than a whisper. "Said he woke up in time to see a horse galloping away. Thought there were two people on it, but it was too far to tell for sure. Then he got up to check on the women and realized Emma was missing."

"I don't know what woke you," Luke told Jonas, "but I thank God for whatever it was."

The Amish man's response was quietly certain. "The source, I know."

Luke didn't have any trouble believing the Lord capable of kicking a man awake at the right time. After all, if He could arrange to have a man tossed out of a saloon in time to lend aid to a stranded Amish family, why not?

"Gather close." The men urged their horses together. Luke looked them each in the eye. Griff, the seasoned cowboy. Charlie, who had shot his first man just this morning. Morris, the quiet flank rider. And Jonas, the man who wore his faith as openly as he wore his bushy beard and funny hat.

Lord, keep them all safe. And help us get

Emma out of there unharmed.

"Here's what we're dealing with. The herd is bedded down, and the rustlers haven't mounted a watch. They are holding Emma in their camp near the entrance to the bowl."

Charlie's gaze fixed on the ridge. "Could we stampede the herd? Come in from behind and run the cattle right over the top of them?"

"Not a bad idea," Griff said. "We spread out and charge in from all directions."

Luke shook his head. "I watched the herd for a few minutes, and I didn't see a single one stir. In the time it takes to wake them enough to get to their feet and stampede, Emma might be in real trouble."

Jonas's expression was no longer impassive. His lips were set in a grim line, and tension had stiffened his back until he sat like a petrified log in the saddle. Fear for his daughter glinted in his dark eyes.

Luke knew how he felt.

"Surprise is a good thought, though." He nodded at Charlie. "The way things are situated, there's only one option. We have to catch them off guard so they don't have an opportunity to use her as cover."

Morris saw where he was going. "Either we charge in and hope to surprise them, or we sneak up on them."

Though Luke would much rather end the situation without bloodshed, if he had to go charging into the camp firing his rifle, he'd do it in a second. As long as he could be sure of Emma's safety.

He closed his eyes, picturing the camp. "Without even a chuck wagon to hide behind, sneaking up on them is going to be hard. On the other hand, I did see some good-sized rocks on some of those hillsides. We might get close enough on foot to take them by surprise." He glanced upward to search the sky, hoping to spot a large cloud in the path of the moon to give them some cover. He found a few, but would they offer enough protection? "I think charging them might be the best solution."

Jonas shook his head. "You *Englisch*. Always barging in with a fight. Always deceiving. 'Deception is a strong pepper that burns the speaker's tongue, not the listener's.' Honesty and openness are the best approach in all things."

Charlie reared back in the saddle to give him a shocked look. "Are you suggesting we march in there and tell them we've come to get your daughter and would they please hand her over without a fuss?"

Jonas nodded, his expression solemn.

"That I will do."

Griff and Morris laughed, but something in Jonas's expression made Luke pause. An idea occurred to him.

"Wait a minute," he said slowly. "You're talking about creating a distraction. You'll approach their camp from one side and draw their attention while we sneak up from the other side and get Emma."

Again, Jonas nodded. "My beliefs prevent me from taking up arms against any man, but words are powerful. I will use my words and leave the weapons to you."

A reckless hope stole over Luke as he pictured the plan unfolding.

It just might work.

TWENTY-ONE

Huddled on the ground, Emma wrapped her arms around her bent knees and drew herself into a tight ball. Though the night was warm, she could not still her shivering limbs. The expressions on the faces of the four men ranged from speculative to eager. The man with black teeth, Lester, kept an evil, hungry gaze fixed on her as he cut large pieces of cooked meat and shoved them in his mouth. She dared not meet his eyes or she would fall apart.

What was I thinking? As if I didn't look foolish enough falling off a horse, sneaking off in the dark when I knew there might be thieves in the area surely proves to Luke that I'm a dull-witted simpleton.

The fact was, she didn't stop to think of the risks before she crept off into the dark. Her thoughts had been fixed on Luke and the idea of him becoming Amish so they could marry. And now she wouldn't be marrying anyone, ever. Would she even be alive to see the sun rise on the morrow?

"We best be up and away from here before sunup," said the one she'd heard the others refer to as Earl. "When they find her missing, they'll come looking."

Another answered with, "This herd's been resting for days. We could rouse them now and head west toward Colorado. We'll deliver them to the reservation, collect our pay, and be on our way to California before anybody can catch up with us. I'll bet we can find someone to give a good price for her too."

"Don't be in such an all-fired hurry to sell her, Porter." Lester fixed glittering eyes on Emma. "A man's got a right to some leisure time first, don't he?" He grinned around a mouthful of food.

A frigid blast of terror washed over her, swamping impending sobs to frozen silence. The hands with which she clutched her knees felt icy, and she was too afraid even to shiver.

Lord, please help me. I'll never be stupid again. I'll listen to Papa and Maummi, and I'll be nicer to Rebecca too. I promise.

Lester shoved a last bite of meat in his mouth and tossed his plate away into the grass. He stood and seemed to grow to

274

giant-size stature when he took a step toward Emma. She squeezed her eyes shut, waiting for a rough hand to snatch her up.

"Pardon me, please."

A voice, not too distant, echoed down from above. For the span of half a heartbeat, she thought it might be the Lord calling to her in answer to her plea. But then she realized the voice wasn't deep and resonant and Lord-like. Instead, it was soft and quiet and intimately familiar.

"Papa!" She didn't mean to shout, but the name tore from her throat of its own accord. Her eyes flew open, and she wildly searched the surrounding hills.

Luke lay flat on the ground behind the ridge, listening to the rustlers' conversation. The circling ridge magnified the sound so he could hear most of the words. Anger built like a hot ball of fire in his gut, but he did not move until he heard Jonas's voice. Only then, when he was sure the rustlers' attention would be elsewhere for a second or two, did he raise his head and look down into the camp. His gaze was drawn to Emma, who shouted "Papa!" in a terrified voice that squeezed his heart in his chest.

He took in the scene before him in an instant. Emma crouched on the ground, just inside the ring of light from a low-burning fire. The three who had been seated leaped to their feet, scanning the opposite hillside for the source of the voice. Lester, the one who had kidnapped Emma, pulled a pistol from the holster at his side.

"Who's there? Show yourself!" Lester shouted.

"I am Jonas Switzer." The answer rolled down the hillside. A dark silhouette rose from the ground and stood upright. "I will fetch my daughter home now, please."

To Luke's right, a quiet crack echoed in the silence as Griff, starting his descent down the hill, crept across a dried root. He froze, as did Morris beyond him. Luke watched the men by the campfire. One head turned briefly to glance around but then fixed again on Jonas.

Lester's arm swung wide as he leveled a pistol on Emma. "I'd better see your weapons tossed down that hill or I'll shoot this here girl."

Jonas's arms spread wide. "I carry no weapon."

With an effort Luke forced his gaze away from the sight of the vulnerable girl huddled on the ground and traced his path down the hill. He could do nothing to help her from here. He needed to be closer. A big boulder ten yards in front of him would provide some cover, and beyond that a shallow crevice in the ground, dark with shadows. Then there was no cover at all for the thirty yards between that and the man who stood with his gun pointed at Emma.

Luke grasped his Winchester in one hand and belly-crawled to the rock as quickly and silently as he could

"You expect me to believe you came after your girl without even a gun to back you up?" A bark of laughter echoed around the bowl. The nearest cattle stirred, and the rumble of bovine voices created a low hum that was repeated from various corners of the herd.

"We are Amish. We do not bear arms against anyone."

Luke didn't pause behind the rock but continued on. He wedged himself into the shallow crevice, lowering his body to the earth inside. To his right he spotted Griff huddled behind a rise in the land, and beyond him Morris lay flat on the ground. A cloud that had provided a moment's darkness blew across the moon, and the hillside was bathed again in white light. Morris was exposed. If one of the men below looked in his direction, he'd be spotted in an instant.

Emma was still thirty yards from Luke.

Fortunately, the rustlers were too busy laughing at Jonas to bother looking over their shoulders.

"That's what they said when we took the wagon with that backbreaking piece of furniture in it," said the one whose voice identified him as Earl. "I didn't believe it then, but I guess it's true."

"I *don't* believe it." Suspicion saturated the voice of the fourth, unnamed rustler. He shouted toward Jonas, "Surely you didn't come here alone expecting us to hand over this here girl just 'cause you asked."

Soundlessly, Luke shifted until he had his feet under him, ready to stand and make a quick dash. Any minute now. He raised his rifle, the barrel pointed in the direction of the kidnapper standing beside Emma.

"No, I did not," Jonas answered.

The rustlers looked at each other. "What's he saying? He's talking in circles."

"I don't know, but I'm tired of foolin' with this idiot." Porter, who stood on the right, closest to Morris, raised his pistol and pointed the barrel toward Jonas.

The next few seconds exploded with rapid-fire action.

A woman's scream ripped through the night. "Papa!" Emma jumped to her feet

278

and dashed sideways, toward Porter, whose gun was trained on Jonas.

A shot rang out from somewhere to Luke's right. Porter fell a moment before Emma reached him.

A second shot answered from the left, from beyond the pass into the bowl.

Charlie! Luke leaped to his feet and sprinted forward, his rifle in his hands. Lester surged after Emma, but he jerked his head around at the sound of thundering hooves. Five horses galloped through the narrow pass, all saddled but only one mounted, as Charlie drove the others before him.

Startled cattle surged to their feet in a wave, beginning with the ones closest to the camp and ending at the opposite end of the bowl.

Another shot, and the unnamed rustler fell. Earl whirled to face the hillside, where Morris, Griff, and Luke ran at full speed. Luke was dimly aware that the rustler's gun rose to point directly at Griff, but he couldn't spare a thought for that. He was heading toward Lester, who had recovered enough to resume his sprint after Emma.

The kidnapper reached her while Luke was still ten feet away. Luke raised his rifle and set the man's head squarely within his sites. In one numb part of his brain he knew this moment would haunt him for the rest of his life.

Then Emma ducked and threw herself sideways. The kidnapper's hand closed on air at the same moment Emma slammed into Earl, knocking the arm that held the gun fixed on Griff. He staggered and his shot went wild.

Lester's back was exposed to Luke, a wide open target. One squeeze of a trigger, and Luke could take the man down.

What kind of cowboy shoots a man in the back, even a low-down, no-good, cattle-rustling kidnapper?

Not this kind.

He flipped his rifle around as momentum carried him across the few remaining feet. Holding the cold metal barrel, he swung the heavy butt like he used to swing a stick at a ball as a kid. It connected with Lester's head. For an instant, the rustler's body stiffened. Then he toppled forward and hit the ground at Emma's feet with a puff of dust.

While Morris relieved Earl of his weapon, Griff approached Luke. The grizzled cowboy stood beside him, staring down at the unconscious man sprawled out in the dirt.

"Well." He took his hat off and scratched

his head. "I never saw a Winchester used that way before, but it sure was effective."

Luke opened his mouth to answer, but he forgot the words in the next instant when Emma flew into his arms. He held her close, his insides quaking with relief while she sobbed.

TWENTY-TWO

When the torrent of tears slowed, Emma became aware of Luke's arms around her. Warmth rushed from her head to her toes, partly from the pleasure of breathing in the earthy, wholesome scent that clung to him, but mostly from embarrassment. What an unseemly show of emotion. If her neighbors back in Apple Grove heard that she'd thrown herself into a man's embrace, she would be the subject of shocked gossip for weeks. Public displays of emotion were not encouraged among the Amish. Papa and Mama, whose love for one another radiated from their eyes, had rarely touched in front of Emma, even within the privacy of their own home.

Her face flamed as she stepped away, and she could not bring herself to meet his gaze. "Thank you for saving me."

"And thank *you,* little gal." Griff approached from behind her. "I had one foot inside the Pearly Gates until you sprang into action."

Emma could find no words to reply. She had attacked a man. Not with a weapon, but by using her body as a battering ram. Of course, if she hadn't acted Griff would be dead. She looked at Earl, whose hands were being tied by Morris, and then at the still unconscious form of Lester. Beyond them lay the bodies of the two rustlers who had been killed because of her foolish behavior, sneaking off into the night and getting herself kidnapped.

What lay heavy on her soul, though, was the fact that she couldn't find it in herself to feel sorry for them. Nor for her act of violence in order to save Griff's life.

Papa approached them, his chest heaving from his sprint down the hillside. Never had she been so glad to hear a voice in her entire life as when his rang out in the night. The urge to throw her arms around him and sob was strong, but she knew he would not appreciate such an emotional display, and she had embarrassed herself enough for one night.

He ran up to her, and before she realized what he intended, he gathered her into a strong embrace. "Emma." His rough beard pressed against her cheek. "My Emma. You are safe."

The embrace lasted only a moment, and then Papa pulled back, his hands clutching her arms below the shoulders. Stunned, she searched his face and was astonished to see tears glistening in his eyes. Papa, *her* Papa, who never cried.

His face blurred as salty moisture filled her own eyes. "Papa, I am so sorry. I didn't mean for any of this to happen. I attacked someone. I committed violence against another human being."

Luke let out an exclamation. "You're kidding, right? These men kidnapped you. They have stolen from who knows how many people, including your own family. They killed two of my men and were about to kill more. You saved Griff's life, Emma. How can that be wrong?"

Anger licked at the confusion obvious on his face. Emma searched for words, but how could she explain the Amish belief of nonresistance? Especially when his question stirred up so much confusion inside her. How *could* saving a life be wrong? Killing was wrong; she knew that. But surely acting in defense of another wasn't wrong. If she had to choose again, she would do exactly the same as before. And therein lay the source of her guilt.

Papa had mastered his tears and answered Luke's question. "Christ did not resist, even unto death." He looked into Emma's face. "We both have things to discuss with Bishop Miller when we return to Apple Grove, daughter."

Emma glanced at the unconscious form of her kidnapper and shivered. No matter what the bishop said, she would not be sorry for the mighty bash to the head Luke had given the man. She supposed she'd have to confess that to Bishop Miller too.

But to her father she merely replied, "Yes, Papa."

During the uproar, the cattle's nervousness had increased. The bowl-like shape of the surrounding ridge had kept most of them contained, but about a third had found a way over the hills on the opposite side from the pass and escaped into the night. The rest huddled together, stamping their hooves and uttering uneasy calls to one another.

Once the two remaining rustlers were bound securely and roped to their horses, Luke instructed Charlie and Morris to take them, along with Emma and Jonas, back to camp.

"You want us to drive these along with us?" Charlie gestured to the press of cattle.

Luke shook his head and then jerked a nod in the direction of the bound rustlers. "Let's get those two back to camp first. They'll be watching for you to get distracted, and I don't want to give them a chance to escape. I'm going to enjoy handing them over to the sheriff in Hays." He glared toward Lester, who had regained consciousness and was littering the air with foul curses about the pain in his head and the indignity of being tied sideways on his horse. "Wake Jesse up and tell him to watch them. Then get back here as quick as you can. Griff and I will round up the strays, as long as they haven't run far, and meet you back here."

Looked like sleep wasn't going to happen tonight. By the time they got this rustled herd back to camp and combined with the others, there were likely to only be a couple of hours before daybreak. Not worth the trouble of getting back on his bedroll.

"Got it, boss." Charlie and Morris headed for their horses.

The assignments taken care of, Luke turned to Jonas and Emma, who stood side-by-side next to Jonas's horse. The sight of her downcast head stirred up a storm of conflicting emotions. She actually looked as though she felt guilty for being rescued.

What was wrong with this woman? Didn't she realize how close she'd come to — He shook off the images that had plagued him from the moment he saw her being hauled into the rustlers' camp. The idea that she'd committed some sort of wrongdoing by knocking a man off his feet when he was about to shoot a friend was so foreign to Luke's thinking he couldn't get his mind around it. The whole thing made him angry.

"Charlie and Morris will make sure you get back safely. This horse can ride double, no problem."

Jonas stepped forward and extended a hand. "Once again, the Lord has used you to help my family."

Luke stared at the outstretched hand for a moment. Jonas's beliefs might be a little more than he could handle, but Luke couldn't help respecting the man. He lived what he talked.

He clasped the work-roughened hand. "The diversion was your idea. A good one too."

A step sideways and he stood in front of Emma. "Here. Let me help you up."

As he stooped to clasp his hands for her to step into, he realized she was not wearing Jonas's trousers. She must have taken them off before going to sleep. Instead, he placed his hands around her middle to lift her up into the saddle. His fingers circled her waist, which was much tinier beneath that bulky black dress than he'd realized. Her arms rose and she placed her hands on his shoulders, lifting her head as she did so. Her face was mere inches from his. Twin moons reflected in the eyes that searched his, and glowed on the even white teeth he glimpsed between her parted lips. Anger evaporated, replaced by the almost overpowering urge to pull her close and cover her mouth with his. The memory of her arms around him when she was rescued returned so strongly his hands trembled at her waist.

Beside them, Jonas cleared his throat and shifted his weight from one foot to another.

Exercising a will he didn't know he possessed, Luke lifted her up into the saddle. Before he released her, she spoke, her voice low and earnest. "I'm sorry I acted foolishly by leaving the camp and putting everyone in danger."

So that was the cause for her guilt. She felt responsible. Sort of like he'd felt responsible for Willie and Kirk's deaths yesterday. Well, and in a way, she was.

"Why did you do that, Emma? You're not usually reckless."

Her eyes flickered sideways, toward Jonas,

before returning to his. She spoke in a whisper so low he almost didn't hear. "I wanted to talk to you alone."

She removed her hands from his shoulders and leaned back, balancing her weight on the horse's back. Luke couldn't tear his gaze away as he stepped back to let Jonas mount. A girl sneaking away from her family to meet up with him in the middle of the night? Jesse would rib him forever if he found out.

But this wasn't any girl. This was Emma.

Jonas dug his heels in, and the horse trotted away. Charlie and Morris, each leading a second horse with a prisoner lying crosswise over the saddle, fell in behind them. Luke watched until they entered the pass and disappeared behind the hills.

Griff came up beside him leading their horses. He tossed Whitey's reins at Luke's chest. "We'd best get to rounding up those strays."

Luke tore his gaze away from the empty pass to find Griff grinning at him. The old cowboy pushed his hat back on his forehead. "Women, huh? There's no figuring them."

"Especially that one," Luke said as he swung himself up into the saddle.

TWENTY-THREE

The human component of the camp was awake when Emma and Papa arrived. The campfire blazed as bright flames licked the sky. Emma caught sight of *Maummi's* familiar form stooped beside it. Rebecca stood in the back of the wagon, dwarfed by the hutch that loomed over her. As Emma watched, her sister caught sight of them and began jumping, her hands waving in the air. A whoop of joy reached Emma's ears as Rebecca leaped over the side of the wagon and ran to meet them.

"You found her! Oh, Papa, I prayed you would find her, and you have!"

Papa halted the horse with a gentle pull on the reins. For a long moment, his arms remained in place, one before and one behind Emma, holding her securely on the horse's back. The ride had been made in silence, and Emma fretted that he was angry. Doubtless he had heard her words to

Luke and was scandalized that his daughter had crept away to meet a man in the night. Explanations formed in her mind, words that would convince him that there was no sin in her intent, but she hadn't the nerve to speak, and even came to dread the moment when he would.

"Thanks be to God," he said.

In that moment, while his strong arms formed a safe barrier around her, she felt a tremor in his muscles that she knew was not anger. He was deeply glad to have her restored to him. She leaned her weight against his arm in a private embrace.

Then he released the reins, dismounted, and raised his hands to assist her. Emotion washed over her as she leaned over and entrusted her weight to Papa. Different feelings than when Luke's hands had grasped her waist bubbled up within her, but joyful just the same.

The minute her feet touched the ground, Rebecca caught her in an uninhibited hug, bouncing in a circle that would surely have set their Amish neighbors buzzing with disapproval. For the second time today, Emma shocked herself with the realization that she didn't care what her Amish district would say, which was surely a sinful attitude. Regardless, she returned her sister's embrace with enthusiasm.

When Rebecca released her, she looked into *Maummi's* impassive countenance.

"We are glad for your safe return, granddaughter." Her face came close and she spoke in a low voice that was heavy with emotion that did not show on her face. "You are unharmed?"

The question sent a rush of love through Emma's chest. Those who thought her grandmother gruff and uncaring didn't know her at all. "All but my pride at having my foolish behavior made public."

"Eh." *Maummi* dismissed that with a wave of her hand. " 'Pluck a proud peacock and he looks like a turkey ready for the pot.' "

Emma laughed. *Maummi's* unending store of proverbs and wise sayings sometimes irritated her, but at this moment she would relish a whole sermon full. And she did feel a little like a plucked peacock reduced to turkey status.

"What is this?" The wise gaze slid to a point behind Emma's head, to where Charlie and Morris approached with their charges.

"These are the low-down, good-for-nothing rustlers who took Emma," Charlie said, with a jerk on the reins of the horse he led. "What's left of them, anyway."

A commotion in the wagon drew their attention to Jesse, who was trying to struggle to his feet. "Bring them over here so I can wring a couple of scrawny necks."

Maummi pointed a commanding finger at him. "Down with you! Would you undo all the good the day's rest has brought?"

Morris respectfully took his hat off to address *Maummi.* "Uh, ma'am? Luke sent word to have Jesse guard these two prisoners while Charlie and me go back to help bring up the rest of the herd. Would that be okay?"

With a regal dip of her head, *Maummi* consented. "He can do that while sitting."

Emma hung back while the rustlers were lowered from their horses, seated on the ground, and tied back-to-back. *Maummi* instructed that her rocking chair be placed nearby, along with a crate from the wagon to prop up Jesse's injured leg.

"Move that chair a little closer," Jesse directed from the back of the wagon. He drew his pistol and pointed it at the bound pair, squinting to line up the sights. "And put their hats on their heads. I might take a notion to have me a little target practice, and I'm not too good a shot at night."

Lester scowled, but Emma couldn't help grinning at the wide eyes and audible gulp from Earl. She was *fairly* certain Jesse was only joking and wouldn't really shoot the hats off their heads.

When Charlie and Morris rode off to help Luke and Griff bring in the other cows, Papa mounted his horse and quietly announced that he would lend a hand helping McCann and Vic guard the herd. Apparently no one was interested in sleeping. *Maummi* disappeared around the back of their wagon, and shortly Emma heard the scrape of items being slid across the wooden bed.

Rebecca resumed her favorite activity — mooning over Jesse. She hovered beside his chair.

"Is your leg comfortable? I can bring a quilt to cushion that crate if you want."

Emma started to protest. The only quilt they had was Mama's, and that was *not* coming out of the chest until they got back home and it could be returned to its place on her bed.

Jesse shook his head. "I don't want a quilt."

From the ground Earl spoke up. "I'll take a quilt. This ground's a might hard."

Rebecca cast a startled glance at him, and Jesse raised his pistol in a threatening manner. "You shut up. You don't get a quilt or a blanket or anything else. You're lucky you get to breathe."

The man fell silent. Rebecca stood with her hands clasped behind her back, staring at Jesse's profile.

"Would you like a drink of water? I can fetch you one."

He rolled his eyes. "Isn't it past your bedtime or something?"

"Rebecca." *Maummi*'s sharp voice called from behind the wagon. "Help me here."

A loud sigh of relief sounded from Jesse when Rebecca reluctantly obeyed. He cast a scowling glance after her. "I don't know what I did to attract that girl's attention, but if somebody would tell me, I promise I'll never do it again."

Emma gave him a sympathetic smile. "She is young and has not known many *Englisch* men."

He gave her a sideways scowl. "Yeah, well you *Aim*-ish should get out more. Then you wouldn't be so apt to fall for the first cowhand who comes along."

His words tossed icy water into Emma's soul, and her smile melted. Was he talking about Rebecca or about her? Surely he wasn't saying she went about mooning after Luke the way Rebecca showered attention on him. Or was he?

And more importantly, was he right?

Apparently she'd made a fool of herself by staring at Luke, watching the easy way he rode and admiring his profile when she was sure he wasn't aware. Did he think of her the way Jesse obviously thought of Rebecca, as a child and a nuisance?

Face flaming, she whirled on her foot and went to help *Maummi* and Rebecca.

Though the sun was not yet in evidence, the eastern sky was a lighter blue than the western half by the time Emma spotted a herd of cattle heading in their direction. Before she could stop herself, she searched the mounted riders until she spotted Luke's familiar figure atop a white horse that reflected the predawn light. Then she remembered her resolve. She would *not* humiliate herself and her family by mooning after him like a lovesick youth. With deliberate resolve she turned her back to the approaching group and bent over the cook fire, feigning indifference. She did peek behind every so often, but only to watch the convergence of the two herds.

The approach of the new cattle caused a stir among the existing ones. As the lead steers came into sight, the sleeping herd awoke and staggered to its feet. Luke and the other wranglers rode into the fray to break up confrontations before they gave way to aggression. The men worked as a team, even Papa, by forming a constantly moving barrier around the whole, gently but firmly urging them to spread out into the sweet green grass that surrounded their bedding ground. By the time the first rays of light streaked into the sky from the still-hidden sun, the two herds had merged into one and set about grazing peacefully side by side.

The riders approached camp at a gallop. McCann broke off when the others headed for the remuda to turn in their tired horses. He came straight to the chuck wagon.

"Whew, what a night," he called toward Jesse as he dismounted. "Been a while since I spent that much time in a saddle. I've got to get some breakfast going to feed this —"

He stopped short when he caught sight of *Maummi,* who knelt on the other side of the fire pit from Emma, flipping hotcakes on a griddle.

Bushy eyebrows dropped down to rest on his eyelids. "What in tarnation's going on here?"

Maummi slid a long-handled spatula beneath a hotcake and tossed it on top of a giant stack being kept warm on a flat rock.

"You helped with the cows. I helped with the breakfast." She switched her attention to a pan full of sizzling bacon without looking up.

Emma stirred the bubbling pot in front of her, decided the apples were ready, and swung the arm to move it out of the direct heat. She felt the cook's stare burning into her, but she couldn't meet his eye. In this case, she would take the coward's way out and leave him to *Maummi*'s capable handling.

"Hey!" He stabbed a finger toward the extra-long griddle. "That's mine. And that turning fork's mine too. You've been in my chuck wagon!"

He turned and ran toward his wagon. *Maummi* picked up a metal plate, loaded it high with hotcakes and bacon, and then ladled gooey sweet apples overtop. She took it to Jesse's chair and thrust it in his hands.

"Eat." The command was issued with a stern stare that no one would dare defy. Then she turned and issued another command to Emma and Rebecca. "Ready the plates."

Morris and Charlie were still out with the herd, but the rest of the men approached the camp as McCann charged out of the chuck wagon. He glared at *Maummi* and

298

then ran over to thrust his purple face into Luke's.

"That *woman*" — he pointed backward at *Maummi* — "went into my chuck wagon. She went through my fixins' and used my pans." He drew himself stiffly upright to announce her ultimate sin. "She *cleaned.*"

In light of her recent realization, Emma couldn't bring herself to look directly at Luke, but she tensed, waiting for his response.

"Dirt is a poor seasoning," *Maummi* commented mildly as she layered a stack of hotcakes onto a plate.

Every eye was fixed on Luke. He opened his mouth, but his response was preempted by Jesse, who had shoveled in a forkful of hotcakes. "Mm-mmm! You gotta try these, Luke. You never tasted hotcakes like these." Cheeks bulging, he chewed with happy abandon.

Emma held a loaded plate in her hands. She shoved it toward Rebecca with a whispered, "Take this to Luke, quick."

Rebecca did, delivering the plate with a curtsey. Looking a little sheepish, Luke sliced off a bite and shoved it in his mouth. His expression transformed to one of bliss.

"Have you tried this?" he demanded of McCann when he had relished the bite and swallowed.

McCann drew himself stiffly upright, sputtering. "Don't make no difference what —"

"Hey, give me some." Charlie approached Emma, his expression eager. "The front of my stomach's gnawing on the back, it's so empty."

Emma ladled a heaping portion of sweet, thick apples over a stack of cakes and handed it to him. He shoved a steaming bite into his mouth and then went into ecstasies of delight.

"Them's the best hotcakes I ever ate, ma'am." He ducked his head toward *Maummi* before taking his plate to a spot near the wagon and sinking to the ground to enjoy his breakfast.

"I'm up for more." Jesse half turned in his chair to hold his empty plate out in an appeal. "I need my strength to rebuild this bone, you know."

McCann glowered all around as the rest of the crew settled into their breakfast. Emma speared a few chunks of bacon out of the pan to finish off a cake-filled plate and took it to him. She offered it with a quick smile.

"Humph." He grumbled as he took it and

turned away from the fire to try the first bite.

Maummi flipped another hotcake on the griddle and pretended not to watch for his reaction. Emma couldn't be so nonchalant. She saw his expression change from angry to skeptical, and then relax into amazement as he chewed. By the time he swallowed, she knew he'd been won over. And no wonder. *Maummi* wasn't known as the best cook in Apple Grove for nothing.

"Hey, what about us?" The shout came from one of the rustlers tied up in the middle of the clearing. "You gonna let us starve while you stand there shoveling food in your faces?"

"Shut up," Jesse said. "You're lucky I don't blow your Adam's apple out of your throat."

Papa, who had been standing quietly off to the side, took a step toward Luke. "An Amish proverb teaches 'Be kind to unkind people. They probably need kindness the most.' "

Spouting proverbs was *Maummi*'s exclusive domain. Papa rarely weighed in with a wise saying from the deep store that had instructed him his whole life. That he did so now spoke to the strength of his convictions in this situation. Though Emma knew full

301

well he condemned the rustlers' actions, his compassion for them overrode his condemnation. The Lord would have them feed the hungry, regardless of their sins. Love for her father washed over her like a strong, refreshing breeze on a hot summer day. She caught her breath, waiting for Luke's response.

His gaze sought hers. "What do you think, Emma?"

He was deferring to her opinion? These were the men who had kidnapped her, and before that they had stolen her family's belongings. But she could only spare thoughts for Luke. He sought her opinion. Warmth spread through her stomach, and looking away felt like ripping her eyes out of their sockets. But she managed to nod and focus on the task at hand, filling two plates with food.

"Untie one hand each," Luke told Charlie. "We're not the barbarians they are." Then he pointed a fork at Jesse. "But watch them while they eat. If they make a move, you know what to do."

Jesse grinned and patted the pistol that rested in his lap. "Oh, yeah."

When Emma had handed two full plates to Charlie for delivery to their prisoners, McCann sidled up to the fire where *Maummi* stood, an empty plate in his hand. He shuffled his feet and blustered for a moment before he managed to speak.

"I don't like people going through my things." His voice growled. "But those *were* the best hotcakes I ever ate. And I don't know what you did to those apples on top, but I could eat a whole pot of 'em by themselves."

Maummi busied her hands with pulling the hot griddle off the coals and setting it aside to cool. "That's a nice griddle," she admitted, nodding toward it. "A good cook arms himself with good tools."

Emma nearly choked. That was as close to a compliment as *Maummi* was likely to give.

McCann cleared his throat. "We're going to be pushing hard today. By the time we stop tonight, the men are liable to have a roaring appetite. I'd appreciate a hand rustling up the evening meal, if you've a mind."

She cast a narrow-eyed sideways look up at him. "Too many cooks in a kitchen step on each other's toes."

For a moment, Emma thought she'd pushed him too far. He drew himself upright, glanced down at the steaming pot of stewed apples, and then let out a breath. "Then it's a good thing we have the whole outdoors to cook in. Plenty of space for both of us."

A smile twitched *Maummi*'s lips as she scraped the scraps from the skillet. She gave a curt nod. "A good thing indeed."

Emma released her breath. A compromise reached, and a hesitant partnership formed. She found herself looking forward to whatever concoction the two of them paired up to create this evening.

As the men scraped their plates clean, Luke sidled up to the fire to stand beside her. "Are you and your sister planning to lend a hand with the herd today?"

She concentrated on her empty plate. Better to avoid eye contact than to turn an embarrassingly adoring gaze on him. "Do you need us?"

"It's going to be a hard day." His answer was vague, as though he didn't want to impose.

Charlie approached to hand her his empty plate, and she smiled her thanks to him. When she turned from setting it in the dishpan near her feet, Luke grabbed her hand, forcing her to look up at him.

"I need you," he said, his voice low and insistent.

A storm erupted inside her rib cage. From the delving gaze that bore into hers, she knew he referred to more than his need for another cowhand for his expanded herd. Somewhere behind her, she was aware that Papa watched, his stare a weight that dragged her soaring heart back to the ground.

She snatched her hand away and busied herself with the dishes. "If you need us, Luke, then of course we will help."

He didn't move but stood silently beside her, watching her work. Maybe he was listening to the thudding of her heart, which pounded in her ears like Indian war drums. He stood so close she could smell the earthy scent that clung to him, and the memory of his hands at her waist as he lifted her onto Papa's horse snatched at her breath.

After an eternity he moved away, leaving the air around her somehow colder.

When he spoke again, his voice projected to everyone in the area. "We've expanded our herd by almost a third, and we're behind schedule. I figure if we push them hard until midday and then stop for a rest, we'll be able to go on tonight until after sundown. What do you think, Griff?"

Emma glanced toward the old cowhand, who had seated himself against a wagon wheel and was taking his time polishing off his breakfast. "If we call a stop near a good watering hole, they'll do fine."

"That ought to put us in Hays tomorrow afternoon. If all goes well we won't miss the train."

If all goes well. Buried in those words Emma heard a lot of doubt, a lot of worry. Luke's reputation as a trail boss rested on their ability to get this herd there on time. In fact, if he showed up with seven hundred more cows than he started with, and a couple of rustlers in the bargain, surely that would look good. He would have no problems getting more jobs as a trail boss. *If he misses that train, though . . .* Emma refused to let herself complete the thought, but it danced a tantalizing jig in her mind.

Surely life as an Amish farmer was better than life as an unemployed cowboy.

"All right, then," Luke said. "Vic will wrangle the remuda. Morris and Rebecca will ride flank on that side" — he pointed east — "with Griff and Emma opposite." He speared Charlie and Papa with a sympathetic grimace. "That makes you two the drag riders."

"What about me? A day and a night is plenty of time to rest this leg." Jesse made as though to get up from the chair, his face a mask of ill-concealed pain. "Bring my horse alongside the wagon so's I can get on him."

Maummi stiffened, her eyes throwing darts across the camp. Before she could speak, though, Luke answered.

"You're not riding anything but that wagon until the doctor in Hays checks you out. But you have an important job making sure those two don't cause any trouble today." He jerked his head toward their prisoners. "If they try anything, you don't need a good leg to fire a gun."

Appeased, Jesse fixed his charges with a cold smile and patted the pistol in his lap.

Luke took a final look around. "Let's break camp and get at it."

His words spurred everyone into action. The men began readying the wagons to leave. Griff, empty plate in hand, swung wide so his path would take him by the fire, where *Maummi* crouched beside the long iron griddle, scraping it clean.

"Ma'am, that was the best meal I've had in years. Maybe ever."

Maummi inclined her head like a queen accepting her due. *"Danki."*

Griff didn't move on. Instead, he shuffled his weight from one foot to the next and glanced around the area. His gaze settled on Emma for a moment, the only person close enough to hear his words.

He cleared his throat and watched the

coals in the cook fire as he spoke. "Ma'am, I've spent almost twenty years in the saddle. I figure I've got a few good ones left in me, but a man can't run cattle forever. Someday he has to hang up his spurs."

Emma couldn't agree more. She hoped Luke didn't want to stretch his trail driving days out for twenty years.

Stooping on the ground beside the fire, *Maummi* turned her head to look up at him sideways, the creases between her eyes clearly urging him to get to the point and let her get on with her work.

Griff cleared his throat again. "And when he does, it sure does help if he has a good woman waiting for him at home. Now, I never had time for a wife, but if I quit the trail, I'd want to find me a woman with some spunk in her. One who speaks her piece." He toed a good-sized rock into the fire, his gaze fixed on his boot. "One who can cook."

His meaning stole across Emma, leaving her numb. No, surely she was mistaken. Was Griff asking to *court* her grandmother? But, *Maummi* was sixty years old! Of course, Griff was probably close to the same age.

"Anyway, I do have a few good years left in me," he repeated. "Something for you to think about."

With an awkward movement, he thrust his fork and empty plate toward Emma and then strode away quickly, like a man bent on escape. Still crouching on the ground, *Maummi*'s mouth gaped open as she stared after him.

It was the first time in her life Emma could remember seeing her grandmother rendered speechless.

Twenty-Four

Riding lead, Luke set an aggressive pace. At first the herd was reluctant. They were accustomed to an easy, sauntering stride while tearing up a mouthful of grass every few steps or so. He targeted a few of the lead steers and stayed on their heels. By mid-morning the herd had spread out wide and settled on an acceptable speed, though he kept a close eye on the sun's position as they passed familiar landmarks. The longer they took to get to the bedding ground he had in mind, the less sleep he would allow tonight.

The oxen pulling the Switzers' wagon easily kept pace alongside McCann and the chuck wagon in front of the remuda. Luke kept watch on the occupants. If it turned out there was a reward for those rustlers, dead or alive, by rights it belonged to everyone. He planned to suggest instead that the money be turned over to Willie and

Kirk's families. He would take a vote later, but he was pretty sure the men would agree with him.

At the sight of that wagon, with its hulking wooden hutch, a chuckle rumbled in his chest. Mrs. Switzer had insisted on driving, while Jesse and the prisoners rode squashed in the back. Every time Luke looked that way, Mrs. Switzer's mouth was moving. What could she be saying hour upon hour? From this angle he couldn't see Jesse's expression, so he couldn't judge his friend's mood. The chuckle turned to a snicker. Served him right. That boy had some growing up to do.

His curiosity finally got the best of him. It was time to check on the outfit anyway. He'd start with the Switzer wagon.

As he neared, he heard the sharp tone of her voice first, and then he was able to make out words.

" 'A handful of patience is worth more than a bushel of brains.' A favorite of my dearly departed, that was. And this one too: 'You can't make good hay from poor grass.' Ah, my Carl. A better man never set foot on the Lord's earth, no matter what the bishop said. He loved to hear my proverbs. Said he could hear the Lord's voice when I quoted. The Bible ones I had to say in English. Carl

311

didn't understand German."

Lester and Earl had been tied back-to-back in the bed of the wagon behind the bench, where Mrs. Switzer sat with the oxen's rope in her hand. The pair were wedged between the sideboard and the hutch, but they were tied up and couldn't move around. The rocking chair had been placed at the back of the wagon. Jesse sat there looking comfortable with a pleasant expression, not nearly as irked as Luke would have thought after being forced to listen to hours of proverbs and Amish wisdom.

Luke's horse approached the wagon as Mrs. Switzer turned her head to fix Lester with a stern look. "Heard this one, have you? 'Cleanliness is next to godliness.' Taking to heart this one would do you good. When next we stop I will beg sody and a toothpick from Mr. McCann for cleaning your teeth."

Earl let out a chortle, and the sour-faced Lester rewarded him with a backward head-butt.

Jesse sat stiffly upright in the rocking chair. "Settle down there." He delivered his warning with a glare, and then he relaxed back into his passive, almost peaceful expression.

Luke slowed Bo's pace to match the wagon and came up alongside Jesse. He readied himself for a string of complaints at being left as captive to Mrs. Switzer and the two rustlers.

"How're you doing?"

"Huh?" Jesse gave him a blank look before reaching up to pull a wad of cotton wool out of each ear. "Sorry. Didn't hear you. What'd you say?"

Luke's laughter rolled over the Kansas plain. "I'm making sure everything's all right here."

"We're fine. Just fine." Jesse swept a hand to encompass the sky. "Pleasant day for an easy ride."

He was stuffing the wool back in his ears when Luke, still laughing, steered Bo away from the wagon. His next stop was to check on the westernmost flank riders.

Emma sat astride her horse like an experienced cowpoke. Well, except for the black fabric of her dress bunched around her thighs, and the black trousers that she had tied in place with bits of twine at the ankles. And her ever-present white *kapp,* which prairie dust had turned into a dingy brown.

The moment their gazes met, she looked away. Luke couldn't tell if the faint touch of color in her cheeks was from the heat or

313

from shyness. They had not spoken privately since her startling revelation that she'd snuck away from camp in the night to talk to him. Here they were in plain sight of everyone, but so removed that no one could hear their conversation.

He nudged Bo with his knees to fall in step beside Sugarfoot. "Everything going okay here?"

His question received a hesitant nod but no comment. She looked straight ahead, giving him a view of a very pretty profile. A man could get used to enjoying this sight every day.

"You look like you're sitting easy in the saddle. Is it feeling more natural now?"

She nodded.

The horses walked along a few yards. Whatever it was she wanted to talk to him so badly about last night sure didn't seem to be so pressing today.

"Emma? You mentioned that you wanted to talk to me about something. This would be a good time."

"It wasn't important." The blush was definitely a darker shade of pink now. "I . . . wanted to thank you again for helping us."

She was clearly avoiding the truth, and he didn't know how to answer. He studied her as he considered a response. A steer not far in front of them started to veer to the west, toward the inviting green prairie grass that waved in the breeze. Like an experienced cowboy she dug in her heels to urge her horse into a trot and cut the wandering animal neatly off. He obediently resumed his former position, and Emma slowed slightly to allow Luke and Bo to catch up.

"You know, you've taken to this easier than most greenhorns I've worked with. If you decide you want a job, I'll hire you for my next cattle drive."

Emma, a cowhand? He caught back a chuckle. The awkward silence was starting to get to him and made him want to fill the void with talk.

At least the ridiculous statement elicited a reaction. She turned to look at him full-on, her expression full of surprise at his ludicrous suggestion.

"No, really," he insisted. He'd look like a fool if he backed down now. "There are women on the trail. Not many, but I've met one or two."

Words failed him as he recalled a female cattle wrangler he met a couple years back. He'd waded into a saloon to fish Jesse out and found a woman matching him drink for drink. It came out later that she'd cleaned him out at the poker table too. Definitely a different class of female than Emma.

"Thank you for the compliment, but I don't think I'd make a very good cowboy." The humor twitching around her lips heartened him. She didn't take offense easily.

"On second thought, the job is a bit rugged for most women."

"You'd probably take to the Amish way sooner than I would to the life of a trail rider." The words were delivered in a comfortable, light tone. So why did he feel like she was waiting for his response so closely?

His shrugged. "Oh, I doubt that."

She fixed her gaze on the herd, her posture slumping. What did he say? Women. He'd never had trouble connecting to one before. Hadn't he saved her life a few hours ago? Why, then, was he stumbling over a simple conversation?

The answer came to him the instant he posed the question. He'd never felt an attraction this strong for any woman. An invisible rope stretched between them as they rode along side by side. Even when he was up at the front of the herd and she back here, he felt the connection. Is that where the term "getting hitched" came from? Did it start with this invisible bond?

"Listen, the other day you mentioned learning how to handle a lasso. If you're still interested I could show you a trick or two when we stop to rest the herd."

A smile curved her lips. He found himself watching her mouth, remembering the almost magnetic pull he'd felt just before he lifted her onto her father's horse in the predawn darkness.

"I would like to learn."

"Good. All right. Until this afternoon, then."

He spurred Bo's sides, and the horse leaped into a gallop toward the front of the herd. Luke refused to look behind him, but he felt Emma's gaze pinned to his back. His mood was curiously light, as if she'd agreed to step out with him for a romantic evening stroll after supper.

It's only a rope handling lesson.

Regardless, he found himself looking forward to the afternoon as eagerly as a kid waiting for a hot cookie.

By the time Luke called a halt for the planned midday rest, Emma had worked herself around a wagon wheel of emotions. His quick denial of her comment about the Amish lifestyle had delivered a crushing blow. Did his answer mean he'd thought about the idea and rejected it? If not, did his offhand manner mean he would never

317

consider becoming Amish?

A relationship between us is doomed. Why do I torture myself?

And what was behind his offer to teach her to handle a rope? Was that a less than subtle hint that she should consider adopting his lifestyle? The idea of her going with him on a trail drive was so far beyond reason that she couldn't believe he'd even joke about it.

It *was* a joke, wasn't it?

The cattle welcomed the stop and immediately spread themselves across the open range, feasting on the prairie grass that grew amid the bristly sagebrush, and quenching their thirst in a watering hole fed by a shallow stream. A few trees stretched sun-bleached branches toward one another to form a sparse shade along the banks of the stream, and soon a cluster of cattle crowded beneath them in search of relief from the blistering July sun.

"We'll give them a couple of hours," Luke told the outfit. "You men might want to get some rest yourselves." He tossed a grin toward *Maummi,* still seated high on the wagon's bench. "And you ladies too."

Emma drew Sugarfoot alongside the wagon and swung her leg over the horse's back. She still hadn't managed to climb into the saddle on her own successfully, but gravity worked with her on the dismount. She landed on her feet, a little unsteadily, and then hurried to help *Maummi* down from the wagon. As she did, she spared a quick glance at the captive rustlers. Lester straightened upright as much as his bonds would let him, scanning the activity nearby.

His gaze rested on McCann, and he raised his voice. "You, Cook! You got room in the chuck wagon? Let me ride with you. Tie me up, gag me, I don't care. I give you my word I won't try nothing." He tossed an anxious glance toward *Maummi*. "Just get me away from this woman."

"Quiet, you." From his perch in *Maummi*'s rocking chair, Jesse growled his warning at the kidnapper. "Your word is worth less than your spit."

Maummi paused in the act of stepping to the ground, her hand on Emma's shoulder. She spoke calmly to Lester. *"Die Ruchlosen verachten Weisheit und Zucht."*

"Did you hear that?" Lester's shout toward McCann held a touch of desperation. "She never dries up! I don't even know what that means."

Rebecca arrived, reining her horse to a stop and swinging to the ground with ease. "I can tell you. I hear it all the time. It means only fools hate wisdom and instruction. It's from *Die Bibel.*"

"She's calling me a fool?"

Jesse growled. "You *are* a fool. Now have some respect and shut your piehole before I shut it for you."

Vic rode up then and took charge of Emma and Rebecca's horses. He would switch their saddles to fresh mounts before the afternoon march began. McCann put out the fresh water barrel, and the girls quenched their parched throats with a lukewarm drink. At least it was wet.

When Emma finished wiping her hot face with a dampened edge of her apron — which was in a shocking state but better than nothing — Luke approached from the direction of the remuda, Papa by his side. He walked up to Emma, his smile as refreshing as a cooling rain.

"Ready?"

Rebecca lowered her cup from wet lips. "Ready for what?"

The answer fluttered in Emma's throat, and she found she couldn't look Luke in the face without giving in to a flush that hovered in the vicinity of her collarbone. "Luke has agreed to teach me how to throw a rope." She glanced at Papa. "If it's okay."

Rebecca rose up on her toes and bounced.

"I want to learn too. Papa, can I?"

The scrutiny of Papa's gaze made Emma want to look away. Instead, she straightened her shoulders and stared calmly back at him, careful to keep her gaze clear of guile.

He gave the barest of nods. "Perhaps I may learn as well."

Luke cast a quick glance at her, and she saw understanding in his gaze. He'd reached the same conclusion as she. They both had hoped for time alone. Papa didn't care a thing about learning to lasso a cow. He merely wanted to stay close while his daughter was in the company of an oh-so-appealing *Englisch* cowboy.

Feeling a tiny bit thwarted, Emma managed a small smile. This was the very reason Amish youth kept their romantic intentions to themselves.

"All right, then." If Luke's smile looked a little insincere, at least he covered it with an enthusiastic tone. "Let's go to the other side of the wagon, where there's a couple of good-sized stumps we can practice on." He turned his head and raised his voice to be heard by those in the vicinity. "Anybody have a lariat we can borrow? We're going to do a little practicing."

"This I gotta see." Jesse's voice from the back of the wagon hinted skepticism.

Griff approached Emma with a grin and a coiled length of rope. "Show 'em what you can do, gal."

He crossed over to the wagon, sat, and pushed his hat back off his forehead, looking as though he was waiting for a show to start. Others did the same, and before long everyone in the vicinity was scattered around the area, their gazes trained on the roping lesson. The flutter in Emma's stomach erupted into full-blown nerves. This was not how she'd envisioned her personal lesson with Luke progressing.

When Papa and Rebecca both held borrowed ropes as well, Luke walked them a little ways off. The area was free of trees, though several dead stumps rose out of the sagebrush-covered ground, as though a storm had sheared a thicket in years past. Luke took up the end of his coiled rope and held it up. The end formed a ring.

"This is called the honda," he explained. "Uncoil a few feet of rope and slip it through the honda to form a loop, like this."

Emma mimicked his actions and adjusted her loop until it was the same size as Luke's. It looked like a giant noose. Beside her, Rebecca and Papa did likewise.

Luke eyed all three and nodded. "Good. Now, leave yourself a few feet of free rope.

You'll need it when you start swinging. What you're going to do is swing the lariat over your head a few times until you get a good feel for the rope and where it's going."

He demonstrated as he spoke. He raised the loop above his head and swung it around from right to left, the other hand holding several feet of loose rope and the coils looped over his arm. "Keep your wrist loose and let it do the work. It should swing like a wheel going around and around above your head."

The loop grew larger as he swung, and it opened up, like a wide, yawning mouth.

"It's taking a long time," said Rebecca. "If you were doing this for real, hasn't the cow already run away by now?"

Someone behind them snorted, and Luke grinned. "Once you get the feel for your rope, you won't have to swing it so much. But for now we're taking our time, making sure we have control." The lariat continued to circle above his head as he spoke. "Don't forget to keep an eye on your target. I'm looking at the stump on your right. When you're ready —"

He took a quick step forward and released the rope. The loop sailed through the air without losing its circular form, pulling a couple of coils of rope off his arm like a tail, and landed neatly around the gnarly stump. He stepped back and pulled the rope. The noose tightened around the stump with a snap.

Applause and cheers broke out from their audience.

"Not bad, Luke," Jesse called. "Maybe you could get a job as a cattle wrangler someday."

The jab was met with good-natured laughter. Emma tried to ignore their audience, which had grown to include almost the entire outfit. Was she about to make a fool of herself again? Well, if she did, at least she'd have Rebecca and Papa as fellow buffoons this time.

"All right, who wants to go first?" Luke looked directly at her, but Papa stepped forward.

"I will."

"Fine." Luke gestured for Emma and Rebecca to step back. "Give him some room, ladies. Okay, Jonas, now grab the loop about a foot or so away from the honda. Give yourself plenty of loose rope in the other hand. Looks good." Luke backed away. "Start swinging."

Papa raised his hand, and the noose began to circle in the air above his head. Within a few swings it opened up like Luke's.

"Good job, Jonas." A note of surprise filled Luke's voice. "Now get the feel of the rope and let it swing until you're —"

Before he finished speaking, Papa let loose his rope. The loop sailed through the air and landed half-on and half-off the stump. He gave the excess a jerk, and the noose tightened and held.

"Papa, you lassoed a stump!" Rebecca's squeal joined the applause of the group behind them while Luke stared.

He recovered himself. "You've done this before, haven't you, Jonas?"

Recoiling the rope carefully around his arm, Papa lifted a shoulder. "Once or twice."

"Uh-huh." After a slap on the back, Luke pointed. "You can go over there and pick another stump to practice on. This one is for beginners."

Papa stepped back but didn't move away. Apparently he wasn't about to let the lesson continue without his watchful eye.

"Who's next?"

Luke glanced at Emma, but before she could speak Rebecca ran forward to take the spot Papa had vacated.

"I am. Show me one more time."

Under the guise of watching the lesson, Emma was free to stare at Luke all she wanted. He'd taken off his hat, and the breeze ruffled through the waves of his hair. The sun had tanned his skin to a warm shade that made his dark eyes stand out. When he raised his arm above his head to demonstrate, the fabric of his shirt stretched across muscles strengthened from years of hard work on the trail. And his hands, the very ones that had circled her waist —

With a start, Emma jerked her mind away from that trail. Perhaps there was nothing wrong in looking, but the Lord surely wouldn't approve of thoughts that lingered on touching.

"Good, Rebecca." He took a step backward to give her room. "Now swing the loop above your head, right to left."

Rebecca raised her arm and swung, with little effect. Instead of rising into the air, the limp rope circled her body. Frustrated, she dropped her arm to her side with a slap against her leg. "I think this one is broken."

A guffaw sounded from the direction of their wagon. Jesse.

Luke ignored him. "It's fine. You just need to put a little more energy into it. Swing harder."

A sigh came from her lips as she reset her stance and tried again. At first the loop behaved the same, but at Luke's urging Rebecca increased the speed of her arm. Slowly, the loop opened. Not a perfect circle, as Papa's had been, but it was at least recognizable as a lariat.

"You're doing great." Luke's approval brought a quick smile to Rebecca's face, which immediately returned to an expression of fierce concentration as the lariat swung round and round above her head.

His words kindled a fierce desire in Emma to hear the same encouragement. She watched her sister, noting the placement of her feet and the speed of her swing.

"Move your arm a tiny bit and feel the rope react."

"I feel it." Rebecca's head faced toward the stump, but her eyes turned upward and circled with the rope.

"Focus on your target," Luke said. "When you're ready, release the noose as it swings forward. Drop your wrist down and then let your palm swing open."

She did so, and the noose went flying through the air. It hit the ground at least ten feet short of the stump.

Rebecca's lower lip protruded. "I missed."

"But that was a good try!" No one could doubt the sincere enthusiasm of Luke's praise. "That's one of the best first throws I've ever seen. It took Jesse a week to get that close to the target when he was learning."

"Hey!" Jesse yelled, protesting from his chair. "I was six years old."

"Yeah?" Charlie's shout was tinged with laughter. "So what's your excuse for missing that calf last week?"

Several others joined in the teasing.

Jesse took the ribbing with good humor. "You wait till this leg of mine heals. Then we'll see who can out-rope any man in this outfit."

Nerves skipped across Emma's muscles, leaving them tense and her stomach uneasy. She watched closely as Rebecca threw four more times, each time her aim improving and her rope coming closer to her target. Her sister had always been the more active of the two, even besting boys in games and races. What if Emma couldn't manage to do as well? Her little sister would show her up in front of Luke and everyone else.

After a few tries, Luke said, "You're trained, Rebecca. All you need is practice. Go on over there and pick out a stump of your own."

When she ran off with the coiled rope draped over her arm, he raised his eyes to Emma. "Your turn."

She couldn't manage to force a sound out

of her tight throat, so she nodded. Feet dragging in the dust, she made her way to stand in the place her sister and father had taken. This was supposed to be fun, wasn't it? Why did her stomach churn as though she might be sick?

Luke's smile calmed her nerves a bit. She managed to return it as she positioned herself the way the others had.

He examined her stance. "Place your feet a little farther apart, about the width of your shoulders, and one slightly in front of the other." His hands on her arms as he positioned her sent her nerves dancing again. She ignored them and tried to concentrate on following directions.

"You have your noose, right?"

Swallowing, she nodded and held it up for inspection.

"Hold it right about here."

He slid her right hand into position. The shock of the skin-on-skin contact almost made her drop the rope, and she found she couldn't quite look him in the eye. Did he feel that too?

"Good. Now, let out about six feet of rope off the coil. For a reference, that's about how tall I am."

Though he no doubt meant to be helpful, her thoughts were momentarily pulled off task as she took in his height. Standing next to him like this, the top of her head came at nose level to him.

Focus, Emma!

"That's right. You're ready to start swinging."

When he'd stepped back, she raised her arm and swung the rope. "Like this?"

"No, swing it the other way. From right to left."

She dropped her arm too fast. The momentum of the rope continued, and circled once around her neck. The end of the loop caught her in the face.

"Ow!" She couldn't help gasping at the stinging slap.

"Are you okay?" Luke's concerned eyes scanned her face. "That's gonna raise a welt."

Terrific.

She managed a smile. "I'm fine. Let me try again."

As he backed away once more, she untangled the rope from her neck and recoiled it around her arm. She checked the size of her loop and grabbed it in the same place he had instructed. This time when she raised her arm, she swung the rope right to left, the way he said. The rope whirled above her head.

"You got it." Luke's encouragement heartened her. "Swing a little faster."

She did as instructed. The loop failed to open, stubbornly remaining shut. She might as well have been swinging a clothesline over her head.

"Your wrist is locked, Emma. Loosen it up." Luke's voice, raised enough to cover the distance between them, sounded every bit as patient as it had a moment before. Why, then, did she feel like an unteachable dunce?

Rebecca's shriek of success pierced the air. "I did it! Look, Luke. I lassoed my stump!"

The watching men responded with applause and whoops of congratulations. Luke turned to award her a big grin. Emma let her rope drop again, but this time she released the other side and covered her face with her hand. One welt was too many already. As the rope lost momentum, it wrapped around her body.

Wonderful. I've managed to hog-tie myself.

The expression on Luke's face when he turned from Rebecca back to her was carefully clear of pity. She flushed hotly. The complete lack of visible emotion said it all. Behind her, the audience fell silent. The fact that they didn't laugh at her expense was

331

probably meant kindly, but their silence was even more humiliating than their jokes.

"I guess I'm better at cooking and sewing than roping stumps." Her gaze avoided his face as she unwound the rope from her body.

"It takes practice." He took a step forward to help her recoil the rope. "Come on. Try it one more time."

Giving up and slinking off to nurse her embarrassment alone sounded like a much better option, but Emma bit back a sigh and repositioned her feet.

"That's good. Take hold of the noose here."

When he positioned her hand this time she was too miserable to feel a single tingle. She did as instructed, gripped the rope in exactly the right place, and when he stepped back she swung the loop up above her head, right to left. Her wrist was loose. Her body swayed slightly on her feet in motion with the circling rope.

"That's it! You've got it going."

Griff and Jesse and the others echoed Luke's cheer. Emma risked a quick upward glance and saw that her loop had, indeed, begun to open up. Not a wide circle like Luke's, but sort of a long oval in the shape of a giant cucumber. She increased the pace of her arm, remembering to keep her wrist loose, and the cucumber became a watermelon.

"Good," Luke shouted. "Can you feel how your movements affect the lariat?"

"Yes, I feel it." She focused more on making her wrist work like the axle of a wagon and the lariat the turning wheel.

The watermelon became a pumpkin.

"Now look at your target. Take aim, and when you're ready, you'll release the lariat when it swings around to the front. Keep your movements smooth. Have you got your eye on your target?"

A movement a little ways beyond the stump drew Emma's attention. A line of steers wandered past on their way to the watering hole. An idea took shape and bloomed in an instant. Leave the stumps to Rebecca. She would lasso a cow.

An oblivious steer stopped and lowered its head to tear up a mouthful of grass.

"Yes," she shouted back to Luke. "I see my target."

"Okay. Whenever you're ready, let her fly."

She did. The release wasn't quite as smooth as she planned, but at least the lariat sailed through the air and didn't slap her in the face. The pumpkin shriveled back into a cucumber, and the long loop wavered unsteadily before dropping toward the ground.

When it landed, Emma could hardly believe her eyes. The loop had managed to snag on the point of one long steer horn. Startled, the animal raised his head, and the rope slid all the way over the horn.

With a shriek of victory, Emma pulled the rope tight. She turned her head to grin at Luke.

In the next moment she was jerked off her feet. Instinctively, she grasped onto the rope and was pulled face first across the ground as the startled steer took off in a run.

"Emma!"

Luke's voice sounded from somewhere behind her, but she couldn't look back at him. Her eyes squeezed tight as she was dragged across tall grass and prickly sagebrush bushes. She was dimly aware of other voices joining Luke's — Rebecca and Papa's — and farther away, Jesse and Griff's.

Her body sailed over dips and ripples in the land like a stone skipping across a pond. Her shoulders felt as if they had been pulled from their sockets with every ditch. The shouts behind her persisted, and she managed a backward glimpse.

A parade of people ran after her. In the lead, Luke's face shone blood-red, and his hands cupped his mouth as he shouted. Behind him, Rebecca had gathered her skirts above her knees and seemed intent on proving that she could still outrun the boys. Papa was close behind Rebecca, and Charlie brought up the rear. Every mouth was open as they screamed in her direction.

Finally, Luke's voice rose above the chaos, and she heard what he was saying.

"Let go of the rope! Let go!"

Until that moment, she had not realized that she still clutched the rope in a death grip. Well, of course. What a dunce.

She let go with her left hand first, and dropped her arm behind her back. When she'd freed herself from the coil of rope, she released her right hand. Her wild ride across the prairie ended abruptly, with her face planted in sagebrush.

Luke caught up with her first. She found herself being lifted off the ground by strong hands, and in the next instant her body was turned and crushed to his. His arms encircled her with such force she couldn't manage to get air into her lungs.

She didn't care in the least.

"Emma!" She heard his voice break. He relaxed his hold and held her at arm's length. "You scared the dickens out of me! You could have been killed." His eyes moved as he searched her face. "Are you okay?"

Okay? Well, mostly yes, except for her head ringing from his embrace. She took a quick inventory. Her hands stung from where the rope had burned them. Her shoulders ached. Where was her apron? Gone somewhere. Grass and dirt and even sticks clung to her dress, and a large rip along the side seam showed that Papa's trousers would need to be mended as well. Her face stung as though she'd scrubbed it with a thorny rosebush. But all her bones appeared to be in one piece.

"I'm not hurt," she said as Rebecca arrived, followed shortly by Papa, huffing and puffing and scanning her head to toe for signs of injury.

A huge sense of victory welled up inside her as Charlie arrived. She grinned at Rebecca, and then she turned a look of triumph on Luke.

"I lassoed a cow." She didn't bother to filter the pride out of her voice.

Luke grinned, and Emma's heart twisted in response. "Yes, you did. But your technique needs a little work before you try that again, okay?"

"Okay," she agreed, and then she allowed him to lead her back to the wagon.

At least she'd proven she wasn't a complete fool.

TWENTY-FIVE

Luke hovered nearby as Mrs. Switzer attended to Emma's wounds. She sat on the tongue of the chuck wagon, her posture stiffly erect, and winced as the scrapes on her face were washed with a clean cloth dipped in a cup of murky liquid.

"What is that stuff?" he asked.

Mrs. Switzer answered without looking away from her task. "Violet tea."

"You mean, like the flower?"

The woman nodded. "The leaves. Keeps infection away."

"Doesn't do anything thing for the pain, though." Emma winced again as the cloth scrubbed at a scratch on her cheek.

McCann stuck his head out of the chuck wagon's canvas cover. "It's an old granny remedy. Won't do a thing to help. The only person who feels better is the granny who uses it."

Creased lips tightened into a line as Mrs.

Switzer daubed at the last remaining abrasion, but at least she didn't snap back a reply.

With the dirt washed away, the wounds on Emma's face didn't look nearly as bad as Luke had feared. When she stood, he saw that she had changed into a different dress, this one with obvious signs of mending. It must have been one recovered from the rustlers' attack and stitched up by Mrs. Switzer. Strips of cloth were wrapped around each palm.

"Rope burns?"

When she nodded, he cringed. Nothing was more painful than a rope burn.

Griff sidled up to join them and peered into Emma's face. "You okay, gal?"

Emma replied without hesitation. "Yes. Sore and stiff, but everything will heal."

A chuckle started down deep in his belly and twitched at his lips. "I'll never be able to get that picture out of my mind. That steer running scared, and you dangling along behind him at the end of that rope. And you." He slapped a hand across Luke's back. "You running after her screaming your head off, and the other girl after you, and then their pa, and then Charlie bringing up the rear." All effort to suppress his mirth evaporated, and Griff gave himself over to laughter. He bent over, hee-hawing and slapping a hand on his thigh. "That was the funniest thing I ever saw in all my born days."

Luke's first instinct was to flare up on Emma's behalf. But then he saw her laughing right along with Griff, even bending over with a hand across her middle. The sound of her laughter bubbled like water over a rocky creek bed, and for a moment all he could do was listen. Even Mrs. Switzer was having a hard time not joining in, her lips twitching like an antsy child that itches to break free from the firm grasp of his mother and run for the open.

Actually, the whole thing was kind of funny, now that he thought about it. He joined in with a chuckle.

Griff managed to recover himself. "Well, I'm glad you're okay, gal. Good job lassoing that steer."

"Thank you."

Still chuckling, he wandered off, taking the laughter with him and leaving an awkward silence in his wake. Mrs. Switzer hung close to her granddaughter's side, while Luke cast about for something to say. The sight of the scrapes on Emma's smooth skin, and the slightly purplish welt on her cheek, bothered him. All his fault, of course.

The rope lesson had been his suggestion, and a stupider one he couldn't imagine. And what was the point? An excuse to get closer to her for a little while, and look what came of it.

The funny thing was, those scrapes and bruises didn't detract from her beauty even a mite.

Aware that Mrs. Switzer's eyelids had narrowed as she watched him, he tore his gaze from Emma's and nodded toward her hands. "Those have to hurt."

Her head dropped as she looked at the bandages, and her shoulders lifted in a shrug.

"Well, obviously you don't need to worry about riding the herd anymore. You can take the wagon beside your grandmother. Griff can handle the left flank by himself."

With a jerk, her head rose and her gaze snapped to his. "But I want to ride."

His eyes squinted as he took in her scratches and her patched dress. "You've had quite a ride already today, Emma. By nightfall you're going to be sore and bruised all over. You ought to take it easy."

"On a wagon?" She scoffed. "The wheels going over bumps and ditches jar me straight through to my bones. A saddle will be far more comfortable."

Mrs. Switzer wrung the cloth she'd used to bathe Emma's wounds and remarked casually, "A folded quilt will cushion the hard bench."

Emma's forehead creased as she watched her grandmother snap the cloth straight and fold it into a neat square. Then she turned to look directly into Luke's eyes. Her chin rose.

"I want to ride the horse." Her tone left no room for argument.

For some reason, Luke couldn't stop a slow-spreading grin. There was something extra appealing about a woman who knew what she wanted and insisted on getting it.

After another hour of rest, Luke gave the orders for the outfit to get the cattle moving. The herd had spread out as they grazed, so the riders urged them into a tighter pack and set out on another long march. Shallow streams snaked throughout this part of the Chisholm Trail, so the cattle stayed well watered even though they were not given time to graze.

A few hours into the afternoon, Luke spotted a couple of long land swells in the distance. Between them lay a fairly narrow pass. They could easily navigate around the low hills, but he decided to take the opportunity for a head count. They would arrive in Hays tomorrow evening with their expanded herd, and he wanted to have a good number to report.

Signaling to McCann to follow, he applied his spurs and his horse leaped forward. The chuck wagon surged after him, the cook applying his whip to the team. The others would know exactly what he intended and lead the herd appropriately.

When they approached the pass, McCann pulled the wagon to a halt on the left and climbed down from the bench.

Luke pointed to the hill and said, "You take that side."

McCann climbed to the top while Luke directed his horse toward a position across from the cook. They were in place before the front edge of the herd arrived. Then the count began. With part of his mind, he wished that they could have hauled that rocking chair up here and set Jesse to counting so he could be down there in the lead. But that thought was quickly forgotten as he concentrated on keeping track of the number of cattle that surged past him down below.

Griff and Morris had galloped ahead to take the point positions. Between the two of them they kept the herd moving through.

Jonas's oxen blended in obediently and marched through. When Jesse passed below, he folded his hands behind his head and stretched out long, a leisurely, teasing grin on his face. Luke took a moment to grimace at him and then kept counting. He heard Griff calling instructions to Emma and Rebecca, and the girls moved through the pass in the midst of the cattle without incident.

When the last steer was north of the pass, Luke called across the gap. "How many do you make it out to be?"

The reply was instant. "Two thousand five hundred and twenty-four."

"Twenty-one," he corrected with a shout.

McCann shook his head. "You must have blinked."

Laughing, Luke swung up into the saddle. They had started out back in El Paso with two thousand and fifteen head of Triple Bar beef. It wasn't unusual at all to add or lose a few head along the way, as less hearty cattle succumbed and range cattle joined the herd unnoticed. But they had increased their count by twenty-five percent. Some had been rustled, of course, but because their brands had been sliced off, the proper owners couldn't be identified. And he had custody of the rustlers to prove his outfit innocent.

He kneed his horse down the hill and followed the chuck wagon through the pass. On the other side, a horse and rider waited. Jonas urged his mount forward to fall in step with Luke's.

His mood light, Luke awarded the man a smile. "Well, Jonas, it's almost over. We'll be in Hays by tomorrow evening."

Jonas's serious expression did not lighten. "And then?"

"Then you can go home. You said your farm isn't too far from there, but if it's late you'll want to stay the night. My treat," he added. "I'll buy your supper too."

The man did not turn his head but kept his stare fixed ahead. "What happens then for my Emma?"

Jonas's meaning slammed into Luke. If he'd been walking, he would have stumbled. This wasn't a friendly conversation between men. This was a father determined to discover Luke's intentions for his daughter. And judging by the look on Jonas's face, he wasn't too happy to be having it.

"What are you talking about?"

A stupid answer that made him look dim-witted, but it gave Luke a few seconds to gather his thoughts.

"I see the way she watches you, the way she smiles when you smile."

Emma's image rose in Luke's mind, that engaging smile on her lips and reflected in her eyes.

Jonas turned his head and caught Luke in a direct glance. "You watch her the same."

He couldn't deny the words. From the moment he opened his eyes back in Gorham and found himself looking up into her face, he couldn't stop watching her, trying to figure out what went on behind that impassive expression that she obviously learned from her father. But when she let an emotion peek through, he felt it all the way to his core.

"I suppose I do," he admitted.

Saying the words gave them extra weight. Jesse had sensed it from the very first, and though Luke denied any attraction between them, he'd known. He'd chosen to ignore it until his responsibility for the Triple Bar herd, and the men of his outfit, were met.

"My Emma, she is a Plain girl. Do you know what this means?"

"I know she's Amish, Jonas. Anybody can tell that by looking at her."

He shook his head. "Being Plain is more than our dress. It is more than the *kapp* our women wear, or the beard our men grow when we marry. It is more, even, than the church we attend. Being Plain is our life.

We dedicate every action, every thought, to the Lord who saved us. We agree to live by the *Ordnung* under the direction of our church leaders." The gaze he fixed on Luke became compassionate, almost pitying. "Being Plain is something you will never understand, and Plain is what my Emma is."

A protest rose in his mind. *No. Emma is so much more than that.* But he found he couldn't form the words, not in the face of Jonas's stare. So he merely nodded and said nothing.

"You are a good man, Luke Carson." Jonas's voice dropped low. "But you are not a good man for my Emma."

The words hit him like hailstones pounding the prairie during a storm. He'd barely become aware that the feelings he had for Emma might be something deep, something lasting, and already he'd been rejected by her father. A man Luke respected enormously.

Jonas urged his mount forward to take his place in the drag position at the rear of the herd. Luke allowed his horse to slow to a creep. The sun overhead did nothing to pierce the misty gloom that muddled his thoughts.

As the distance between him and the herd lengthened, he couldn't help seeking out the form of the black-clad flank rider who had somehow managed to capture his heart.

TWENTY-SIX

Though she was too stubborn to admit it, Emma knew she'd made the wrong decision the moment she climbed into the saddle. Even picking up the reins with her sore hands made her suck in a hissing breath. But pride won out over pain, so she clamped her teeth together and took her place at the herd's western flank. Thankfully, the cows under her charge behaved themselves, so she spent the long afternoon and evening hours in the saddle trying to move as little as possible and letting the horse have her way. When Luke finally called a halt for the night, she rallied enough to help put the cattle to ground, and then she fell onto her bedroll without even a thought of supper.

The next morning was worse. The first thing she became aware of, even before the last tendrils of sleep had unwound themselves from her conscious mind, was her stiff, aching muscles. The skin on her face felt tight and raw. Lifting an arm to peel away the bedroll brought so much pain she couldn't suppress a groan.

"Rope another cow today, will you?"

She cracked open an eye to find *Maummi* standing over her, a cup in one hand and a cloth in another. The smirk on her face elicited another groan from Emma.

Maummi sank to her knees and helped Emma rise into a sitting position. She dipped the cloth in the cup, and began gently washing the scrapes on Emma's face. The scent from the water was clean, fresh, and faintly grasslike. More violet leaf tea. Was the cook right, and it was nothing more than a granny recipe? Perhaps, but much good would come of keeping the wounds clean regardless.

"Consider this, granddaughter." *Maummi* blotted as she spoke. "Which is more comely, a deer gliding through the twilight or a clucking chicken strutting in the glare of the day?"

Emma winced, and not because of her stinging scratches. This lesson was one *Maummi* had used to teach Rebecca, who always tended toward rowdy and loud rather than soft-spoken and gentle, as befitted an Amish woman.

"A graceful deer," Emma answered sullenly, plucking at a loose thread where her dress had been mended.

"And do deer lasso cows?"

Emma wanted to retort that chickens didn't lasso cows either, but she held her tongue. "No, *Maummi*."

Her grandmother nodded. "When we are back in Apple Grove, you will leave the saddle horses and cattle and ropes behind, *ja?*"

Emma didn't answer. The question asked far more than the words implied. Was she ready to step back into the role she'd left behind a week and a lifetime ago? She and Rebecca had certainly not led the lives of typical Amish women the past few days, wearing Papa's trousers and straddling horses and working alongside *Englisch* cowboys. Watching the men and listening to their talk of their families and tales of trail life was far more interesting than listening to Mrs. Miller drone on about the virtues of her husband and son, or the tally of the pickles she'd put up the week before. Plus, Emma had enjoyed a strange sense of satisfaction that came from doing the work of a cowboy without the disapproving scrutiny of their Apple Grove neighbors.

And yet she loved her Plain life. She had

never wanted anything else.

Until Luke.

A painful lump rose in her throat. When she returned home, she would no longer be able to look ahead and see him at the front of the herd, to admire the way he led. Never again feel the giddy flip-flop in her stomach when his gaze connected with hers across the campfire. In fact, today would likely be the last time she saw him, ever.

Unless he agreed to become Amish, to live by Christ's teachings and the *Ordnung*. Long hours in the saddle yesterday afternoon had given her time to consider their discussion over and over. He hadn't made a firm decision. In fact, she hadn't actually asked the question. Surely the feelings she felt for him weren't one-sided. There might still be a chance that Luke would embrace the Amish lifestyle if he really loved her.

Maummi's hand hovered in the air, the cloth several inches from Emma's face, her eyes probing as she waited for an answer.

"Maybe . . ." She clamped her teeth down on her lower lip. She couldn't say the words, couldn't bear to see denial, or maybe pity, in her grandmother's eyes. Instead, she shook her head. "I don't know, *Maummi*."

One thing she did know. She would not give up hope that Luke would profess his love for her and join her in the faith, not until she heard it from his own lips. And she had until tonight, in Hays, for that to happen.

The last leg of the trail was the hardest of all for Emma. The cattle seemed intent on spreading out as wide as the entire prairie, and the farther they roamed from the main body of the herd, the slower their pace. Emma actually forgot her own pain for long stretches of time, so determined was she on keeping the western flank in hand. Behind her, Griff was having a similar experience, while on the far side, Morris and Rebecca rode with a stream on their right, which their cows seemed to consider as a natural barrier not to be crossed.

Even worse, Luke maintained his own position in the lead. Hours passed without him circling the herd to check on his cow-hands. When she wasn't chasing steers, Emma stared at the back of his head in hopes that he would turn toward her and she could get his attention. If he would only come back and ride a short while with her, she would find some way of turning the conversation in the direction she wanted.

Not only did he not look toward her, he didn't stop the herd at noontime either. She kept watch for signs of a halt, but he seemed intent on pushing the cattle and the riders to the ends of their endurance. When the sun started its descent, she twisted impatiently in the saddle to catch Griff's eye. He urged his horse into a gallop and soon drew alongside her.

"You doing okay up here, gal?"

"We've been a long time without a rest." She swept a hand toward the cattle. "They are starting to look tired, and they seem hungry. They keep wanting to spread out and graze."

He shrugged. "They'll be okay. It won't be much longer now. I've traveled this trail a half dozen times, so I know what Luke's doing. He'll push to get to a grazing field an hour this side of Hays, and then we'll stop and let them eat and drink their fill. That way they'll be at full weight when we arrive." He peered more closely at her. "This is a cowhand's life. We grab a bite in the saddle and keep moving. The beef will be okay, but how 'bout you? Belly empty, is it? I have some jerked beef you can chew on."

She eyed the unappealing strip of shriveled meat he extended. That was one part of trail life she could never get used to. Meals were not meant to be gobbled on horseback. They were meant for sharing with family and friends. Even if she were starving, she doubted she could choke down that dried-out hunk of beef.

"No, thank you." Instead, she picked up the canteen that hung from the saddlebag and drained the last of her water.

A pair of steers chose that moment to make a break for the open. Emma felt sorry for them, held to an unyielding pace, crowded in with the others, and forced to follow in the footsteps that hundreds of other cows had trampled before them. If she were a cow, she'd be tempted to run away too.

But she wasn't. She was an Amish girl, and her job was to make sure they followed the herd. She urged her tired horse ahead to cut off their escape.

The afternoon was half over when Luke called a halt. Finally, Emma could let up her vigil and let the cattle under her charge wander into the wide, open plain. They did so, tearing up great mouthfuls of grass along the way, stopping only to drink their fill from a half dozen small streams that crisscrossed the prairie.

Griff rode up from behind. "Let's head in, gal. I'm ready for a good, long break.

The railhead at Hays isn't more than an hour's easy traveling from here."

She nudged Sugarfoot ahead to keep pace with him as they rode toward camp, where the chuck wagon stood sentinel on one side, and the Amish wagon with *Maummi's* giant hutch on the other.

"Griff, what will you do when we get to Hays and this cattle drive is over?"

The old cowboy pursed his lips and thought a second before he answered. "I'll probably hang around there for a while to see if I can rustle up another job. There's still time to get back down to Texas and start another drive before cold weather sets in. If I don't find anything in Hays, I'll head on over to Abilene. There's always something going on there."

They rode on a few paces. Was that what Luke planned to do too? Drop off this herd and immediately find another one to lead?

"You mentioned the other day that you might want to settle down sometime." Though she didn't look at him directly, she watched for a reaction out of the corner of her eye. "Did you mean it?"

"You know, if I could find me a good woman, I would." A grin twisted his lips. "But I don't think your grandma will have me."

Though his tone was light, Emma detected a note of regret in his words. And he was right. *Maummi* was as entrenched in the Amish life as her son and granddaughters.

She chose her words carefully. "If you decide to become Amish, I think she would welcome your attentions."

The laughter she received in response hammered at her hopes. Is this how Luke would react to the same suggestion?

"Trust me, gal, I'd be the worst Amish man ever. I've been riding a horse way too long to start hitching up wagons or buggies now." He shook his head, still chuckling.

"Still," she persisted, "some do convert to Amish. It is a good life, a peaceful life."

The sideways look he gave her held a touch of sympathy. "I know what you're thinking, gal." His eyes softened. "He won't do it. Even when he gives up the trail, he doesn't have it in him to give up the life of a cowboy."

He sounded so certain, so sympathetic, that Emma's eyes stung with barely restrained tears. She couldn't muster a reply, and instead fixed her gaze on the remuda, which Vic had stopped beyond the two wagons. Luke was there now, changing his saddle from Bo to a fresh horse.

He does have it in him. If he loves me, he

will do it for me.

She managed a noncommittal nod for Griff and then kneed Sugarfoot forward. There were only a few hours left between now and the time they turned the herd over to the agency in Hays. She had to talk to him before then.

But when she reined Sugarfoot to a halt beside Luke, his greeting wasn't as warm as she had hoped. A smile brushed across his lips but failed to stay in place. His gaze lit on her face briefly but then swept the landscape behind her.

"I hope the ride wasn't too long for you. You did a great job. Thanks." He bent down to fasten the cinch strap beneath the horse.

How does he know if I did a good job or a bad one? He hasn't looked at me all day.

The thought almost shot out of her mouth, but she bit it back. "I was hoping to talk to you alone, but you never came back to ride with me."

"Yeah? Well, I have a minute right now before I leave." He kept working as he spoke, his eyes fixed on his hands.

"Leave?" Sugarfoot pranced sideways when she stiffened in the saddle. "You are leaving?"

"While the cattle eat their fill, I need to ride ahead into Hays to let them know we're here and check on the train. It'll take a couple of hours."

He straightened, but the face he turned up to her wore the polite expression of someone whose mind was elsewhere. Emma's words knotted in her throat. The kind, searching eyes of the Luke she loved had grown distant since this morning.

"What did you want to talk about?"

The sound of hooves from behind announced someone's approach. She glanced back to see Papa riding toward them, his gaze fixed on her. He halted his horse directly beside her. Luke glanced at him and then turned back to the horse to check the position of the cinch straps.

"Emma, *Maummi* has need of you and Rebecca to help with the cooking. I will care for your horse."

How did he know what *Maummi* needed? He'd just come in from the rear of the herd, where he'd been all day. She glanced toward the camp, where her grandmother knelt before Jesse's chair, checking on his leg.

He is trying to separate me from Luke.

Knots tightened in her middle, and she had to bite back a frustrated retort. Though her lips were clenched shut against disrespectful words, she didn't bother to school the resentful glance she turned on Papa. He returned it calmly, without the slightest sign of backing down.

Finally, she lowered her head. "Yes, Papa."

She swung out of the saddle and landed a little unsteadily on the ground before placing the reins in her father's hand. With one last longing glance at Luke, who did not look up, she headed toward the wagon to help her grandmother.

But she did stomp puffs of dirt with every frustrated step.

TWENTY-SEVEN

The main street of Hays bustled with activity. Down the center of the wide street lay a long stretch of railroad tracks, with train cars lined up from the edge of town past the stockyards. On the south side of the tracks the train depot stretched almost the full block. The buildings that lined the north side had all been built in recent years, since fire had destroyed much of Hays a few years back.

Not much had changed since Luke's visit the previous year, when he'd ridden point for Pa in a drive from Laredo. Lively music poured from the open doors and windows of a handful of saloons and gaming houses, none of which lacked for customers. As he walked past Tommy Drum's Saloon, a roar of cheers went up inside, probably a winning poker hand that had caught the rowdy crowd's approval. Snatches of conversation reached him, more than a few in German, thanks to the German-Russians who had settled in the area at the urging of the Kansas Pacific Railroad. Down at the end of the street, past Krueger's Dry Goods and Groceries, a group of cowboys stumbled out of Kate Coffey's Saloon and headed toward the Sporting Palace, one of several brothels that also served as a crib for soiled doves.

As he rounded the corner heading for the stockyard agent, he resolved to keep the Switzers away from this part of Hays.

At the reminder of Emma, Luke's step slowed. All day long she had plagued his thoughts. One of the hardest things he'd ever done was not turn around to see how she was faring during the longest haul of the journey. But he knew that Jonas, bringing up the rear, was sure to be watching, so he had to trust that Griff would keep an eye on her and give her a hand if she needed it.

Hours in the saddle had given him plenty of time to consider Jonas's words. The conclusion burned like acid in Luke's gut, but he couldn't deny the truth. Jonas was right. Emma was raised in a world he could never understand, nor could he ask her to give it up. He had nothing to offer her. No home and not much money. The only family he had left was his pa and a couple of brothers who were spread out between here and New York, surely no substitute for the father and sister and grandmother she would have to leave behind.

Emma deserved a better life than the one he could give her.

"Hey, look who finally showed up!"

The shout jarred him out of his gloomy thoughts. He raised his head and saw a familiar figure. He grinned. "Pa!"

He quickened his pace and exchanged an enthusiastic handshake with his father. "What are you doing here? Last I heard you were taking a herd of Longhorns to Abilene."

"Delivered them a week ago and decided I'd ride on over here to see how my son came out on his first job as trail boss." His eyebrows slanted askew. "You cut it close, boy."

"Train's still here, isn't it?" Luke jerked his head down the street. "Like you always said, as long as you make it before the train leaves, you're on time."

"No, I always said better early than late." His grin became a smirk. "So, you still have life all figured out, do you? Got it lassoed and hog-tied into a tidy bundle?"

Luke couldn't meet his pa's eye. "Well, I might have learned a thing or two."

Pa's laugh rang down the street. "But you

made it, and that's what counts. C'mon. Let your old man buy you a drink to celebrate."

Luke laughed off the offer, as he'd grown accustomed to doing whenever Pa wanted a drinking partner. "Thanks, but I just rode into town to make the arrangements. My outfit's grazing the herd a few miles south of here, and they are eager to be free of them." He grew grim. "It's been a rough ride the past week."

Pa's expressive eyebrows arched. "Rustlers?"

"Yeah. I lost two good men and picked up a pair of prisoners to turn over to the sheriff." He brightened. "I also gained an extra five hundred head of beef."

"That *is* something to celebrate." A firm hand thumped him on the back. "You go on and take care of business. I'll be hereabouts later on, so we can meet up then."

"I'll find you."

Luke watched his father saunter down the street, his gait as cocky as ever. When he reached the entrance of a saloon, he turned. "Luke?"

Luke stopped in the act of entering the railroad agent's office.

"I'm proud of you, son. You did a good job."

That was one of the few words of praise Luke had ever heard his father utter. He flashed another grin. "Thanks, Pa."

Luke returned to the herd accompanied by two of Sheriff Charles Howard's deputies. A mouthwatering aroma rising from various pans on a large fire greeted them before they had dismounted.

Ramsey, the older of the two men, raised his nose in the air and drew in a long, appreciative sniff. "I don't know what that is, but I sure hope I'm invited to stay to supper."

The other man, Hamilton, agreed. "Who's your cook on this drive, Carson?"

"I am." McCann came around the chuck wagon at that moment, water sloshing from a full bucket at his side.

Ramsey's face broke out into a grin. "I knew by the smell it would be somebody good. How you doing, McC—"

The name was cut off in a gulp as Mrs. Switzer rounded the wagon behind him carrying a stack of tin plates. How she'd managed to keep her *kapp* and her apron as white as the day she started, Luke didn't know. Or maybe she had a store of clean ones tucked away in that hutch of hers. The *kapp* bobbed up and down as she dipped a silent nod to greet the newcomers and bypassed McCann on her way to the campfire.

Two horses approached from behind, and Luke turned to see Emma and Rebecca rein their mounts to a stop near the remuda. They both slid out of the saddles and took a moment to settle their bulky skirts around the black trousers they had lashed close at the ankles. Jonas chose that moment to approach from the opposite direction, leading two of his four oxen by rope halters. As he neared, he drew the watchers' attention to the hulking hutch in the back of the ox wagon.

Both deputies gawked, their jaws slack and their eyes bugging.

Hamilton found his tongue first. "Carson, your outfit is crawling with Amish."

Luke hid a grin. "They have been lending a hand since we were attacked by rustlers. We were lucky they came across us when they did."

"Speaking of rustlers, I hope you fellows are here to take charge of these two." Jesse's voice cut across the distance. His chair had been lowered to the ground behind the wagon, where he kept watch on his prisoners. "I've looked at their ugly faces so long I'll probably have nightmares for months."

The deputies went to take a closer look at the captives, and Luke with them. He was aware of Emma's gaze fixed on him, and also of Jonas's sharp-eyed stare from the other side of the wagon. By mustering an enormous amount of strength, he managed to keep his step straight and his eyes forward. He knew that if he even glanced her way, his resolve would crumble.

"Well, look who we have here." Ramsey bent over at the waist and made a show of examining the rustlers. "If it ain't Lester Aims and Earl Bishop. Boys, Sheriff Howard is gonna be mighty glad to see you two. He has a list of complaints against you twice the size of a Texas steer's horn."

"We'll take them from here," Hamilton told Jesse. Then he cast a hungry look toward the fire. "But there's no hurry, is there? We have time for some grub if someone was to invite us."

McCann poured a dipperful of water into the big pot suspended over the low flame. Mrs. Switzer stirred the contents, brought the spoon up to her lips for a taste, and then gave a satisfied nod. With ceremony, McCann bent over, picked up a metal triangle, and held it aloft to run the striker around the inside.

"Come and get it." His familiar bellow

rolled over the prairie. He lowered his gaze to the deputies and grinned. "Guests are always welcome at the McCann-Switzer chuck wagon."

If the two thought that anything was odd in the addition of an Amish woman's name to the reputable trail cook's, they didn't waste time saying so. Soon they were tucking away stew and biscuits as though they hadn't eaten in a week.

McCann sidled up to Luke. "You'd barely ridden out of sight when Jonas spied a couple of jackrabbits and set about laying snares. Before I knew it, he had a half dozen of the scrawny things. Ordinarily I would have spitted 'em and roasted 'em, but Miz Switzer insisted on stewing them. You won't believe how good stew can be until it hits your tongue." He lowered his voice and spoke out of the side of his mouth. "I watched how she did it. Can't wait to try it myself. And the peach cobbler she cooked up. Mm-mmm." He stepped away to oversee dishing up generous portions of rabbit stew.

Luke turned his back to the activity around the fire and gazed out over his cattle. The job was almost done. Nothing left but the counting and weighing and collecting his pay. The stockyard agent had assured him that the extra cattle would be counted as part of the Triple Bar herd unless they had traceable brands. Hancock would make a tidy profit, and Luke would no doubt have his pick of jobs once word spread.

Why, then, was he fighting a melancholy cloud that threatened to settle over his soul?

Someone approached from behind. Clearing his expression, he turned and found Emma standing no more than an arm's length behind him. The angry scratches on her face had settled into a spray of tiny scabs, and the welt had become a faint bruise that marred one perfectly smooth cheek. She was, if anything, more beautiful to him than ever.

Her eyes searched his, and his resolution to honor her father's request wavered. How could he say goodbye to her when what he really wanted to do was sweep her into his arms, throw her on his horse, and ride hard for Texas before anyone could stop them?

"I brought your supper." She thrust a plate of thick, delicious-smelling stew into his hands.

He automatically took it. "Thank you. I . . ." He cleared his throat. "I heard it's really good."

The dusty ground must have held some special fascination for her, because she studied it with rapt attention. The silence between them became electric, full of unspoken sentiment and suppressed feeling. Around them, the men's talk swelled with praise for the food and admiration for the two cooks who had produced it, but the noise seemed to bounce off an invisible barrier that surrounded Emma and Luke.

But that same barrier stood as firm as a stone wall between them.

Her shoulders rose as she drew in a breath. "Luke, I've wanted to say something, but I'm afraid you'll think I'm forward."

The idea brought a smile to his lips. "I can't imagine anything you could say that would make me think you forward."

She looked up, her eyes full of an unnamed emotion that caused his insides to quiver in response. "I wanted to say —"

"Emma!"

An outside voice ripped through the fragile connection between them. A guilty flush tinged her scraped cheeks as she turned toward her sister, who approached at a trot.

"Papa says to come and help with serving the cobbler." Rebecca dimpled as she cast a sideways grin toward the occupant of the rocking chair. "*Maummi* heard peach was Jesse's favorite and made it special for him."

Luke raised his gaze and found Jonas staring at him from across the laughing, relaxed crowd of cowboys. A look of meaning passed between them, and Luke remembered his resolve. This little Amish girl was not for him. She had a place waiting for her back in Apple Grove, far from anyplace he'd ever thought of as home.

"Go help," he told Emma, handing her his plate. He hadn't touched his stew. "I need to check on my herd."

Hurt darkened her eyes, but he tore himself away from the silent plea. Like a prisoner escaping a death sentence, he strode for his horse to escape to the wide Kansas plain and the twenty-five hundred cattle that were much easier to deal with than one sad-eyed Amish woman.

TWENTY-EIGHT

The herd arrived in Hays before sunset, when the sky was still a bright yellow-orange and the breeze that blew off the prairie was still hot from the long summer day. Emma could muster no enthusiasm for the town that loomed before her. How could she enjoy the end of the trail, when it also meant the end of her hopes for a life with Luke?

They approached from the west. As Luke and the lead cattle passed the first of the long rail-lined pens that made up the stockyard, the chuck wagon veered off toward the north and drew to a halt above the curve of the trail, where the cattle veered right toward town. *Maummi* led the oxen in behind, and a tight line of cattle filed past, following their leaders in a parade of high-priced beef. The buildings emptied their occupants in a trickle of spectators who lined up to watch the familiar process of funneling cattle into the stockyard stalls to await counting and weighing. Above the noise of bovine hooves shuffling in the dust and anxious cattle grumbling, saloon music carried down the street on the dry afternoon heat.

Emma had received instruction from Griff on this final stage of the journey, and she kept a firm hold on the reins as she urged the cattle ahead. On the other side of the narrow column of cattle, Morris and Rebecca forced their charges to merge with their herd mates, always advancing. Griff pressed close behind her, a comforting presence in this unfamiliar task of pushing steers toward small fenced-in pens. Up ahead, Luke had been joined by a half-dozen cowhands who shooed the cattle into the stocks with much shouting and waving of arms.

One by one, the keeps filled as an unending current of beef flowed like a river down narrow stockyard aisles and into pens that accommodated far more cattle than Emma would have dared press together. The townsfolk formed a line at the edge of the yard, calling out encouragement to the workers and congratulations to Luke, who sat tall in his saddle to oversee the operation. Emma found herself hard-pressed to focus on the task at hand, her gaze drawn to him like a honey bee to fragrant spring blossoms. Time had almost run out, and still she had not spoken her mind.

She would, though. Before this day was over, she would find a way to speak with him alone and lay out her request.

A voice rose above the buzz of the crowd, tinged with indignant shock that boosted its volume to drown out every other sound.

"It's our Emma!"

Her gaze snapped to the edge of the crowd of onlookers, to a pair of black-clad men with unmistakable bushy beards and round straw hats. Her jaw slackened and her mouth hung open when she recognized them both. Amos Beiler and Bishop Miller.

The bishop drew himself upright, sparks from his disapproving eyes snapping at her all the way across the river of cattle. "Emma Switzer, down from that animal you will get and come with me now."

Her heart sank into her shoes.

Emma stood beside their wagon, her head bowed and her hands folded quietly before her while Bishop Miller spoke in an even but stern tone to Papa. Beside her, Rebecca had adopted the same pose, though *Maummi*'s chin tilted defiantly upward and her lips were pursed. Cattle continued to file past them, though the end of the stream was now in sight. Slightly behind the bishop stood Amos, his face a mottled red and his gaze fixed on the hard-packed dirt in front of his feet. Emma shifted her weight. How embarrassing to have him witness the verbal discipline of her family.

"And what witness did you bear, Jonas?" The bishop's voice, though disapproving, remained soft and controlled. "Representatives of Christ we are. Did Christ allow His women to ride about on horses with their . . ." He closed his mouth and drew a slow breath through his nose. "It is unseemly, and not worthy of our Lord or our Amish district."

A protest rose in Emma's mind, a reminder that the Lord's mother rode a donkey. But she kept the thought to herself because there was certainly no evidence that Mary had herded cattle or dressed in men's trousers on her way to give birth to her blessed Child.

"We owed a debt. I judged our assistance appropriate repayment." How Papa managed to keep his tone mild and return the bishop's stare without looking away, Emma couldn't imagine. A spark of pride in her father flickered to life, but she squelched it immediately. Such feelings were surely sinful because they were clearly at odds with their church leader.

Bishop Miller's eyebrows edged upward until they disappeared beneath his hat brim. Behind him, Amos shuffled his feet and inspected the wagon wheel carefully.

"I think it will be best to continue this conversation later in private," said the bishop. "Amos and I have business here in the morning, and then we will return home. Jonas, I will pay a visit to your farm on Tuesday."

His eyes moved as his gaze swept the group. Though she kept her eyes downcast, Emma felt the weight of his stare when it rested on her. She did her best to remain stiffly erect and not flinch. With a final sad shake of his head, Bishop Miller headed in the direction of the town.

Before he followed, Amos sidled up to Emma. "I'm glad you're coming home to Apple Grove."

She couldn't force herself to return his gaze but merely nodded mutely.

"We will talk later. Yes?"

She managed another nod, though as far as she was concerned there was nothing unsaid between them. Now that she'd seen him again, her resolve was stronger than ever. She would *not* become Mrs. Amos Beiler.

Left alone, no one spoke. The Switzers stood in silent commiseration, each one bearing the weight of disapproval. Emma knew the fault lay entirely with her. She had pushed Papa to help Luke, convinced him that their duty was to lend aid to the one who had aided them. Would they be disciplined, perhaps even rejected, by their Amish neighbors? She couldn't bear being responsible for that.

Jesse's voice interrupted the gloomy silence from the other side of the hutch. "Sounds like somebody slipped a burr under his saddle. Don't any of you *Aim*-ish people have a sense of humor?"

His observation acted like a tonic. Papa's stiff posture relaxed. Emma raised her head in time to see him spare a small smile toward the wagon.

"We opt, instead, to teach our children manners." *Maummi* addressed her scold toward the wagon. "Respecting one's privacy is the first lesson they learn."

"Hard not to overhear with all that shouting going on a few feet away."

Because it was impossible to imagine Bishop Miller shouting at anyone, Emma couldn't help smiling.

"Can somebody give me a hand down from this wagon? I'd kind of like to head into town."

"Not until we find the doctor." *Maummi's* tone brooked no argument as she marched toward the back of the wagon. "Jonas, will you see to it? Find one who has not spent the day in a saloon, if such a thing is possible in this rowdy *Englisch* town."

"I will send the doctor to you and then find a place to spend the night," Papa said. "Perhaps in the morning we will travel back to Apple Grove in the company of the bishop. We can pass the hours on the road in prayer and conversation."

As she watched him head for the town center, Emma's spirits plummeted even further. No doubt Papa would insist on riding in the bishop's buggy so they could converse privately. The time would be spent in defending their actions and convincing Bishop Miller of the Switzer family's devotion to their district and the *Ordnung*. She had no doubt that Papa would succeed in the end. But of course that meant the entire journey would be spent with Amos on the wagon bench beside her.

And Luke would stay behind in Hays.

A sudden fierce desire arose in her. When Papa returned, he would shepherd them into town and hover over them with the vigilance of a sheriff guarding a prisoner. He would linger near and purposefully thwart her attempt to speak privately with Luke. Her gaze sought him and found him easily, riding in the saddle above the moving mass of cattle. This might be her last opportunity.

Though Sugarfoot waited nearby, saddled and ready, she didn't dare mount the horse. Forgiveness might be granted for her riding thus far, but if she expressly disobeyed the bishop mere minutes after his reprimand, she would be disciplined for sure. Her gaze scanned the stockyard. A wide aisle lay between each long row of pens. As the cattle streamed down the aisle to fill each row, Luke moved his sentinel position forward, a guiding figure that served as the end point for the cattle's journey. If she skirted around the edge of the herd in Papa's footsteps, she could cross the street and approach Luke from the already filled pens behind him.

When Papa's hat disappeared in the crowd of townspeople, she started after him.

Rebecca's voice stopped her. "Where are you going?"

With a quick glance toward the hutch, which blocked *Maummi* and Jesse from view, she placed a finger to her lips. "I'm going to speak with Luke. I'll be back shortly."

Her sister's head turned toward the cowboy, and when she looked back at Emma, she wore a wide grin. "I wondered when you would finally get around to talking with him. Are you going to ask him to marry you?"

Shocked, Emma reared back. The idea! "Of course not!" She lowered her voice. "But if *he* happens to bring the subject up . . ." She returned the grin.

Rebecca giggled and threw her arms around Emma for a quick hug. "I'll distract *Maummi*."

Heartened by her sister's enthusiasm, Emma followed in Papa's footsteps.

The stocks were only a third full, and the end of the herd had nearly arrived. Cattle pressed close inside each pen, head-to-rump, their sides touching. Cows voiced their confusion, the combined sound so loud they nearly drowned out the shouts of the stockmen. Hugging close to the plank fence on one side, she approached Luke's position. His attention was focused on his herd and on the cowhands directing cattle through the half-filled aisle in front of him. She came to a halt beside him, her back against the rails, and waited for him to notice her.

When he did, he started visibly. "Emma. What are you doing here? I thought you were with Jonas and your grandmother and . . . those other Amish men. I figured they must be friends."

"From our district. The older one is the bishop." She cut her gaze away for a second. No need to describe Amos.

"Ah. He didn't look very happy to see you."

An understatement, but that wasn't what she wanted to talk about. She glanced around. The stockmen were halfway down the aisle, forcing the stream of cattle into an empty stall. Though she would prefer to sit with Luke face-to-face for this important conversation instead of craning her neck to see him up on his horse, time was short. Papa would return soon, and her chance to talk with Luke would be gone.

"I would like to talk to you about something important."

His glance swept the moving cattle before returning to her. "I'm a little busy right now. Can it wait an hour or so?"

An hour? Papa would return in a few minutes. She shook her head. "No. We must talk now."

Reining up, he took off his hat and scrubbed his fingers through his hair.

"Emma, we've had several opportunities to talk but you were never in the mood. Yet you pick now? Your timing could be better." He shoved the hat back on his head.

This was not going as she'd hoped. She turned to scan the town behind her, looking for Papa's hat amid the people on the street. The muscles in her stomach tightened into knots. "I want to know —" Her throat closed on the embarrassing words. With a hard swallow, she tried again. "Luke, will you become Amish?"

His expression closed, and for a long moment he stared at her. A thousand thoughts darted through her mind, each one pressing against the other like the cows that surrounded them. Foremost among them was the realization that the idea of becoming Amish had never occurred to Luke. Which meant he had never considered a life with her.

Which meant she had badly misinterpreted his feelings.

A measure of composure returned, and he slowly shook his head. "Emma . . . I don't . . ." Words appeared to fail him. "I'm not . . ."

Hurt and humiliation rose from a sick ball in the pit of her stomach. "You're not what?" Her tone snapped, and she didn't bother to filter the emotion.

His hand rose, and he rubbed it across his mouth. "I'm not an Amish man. I'm sorry. I have my own beliefs. You are good folk, but . . ."

He didn't have to finish the thought. But she was not *Englisch.* Hot, angry tears sprang into her eyes. No, not angry. Embarrassed. She had offered herself to him, only to be rejected. What must he think of her? She lowered her head toward the ground. Her mind emptied of any response she might make, any words that would restore her dignity and allow her to escape with her pride intact. Instead, she turned blindly to make her exit.

"Emma! Don't!"

She refused to stop, refused to prolong this humiliating discussion any further. Her head down, her vision blurry with unshed tears, she stretched her pace to almost a run.

In the next moment, she was surrounded by cattle. They pressed her on all sides, lifting her up and hurtling her sideways. Her feet left the ground but she remained upright, swept into the stocks in the midst of the herd. She struggled to move, to free herself, but the smelly hides that surrounded her covered hundreds of pounds of solid flesh. They pressed together, and her breath left her lungs. A searing pain stabbed her chest, and she couldn't move enough to gasp in a breath. Somewhere in the distance she heard her name, but panic had a firm grip on her. How could she even think about answering when she couldn't manage to breathe?

Then panic receded as fog settled over her oxygen-deprived brain.

I'm going to faint. And then I'm going to die. They'll bury me on the farm beside Mama.

Dimly, she was aware of shouts nearby. The wall of beef moved. Air entered her lungs in an agonizing rush. She sank toward the ground.

And then strong arms encircled her. The pain in her side sent white-hot stars dancing in her vision as a panic-stricken voice rumbled through a mouth pressed close to her ear. Luke's voice.

"I've got you. Thank God, I've got you."

Twenty-Nine

The doctor's house sat one street over from the center of town, close enough that the noise from the saloons and even the bawling of the cattle in the stockyard carried easily. Luke's boots traced a worn path on the planks of the front porch, walking in the footsteps of many worried people awaiting news of a patient from inside the two-story structure. He stopped in front of the open door to peer inside. The entry hall bore evidence that the doctor was married. A lace cloth draped a small table placed against the left-hand wall, and a couple of fancy glass dishes were displayed on top of it. A wide set of stairs led to the second floor, where the doctor and his missus presumably lived. The only person in evidence was Jonas, who stood at the opposite end of a short hallway next to a closed door.

He did not look up at Luke. He hadn't

spoken to him or met his eye since he arrived.

Not that Luke blamed him. It was his fault Emma had been injured. He'd handled the conversation badly. No wonder she'd been offended and charged off blindly in the wrong direction. She'd surprised him by asking if he would become Amish, and his reaction had obviously hurt her feelings.

And what was behind her question, anyway? He could only think of one reason. If he became Amish, they could marry with the blessing of her family and her church.

Marry.

The word sent dual shivers down his spine, because the idea of him becoming Amish for any reason was so outrageous he couldn't pretend to give it serious consideration. Him, be like Jonas? His faith was nothing like Jonas's, his convictions shallow in comparison. He'd been raised to love the Lord and love the Bible, but the Plain life an Amish man had to embrace? Jonas was right. Luke couldn't begin to understand.

The second shiver came with the realization that Emma would ever consider marrying him. She had put quite a bit of thought into it, in fact, to come up with her idea. That could only mean one thing. She loved him. Not merely that she shared the attraction he felt, but she felt that same invisible bond that had somehow snaked around them and drawn them together.

Emma loved him. And, he realized, he loved her.

The sight of her penned in the midst of those cattle had nearly scared the life out of him. He'd forced his horse into the herd, kicking cows with his boots and shouting to catch the attention of the nearest stockmen. When he finally reached her, after an eternity of frantic, whispered prayers while wading through a sea of beef, he threw himself from the saddle into the press. He still wasn't exactly sure how he'd managed to force those two steers apart to release her. Maybe his panic gave him extra strength, or maybe it was the prayers. But he'd lifted her into his arms and carried her out.

Directed by shouting townspeople, Luke had run — literally — toward the doctor's house while Emma's soft sobs filled his ears. He'd met the rotund little man in the street on his way to examine Jesse, and he immediately turned around so that Luke could follow him back home.

After carrying Emma down a short hallway and gently laying her down on a narrow bed in what was apparently an examining room, Luke was shooed out of the room.

The doctor wouldn't even let Jonas in when he arrived, only Mrs. Switzer and Rebecca, who were with Emma now.

What was taking so long? He strode across the planks to peer inside again. No change, except that now Jonas stood with his head thrown back, his face pointed toward the ceiling with his eyes closed. Praying, probably. Which suddenly sounded like a very good idea.

No prayers came to mind, only a frantic request. *Lord, don't let her die. Please.*

Noise from inside the house sent him scurrying back to the doorway. The doctor emerged from the examining room, followed by Mrs. Switzer and Rebecca. He spoke to Jonas, his voice loud enough to carry down the short hallway to Luke.

"A couple of her ribs are broken. As far as I can tell that's all, though she'll need to stay here for a day or two so I can keep a watch on her. I've wrapped them, and also given her a salve for those scrapes on her face, which will help them to heal without scarring. It's going to hurt to breathe for a few weeks, but I think she'll be fine."

Air left Luke's lungs. He sagged against the doorjamb. She was going to be fine. She wasn't going to die. *Thank You, Lord.*

"You can go on in and see her. I'm going

to have my missus fix her up a broth that will help strengthen her bones." He smiled at Rebecca. "Why don't you come upstairs with me and bring it down to her when it's ready?"

When the two of them had climbed the stairs, Jonas disappeared into the room. Luke stared for a long moment after the door closed behind him. He had no place here. He wasn't family, he wasn't Amish, and it was his fault she was hurt. Jonas wouldn't let him near her, and rightly so.

It was enough to know she would recover.

The blazing fire in Emma's side was somewhat quenched by the tight binding the doctor had applied. She couldn't draw a deep breath without excruciating pain, but at least the bandages allowed her to take shallow breaths without too much discomfort.

A shame her feelings weren't allowed the same comfort and support. The conversation with Luke pierced like an arrow through her heart. He would not become Amish, which meant he didn't truly love her. Though her ribs hurt with every breath, it was the pain in her heart that hurt the most. From that she might never recover.

The door opened and Papa came into the room. The sight of him sent a rush of guilty tears into her eyes. She had shamed him again in front of Bishop Miller, who undoubtedly had received a report of her unseemly behavior in seeking Luke out and getting trampled on by cows in the process.

"Oh, Papa, I'm so sorry," she said, sobbing.

Once the tears started, she could not stop them. They weren't merely tears of guilt. They were tears that came directly from an injured heart.

Papa sat in a chair beside her bed, sought her hand to hold, and waited until the tears slowed.

"For what do you apologize?" His soft words and tender tone made it hard to talk without giving in to painful sobs again.

"I've made a fool of myself and of you." She picked up the corner of the stiff linen sheet that covered her and blotted at her eyes. "I've fallen in love with . . ." More tears interrupted her words. "With a . . ." Another sob, and she buried her face in the sheet. "With an *Englishcher*."

Again, Papa waited silently for her tears to run their course. He even produced a handkerchief and handed it to her.

"And does he return your love, this *Englisch* cowboy?"

"He doesn't. I asked him . . . I asked if he

would become Amish, and he said . . ." Pain pierced her side when she gulped inconsolable draughts of air. "He said no."

Silence met her confession. Her quiet cries sounded in the room until finally they stilled. Only then did Papa speak.

"Luke Carson is a good man."

Emma tried to swallow back her tears. Of course he was. If he were a scoundrel, she would never have fallen in love with him.

"But he is a wild stallion," Papa continued. "The Amish life is a pond, small and contained, with rounded edges. What happens if you put a stallion in a pond, my Emma?"

The truth of his words penetrated, and her tears returned. "He drowns," she answered.

Papa nodded. "He does indeed. A stallion must run in the open air, where a fish cannot live." His voice became softer, and he leaned across the edge of the bed toward her. "And you know what happens to a fish when you take it from the pond and force it to live in the open air."

She nodded. "It dies."

"Yes, she does. What did our Lord say? *Ein Dieb kommt nur, dafs er stehle, würge und umbringe.*

I came that they may have life, and have it more abundantly.

391

The words only made Emma's tears flow harder. The truth in them carved into her soul like a sharp blade. In the past few days she'd lived life on the open plain, enough to know that she would never be satisfied there. She preferred the boundaries and cool waters of the pond.

"He is waiting outside, your *Englisch* cowboy. Will you speak with him?"

His words sent a flood of panic through her. What would she say to Luke? How would she apologize for trying to drown him in a pond full of Plain water?

She had to try, though. There had to be an end. Otherwise, she would forever drive herself insane trying to imagine his parting words to her, and hers to him. Swallowing back yet another wave of weeping, she nodded.

Papa nodded and patted her hand. "Choose wisely, my little guppy."

With that he left the room.

THIRTY

After the doctor and Rebecca had disappeared upstairs, Luke started to turn away, but footsteps coming down the hallway halted him. He turned and waited for Mrs. Switzer to approach. When she did, she tilted her head up to look into his face.

"*Danki* for saving her life."

Bitterness welled up inside him and he shook his head. "Don't thank me, ma'am. It's my fault she was there to begin with."

Her eyes narrowed as she studied him. Then she pointed toward a row of rockers that lined one side of the porch. "We will talk."

Luke didn't even consider denying her request. The fact that someone in Emma's family was still talking to him left him feeling more than a little humble. And grateful. He crossed the porch and sank into one of the chairs.

Mrs. Switzer took the one to his right.

"You speak of fault like one who feels the weight of guilt. Why is this so?"

"Yesterday she told me she wanted to talk to me about something. But when we had a few minutes together, she seemed reluctant and I didn't push her. Then all day today I knew she was trying to get my attention, and I ignored her." He looked straight ahead, at the dim candlelight in the window of the house across the way. "If I'd taken the time to talk to her, she wouldn't have come looking for me and wouldn't have gotten caught between those steers."

"You did not want to talk to her?"

"It's not that." Luke glanced sideways. "Jonas . . . sort of asked me not to."

They rocked for a few moments in silence. Twilight was falling, and the sound of the cattle no longer reached the doctor's porch. The absence of the sun left the air cooler, though still heavy from the heat of the day.

"You see what a good father is my son." Mrs. Switzer's quiet voice joined hands with the dimness to form a comforting pair. "He's always looking out for his girls."

Luke nodded. "Yes, ma'am. I admire your son. I've grown to admire him more every day."

"His father was a good man too." She continued as though he had not spoken.

"But he was not Plain. Not Amish."

His head turned toward her. "He wasn't?"

She shook her head and spoke in a whisper, as though relaying a great secret. "He was *Presbyterian.*" Luke could hear the tender smile in her voice. "A finer man never lived, my Carl. Only a few years we had together, and my papa did not approve. My mama cried herself nearly to the grave. But I would not trade one minute with him." Her rocking stopped, and she turned sideways in her chair to face him. *"Not one minute."*

Her meaning was crystal clear. Love was worth a sacrifice.

But he couldn't ask Emma to make that sacrifice.

Could he make it? Could he become Amish?

An image flashed into his mind. Himself in black trousers, suspenders, and a round-brimmed straw hat. Clean-shaven lips, an untrimmed beard sprouting from his chin. Could he do that? For Emma, yes. He could.

But what about the rest of it? Trading in Bo for a workhorse. Subjecting himself to the authority of the bishop, the man he saw speaking sternly to Jonas and the Switzer women. Standing by, unresisting, while thieves stole his belongings and left his family helpless. Not lifting a weapon to rescue his daughter from cattle rustlers who intended to ravage her and sell her to savages.

No. That he could not do. If he did, his commitment would be so grudging that it would end up destroying any peace he and Emma shared.

He shook his head and spoke into the darkness without looking at Mrs. Switzer. "I can't do it. I can't become Amish. Jonas is right. I'll never understand the Plain life."

A chuckle rumbled deep in her chest. "There is more than one way to cut a cake, my mama used to say."

Before he could consider her meaning, footsteps sounded in the hall and Jonas stepped through the doorway. He came to a stop in front of their chairs and actually made eye contact with Luke. The compassion with which his expression was saturated sent a finger of regret trailing down Luke's spine. Clearly, Jonas had won. Which meant Luke had lost.

"She will speak with you now." He switched his gaze to his mother. "Will you chaperone, please, while I check with the livery on our wagon and oxen?"

Mrs. Switzer bowed her head in acquiescence, and without another word Jonas left the porch.

■ ■ ■ ■

Though tiny, the scabs on Emma's skin showed starkly against the pale white linen pillow coverings. Luke entered the room, his hat in his hand, and hesitated in the doorway. She looked so frail that words were snatched from his chest, and all he could do was stand and stare at her.

Mrs. Switzer poked her head into the room. "The hallway is a good place to wait. I've found a comfortable chair out here."

She disappeared, leaving the door open and them alone.

Luke clutched his hat brim in his hands and found that he couldn't look the pale young woman in the face. "The doctor said you're going to be fine. I'm glad."

"Thank you." Her voice fell softly on his ears. "You saved me yet again."

"No, I only . . ." The words trailed off. "I'm sorry I didn't come talk to you earlier today."

Emma didn't reply. When he finally raised his gaze, he discovered she was staring at her hands clasped on the sheet. Her long eyelashes curved against the backdrop of her scraped cheeks. So graceful, so vulnerable.

While words were still bouncing around in his thoughts, trying to figure out which would emerge, she reached beneath the bed linens and drew forth an item. "I made this for you."

She held a white object toward him. Hesitantly, he crossed the threshold to her bedside.

The gift was a square of soft fabric the size of a handkerchief. The edges had been finished with fine, even stitching. In the center a colorful image decorated the plain white field. When he recognized it, emotion surged up from deep in Luke's soul. It was his brand, the one he had designed as a boy. The one he intended to use one day when he owned his own herd.

"It's beautiful."

"I wanted you to have it," she told him shyly. "For when you start your own cow farm."

He grasped the kerchief between his fingers and met her eyes. "When did you make it? You've been pretty busy on the trail."

"I began the night you told us of your dream to own your land and cattle. Every night I worked a bit . . . until my eyes were too tired to see." She swallowed. "I am glad that you have this dream, Luke. I pray that someday you will have this place of your heart."

He shifted. "Emma, I've been doing some serious thinking." The words, barely acknowledged until this afternoon, welled up from somewhere inside him. He glanced toward the open door, aware that her grandmother was probably listening to every word. What did she say about there being more than one way to cut a cake? He lowered his voice to a whisper. "I'm expecting to get a bonus from this herd. Mr. Hancock is going to make a bundle, and he's known for passing on his profits. If I can make this much money a few more times, I'll have enough to buy back my old family farm in Texas. Then I'll leave the trail. I'll raise a herd of my own, and build a life." He paused and caught her gaze in a meaningful one of his own. "A life for myself and my family."

If only she hadn't mastered her father's talent of masking all her emotions. She stared at him through eyes that seemed so passive as to be indifferent.

"There are Amish cows as well as Texas ones," she finally said.

He couldn't hold steady under her gaze. He looked away. "I can't become Amish,

Emma. I want a simple life, but not a Plain one."

When she looked up again, tears sparkled in her eyes.

"Emma . . ."

"What you say is true, Luke." She looked past him as though he wasn't there. "It is not meant for Amish and *Englisch* to be together."

Maybe so, but his life would never be the same without her. And she might tell herself that Amish and *Englisch* didn't mix, but would her heart believe it?

Did his?

Without another word, he turned and left the room, the handkerchief clutched in his fingers.

Thirty-One

Apple Grove, Kansas
September 1881

Fall had reached its cool fingers into Apple Grove. For the first time in months, the morning sun failed to warm the chill from the air. Emma pulled a pan of biscuits from the oven and set it on the iron surface, glad for the heat inside the small room. She slathered the biscuits with a slice from the roll of butter she had helped *Maummi* churn a few days before.

"Mind that butter, girl." *Maummi's* voice held the same instructive tone she'd adopted for years, ever since Emma could first pull up a stool and reach the surface of the countertops in the family kitchen. "Too much and you'll make the biscuits soggy. And reach for me a jar of strawberry preserves when you finish there."

"Yes, *Maummi.*"

Emma did as she was told, her mind

wandering as her fingers grasped a glass jar from the high shelf opposite the kitchen's deep washtub. Did Luke like strawberry preserves? She didn't know because she'd never had a chance to ask him. They had known each other for a mere week, and that almost two months ago. Why, then, did thoughts of him continue to plague her?

As always, memories of the handsome trail boss tugged on her like melancholy weights dangling from her heart. To say she missed him was a gross understatement. Every thought was saturated with his presence. Where was he now? Probably leading another cattle drive from Texas, making more money to buy his farm. Would he ever leave the trail, or would he end up an old cowhand like Griff, always talking about making a home but never doing it? Sleep eluded her when she laid her head on her pillow at night, her imagination filling the empty place beside her with thoughts of a dark-eyed cowboy. Even her dreams were full of him.

She filled her days with work. Gathering eggs, mucking out the horses' stalls, and maintaining the family garden plot alongside *Maummi* and Rebecca. Every so often Bishop Miller stopped by to check on her and Papa. Though the Switzers had been completely restored to the good graces of their Amish district, the bishop seemed especially concerned for Emma. He had sorrowfully rejected her request to attend the baptism classes that started two weeks past with the explanation that he doubted her readiness to commit to a life of dedication to the Plain way. He'd advised waiting until next year to join the classes. Rather than the bitter disappointment she expected, Emma actually felt a flicker of relief. That would have worried her, had she allowed herself to dwell on it. Instead, she filled her time with the endless tasks of farm life.

In two more days she and *Maummi* would leave Apple Grove and move to Troyer to live with Aunt Gerda. This time a delegation of eight Apple Grove Amish men would accompany them. *Maummi*'s hutch was already loaded on the wagon in the barn, awaiting their departure. Try though she might, Emma couldn't muster any enthusiasm for the journey.

When the hot buttered biscuits had been piled on a platter and placed in the center of the table, a commotion outside drew her attention. *Maummi* rose from her stool in the corner of the kitchen to peer out the window.

She turned a surprised expression toward Emma. "Set two more plates at the table. We have guests."

Rather than obeying immediately, Emma crossed to the window to peek outside. What she saw set her heart to fluttering.

Two horses and their riders drew to a stop in the side yard. Rebecca appeared from the doorway of the barn to investigate the arrival, and she dropped a pail of milk in her excitement. Jesse and Griff called cheerful greetings toward her as they dismounted.

Her heart pounding, Emma retrieved two more place settings and rearranged the table to accommodate their guests. There was no sign of the one cowboy she longed to see, but at least these two might bring news of him. She exited the house after *Maummi* at the same time Papa arrived from the field.

"It is a good day when we can welcome friends to our home," he told them, his smile wide. "You'll join us for dinner?"

Griff placed a hand on his belly and grinned toward *Maummi.* "Can't tell you how I was hoping you'd ask."

Jesse's limp was barely noticeable as he trailed *Maummi* and Papa into the house. He spared a smile toward Rebecca, who looked ready to keel over with excitement, and then took his place at the table. He and

Griff devoured *schnitz* and *knepp,* buttered sprouts and potatoes, and biscuits with jam, answering Papa's polite questions between mouthfuls. Yes, they had gotten along well since the end of the cattle drive in July. Griff had delayed his plans to look after Jesse. No, they hadn't yet taken on new assignments, though they both had multiple offers and intended to head back to Texas soon.

Emma bit her tongue and toyed with her food. Luke's name loomed over the table, an unspoken and unacknowledged presence that she could not stop thinking about. It wasn't until the meal was almost over and *Maummi* had served up heaping portions of apple pie that she finally gathered the nerve to ask the question that had pressed on her mind since the moment she laid eyes on the pair.

She scooped a spoonful of her dessert and held it before her mouth. "And what of Luke? Did he take another job as a trail boss, as he intended?"

Jesse and Griff exchanged a loaded glance before they answered.

"No," Griff finally said. He set his spoon down on the rim of his bowl and speared her with a meaningful stare. "Haven't you heard? Luke quit the trail. He took a mortgage and bought a farm not ten miles from here, just on the other side of Hays. The old Zurcher place. Mr. Hancock was so grateful for the extra profit from our cattle drive that he gifted Luke with a hundred head of longhorns to seed his own herd."

A numb realization stole over Emma. Luke lived not ten miles from here? And he'd given up the trail and his plan to buy his family farm in Texas? She set her spoon down, the dessert untasted.

"I wondered if you knew," Jesse said quietly. "He's been working hard to establish his herd, but his heart isn't in it. It's like . . ." He glanced at Jonas and then back at Emma. "There's something missing. Or maybe *someone.* So Griff and I were talkin', and we think we know what's missing. That's why we're here —"

She couldn't take anymore. Emma's chair scraped across the wooden floor as she pushed back to flee the table. They were all looking at her, and the reason pressed against her like the weight of water against lungs begging for air. Luke had settled a few miles from here . . .

As she exited the house, she heard Jesse's pursuit. She ran to the hitching post where his and Griff's horses were tethered, and then she stopped and turned to face him.

"Why didn't he send word?" she asked,

searching his face for the answer.

Jesse shrugged. "He's a stubborn, mule-headed cowboy, maybe?" His tone grew soft. "Or maybe he's afraid of being turned down. All I know is he's got a big, empty house on that farm, and he's waiting for someone to help him fill it up."

A noise behind Jesse caused him to turn. Papa had also exited the house and approached them with a purposeful stride. His eyes remained steadfast on Emma as he spoke to Jesse.

"A moment with my Emma, please."

With a final look at her, Jesse went back inside.

Emma couldn't return her father's gaze. She lifted a hand to stroke the muzzle of Jesse's horse. The animal tossed his head and whickered softly in response.

Papa's voice cut through the silence that surrounded them. "You still love him, this *Englisch* cowboy."

Painful tears flooded her eyes. It was not a question, but Emma mastered herself enough to nod in response.

He sighed. "On the day of your birth, your mother and I stood gazing down at you in your cradle. We talked. We wished for our daughter a Plain life, a peaceful life. We wanted you to embrace our faith. Our ways.

Our beliefs."

His words sliced deep. "I know, Papa. I have. Really."

Sadly, Papa shook his head. "You believe. But your heart leads you elsewhere."

Silence fell between them, broken only by Emma's quiet sobs. After a few moments, Papa reached out a hand and placed it awkwardly on her arm.

"Peace is not possible without love," he whispered. "Above all, your mother wanted you to have love. I want you to have love. I want you to have it in a Plain life, but . . ."

Emma's heart welled up with hope. Papa would never say the words that approved her rejection of the Plain way of life. But he came as close as he could when he wished her a lifetime of love.

Despite his reticence against displays of emotion, she flung her arms around him and clung to him. Never again would she enjoy this moment with her father, with her heritage and her faith intact. She would not be shunned, because she had not been baptized. But she would be *Englisch.* An outsider. Whispering a sweet and silent farewell, she leaned back and fixed her gaze on his.

"I love you, Papa."

His lips twitched with unspoken words.

Instead, he lifted an open hand and placed it on her forehead. "Go," he said. "And find happiness."

Joy sparked to life deep inside her and quickly flared to a blaze. Luke waited a few miles from here. She needed to harness the horse to the buggy, and quickly, before her nerve gave out.

When she turned toward the barn, her gaze snagged on four pairs of eyes that stood watching her outside the house.

Jesse strode toward her. "Take my horse," he said. "He's fast, and he knows the way."

She looked down at her bulky black skirts. How could she ride like this? And then it hit her. She *could* ride astride now. No one would fault her. No one would condemn her if she did.

Rebecca's grin lit the entire barnyard. That her sister wished her well would never be in doubt. Before Emma turned toward the horse, *Maummi* lurched forward and grabbed her into a hug.

"May you find what I found," she whispered, tears glittering in her eyes. "You have my blessing as a gift for your new home. And something else besides."

Emma laughed at the meaning sparkling in her eyes. Then, with a grin toward Rebecca, she gathered her skirts, climbed into

Jesse's saddle, and pointed his horse toward the old Zurcher farm.

Luke stood out in the pasture, watching a pair of newborn calves frolic in the green grass. The sight of them sent a ripple of satisfaction to his gut. They were his, the first born under the Lazy C brand, and he couldn't stop staring at them.

His gaze swept upward, over the wide open pasture and the herd that grazed within the fenced borders. To his right, the lush plants of the previous owners' garden bore more squash and late red tomatoes than he could pick in a month. And behind him, a house loomed empty and lonely, the only furnishing his bedroll on the hard wooden floor in the biggest bedroom.

The silence of the farm, and the occasional call of a mother cow toward her playful calf, occupied his thoughts. In the dim recesses of his mind he heard the sound of a horse's approach, but he didn't credit it as real. Instead, his inner eyes were fixed on the image of a sweet face, a softly curving cheek, and a pair of lush lips that quirked at the edges and invited his touch.

A weight dropped around his body. In the next instant, a rope tightened, pinning his arms to his side.

He turned to find a haunting, laughing gaze fixed on him. At first his mind grappled to place the beautiful woman whose long hair swung freely around her shoulders, with no white *kapp* to hinder its dance in the Kansas breeze. Then somewhere in the depths of his chest, his heart lurched toward the woman who had lassoed his emotions months ago on the Chisholm Trail. His boots followed and took him to her side.

She lifted her end of the rope, her eyes dancing with humor. "I've been practicing my technique. How am I doing?"

Did her presence here, without her Amish *kapp,* mean what he thought? Was she ready to give herself to him, freely and without encumbrance? He'd longed for this moment through the long days and nights of the past two months. With an impatient hand, he freed himself from the confines of the rope and raised his arms to encircle her. Moving with reverence for the precious treasure he held, he pulled her gently to him.

"You're doing fine," he whispered.

He lowered his lips to cover hers. The moment they touched, a wave of emotion swept from his head to his feet. He felt her go limp in his arms, and he tightened his hold on her.

"I heard you'd given up the life of a trail

boss and settled in Kansas," she whispered when their kiss ended, her gaze locked onto his. "I could hardly believe it was true."

"Yes, ma'am. It's true." He brought her upright and picked up a silky lock of her unbound hair between his rough fingers. "Does this mean you've given up your Plain life for mine?"

Her hand rose to rest upon his cheek. "Why must we choose one or the other? Instead, can't we make a new life together?"

Overcome, he pulled her toward him again. In the moments before their lips touched for a glorious second time, she whispered, "There is something I need to tell you. *Maummi* is giving us a wedding present. I hope we'll have room for it in our house."

A movement behind her drew his attention. He tore his gaze from hers and focused on the unmerciful sight. Pulling from the main road onto his property was Mrs. Switzer in her ox-drawn wagon. Jesse rode on the bench beside her, and *that hutch* loomed in the wagon over their heads. Though he'd thought himself rid of the thing forever, it seemed determined to haunt him.

But it was a fair exchange. *Maummi*'s hutch for Emma's heart. He'd take it.

"That," he said as he lowered his head

again to claim a kiss from the woman he loved, "is a price I'll gladly pay."

DISCUSSION QUESTIONS

1. Today, one of the reasons Amish people stand out is because of their non-technological lifestyle, but no one had technology in 1881. In *The Heart's Frontier,* what set the Amish people apart from others?

2. When confronted by armed thieves, Emma is proud when Papa responds by quoting directly from the Amish Confession of Faith. Why do you think those words came so easily to his lips?

3. Emma is frustrated with her father's reluctance to make a decision about returning home or continuing on to Troyer. Was Jonas's hesitation justified? Is there a point where too much caution is detrimental?

4. When the story begins, Luke is cocky and

sure of himself. What lessons did he learn along the cattle trail?

5. Emma's first impression of Luke is not good. What was the turning point in her feelings for him?

6. Amish parents like to teach their children with proverbs. Did any of *Maummi*'s proverbs teach you something?

7. Luke needs to focus on getting his herd to Hays. What makes him continue to help the Switzers, even at the risk of missing his deadline?

8. Luke felt responsible for the deaths of Willie and Kirk. Was he?

9. Emma feels guilty for acting foolishly when she snuck away from the camp after dark. Was the kidnapping her fault? Why or why not?

10. Why did Luke struggle with shooting the cattle rustlers?

11. Why did Papa try to discourage Luke

from pursuing Emma? Were his concerns justified?

12. *Maummi* didn't want Emma to fall in love with an *Englisch* man, even though she married outside her faith. What were her reasons? What made her change her mind about Luke?

13. What was the message behind Emma's hand-embroidered gift to Luke? Did he take that message to heart?

14. Emma tells Luke that she doesn't want to choose between an Amish life or an *Englisch* life, but a life they can discover together. Do you think that would be possible for them? Do you think that would work as well today for an *Englischer* and a Plain woman?

15. Which character did you most identify with, and why?